PRAISE FOR *SWEETWATER RANCH* AND EDGAR AWARD WINNER GEOFFREY NORMAN

"A TOUGH, FAST-MOVING STORY. . . . He brings events to a dramatic conclusion that another Florida writer, John D. MacDonald, would have admired."
—*Playboy*

"THIS GUY IS TOUGH. AND SMART AND FUNNY. AND HE WORKS A PART OF THE STRANGE STATE OF FLORIDA THAT NO ONE HAS DISCOVERED YET. In prose as lean and gristly as Morgan himself, Geoffrey Norman has told an old tale of revenge, justice, and love in a voice that's as fresh as a breeze off the Gulf." —James W. Hall

"HELL OF A SATISFYING STORY. Norman's private investigator, Morgan Hunt, is a hero in the Travis McGee tradition, and every ounce as cool. More, please." —Christopher Buckley

"*SWEETWATER RANCH* IS AN UNUSUAL DETECTIVE NOVEL: IT'S SMART, MARVELOUSLY SMART, AND TOUCHING. Morgan Hunt is as thoughtful as he is tough, and he reveals a sense of justice that is true to the spirit, not the letter, of the law. This is a wonderful novel, one of those wonders that transcends the genre."
—James Crumley

Sweetwater Ranch

Geoffrey Norman

A DELL BOOK

Published by
Dell Publishing
a division of
Bantam Doubleday Dell Publishing Group, Inc.
666 Fifth Avenue
New York, New York 10103

While a few of the place-names in this book are from panhandle Florida—an actual place—the characters and situations are entirely a product of the author's imagination.

ISBN: 0-440-21219-7

Reprinted by arrangement with The Atlantic Monthly Press

Printed in the United States of America

Published simultaneously in Canada

March 1992

10 9 8 7 6 5 4 3 2 1

OPM

for Jim Norman

Chapter One

Nat Semmes talked while he drove. He kept his eyes on the road because he was driving fast, the way he always did, and because we were on the sort of two-lane where you are likely to come over a rise and find yourself on the bumper of a pickup that is going fifteen miles an hour because if it went any faster, it would fall apart. A generation ago, the pickup truck would have been a mule wagon.

I watched the passing pastureland and piney woods and listened to Semmes. His voice was soft and urgent.

"You wouldn't believe what some of these boys have been through, Morgan," he said.

Sure I would, I thought but didn't say it.

"You get to where nothing much surprises you when it comes to what people will do to each other. But when you see it done to a kid . . ."

Semmes's long jawbone was locked down tight,

and his thin face seemed almost gaunt, hollowed out by the acids of his anger.

"How many are there?" I asked, trying to keep it practical. No point in getting all righteous and worked up out here on the highway, where the only thing to do about it was rave. I prefer action to pointless emotion. Semmes does, too, most of the time. But some things set him off.

He sighed. "He's got forty-five beds and about five kids lined up for every one of them. There are a lot of kids in this world who need a place to go. Somewhere safe—that's the minimum requirement. Just someplace safe."

Semmes downshifted and accelerated through a long curve. The Porsche seemed to glide by the bean fields that flanked the road. The beans had the bleached, withered look they get in the summer. It was the fat part of July, and the heat had been building since daybreak. If any relief came, it would be late in the afternoon in the form of a distant thunderstorm that had been brewing all day long. But until the storm broke, the heat would accumulate steadily, bearing down on everything like some kind of weight.

I felt alert and eager in spite of the heat. I knew that Semmes had not called me just to ride along and keep him company. He had a job and a job meant action. I have a weakness for action. It is an appetite that has ruled my life. It has gotten me into a lot of trouble and nearly killed me more times than I can remember. But in a more important way, action has never let me down. It always makes me feel alive.

Semmes is a lawyer and a good one. He is old school, in it for reasons other than money, and he loves a good fight. He is smart, resourceful, and tenacious as a pit bull. But his skill is with argument, and his turf is the courtroom. I am his eyes and ears. I go where he wouldn't know his way around. What he provides me is the assurance that I am working for a good cause. I haven't always been able to say that.

Semmes and I make a good team. He had been my lawyer and friend when I needed both badly. Without his help, I would still be stacking time, hour by hour, day by day, year by year, at Holman prison, just over the line in Alabama. Semmes had pried a pardon out of the governor's office for me even though the charge was murder, and there was never any doubt that I had done the killing, only some controversy about the circumstances. Now that I had the pardon, Semmes was no longer my lawyer, but he was still my friend.

He was also my employer, from time to time. One of the men who worked for the governor had wondered just what I would do on the outside if they should decide to pardon me. Did I, he asked, have any useful skills?

I had plenty of skills, and in some contexts, they were exceedingly useful. I could set the timing and head space on a machine gun in the dark, for example. I could lay an L-shaped ambush, tie off a bleeding artery, and call an air strike to within one hundred meters of my own position. But those weren't the sort of skills that the man in the governor's office had in mind. Nor were they the sort I wanted to peddle. I'd had enough of all that.

So Nat Semmes told the bristling little clerk who was handling things while the governor was busy cutting the ribbon on a new highway that he would hire me as an investigator and guarantee my employment in writing. That probably wouldn't have been good enough for a common convict. But Semmes had kept my name in the newspapers, and the people in the governor's office were tired of me and especially tired of Semmes, who had a way of not letting go once he put the bite on something.

Since then, I'd done some jobs for Semmes. Still, I was anything but a full-time investigator even though I had my certificate from the state of Florida. I made my living, such as it was, doing whatever came along. Just now, I was rebuilding an old house I'd picked up for next to nothing. In a couple of months, I would be going out West to work as a guide during elk season for an outfitter who was an old friend. I'd had some money saved when my conviction came down, and among the many things I learned while I was doing time were the miracles of compound interest and how to play around in some of the markets. I got to be especially good at figuring where the price of soybeans would be going. When it comes to money, I don't really need much, and it seems like I have plenty.

Semmes still calls me for some jobs. There are other people he uses, but now and then he seems to think he needs me and only me. I suspect he understands that I need the action.

We were on our way to a job now, and Semmes was explaining it in his fashion, which is to start at the beginning, with the people involved. For Semmes, everything begins with personality. "I don't take *cases*," he'd told me once, making the word sound like it described something vile. "I represent people. I don't figure that just *anyone* is entitled to my best defense." Semmes had to believe in you before he'd take your problems on. That didn't mean he had to believe you were technically innocent; I was proof that his standard was more complex than that. It came down to something intuitive: he either believed in you or he didn't. And he plainly believed in someone named John Fearson.

"The kids call him Big John," he was saying, "and they love him. He's what one of my expert witnesses would call a positive male role model. That means he's a better father to these boys than their real fathers ever were." He frowned and studied the dashboard for a second or two. He had a common, bland face like the sort in those old Civil War photographs. It was a country face, I suppose, not sophisticated or devious. Innocent and almost empty in repose. But anger could transform it entirely. When you saw that happen, you could understand how those farm boys who became Confederate infantrymen had been so terrible in battle. When the look was on Semmes, you realized that he was the sort of man who would not be satisfied with merely defeating his enemies. He craved their total destruction.

"But then," he went on, "that's not saying much. Most of John's boys were abandoned by their real fathers. Old Dad got the itch one day and just hit the road; you know how it is." He paused again and rubbed his long chin.

"A lot of those boys don't have any idea where old Dad is or even if he's still alive. That's bad enough, but it's better than what some of them have been through. Dad stayed around to get drunk and beat the living hell out of them."

We rode on, in silence, for a while. Northwest Florida seemed to float by, the way the ground slides under you when you are at altitude. It was scrubby country, the sort that would never make a postcard. Piney woods, mostly, which was good for pulp and for hunting. The understory was palmetto, jack oak, and dogwood. For two weeks in the spring, when the dogwoods bloomed, this woods would be tender green and chaste white and undeniably beautiful. The rest of the year, it was monotonous and monochromatic.

It was an easy place to overlook in general. The map says it's part of Florida, but Escambia County, where Semmes and I lived, is about nine hundred miles away—and a few million miles in spirit—from what most people think of when they hear the word Florida: Miami, Fort Lauderdale, and Palm Beach.

"How old are the boys?" I said.

"All ages. Six up to seventeen. Even John says you can't do much with the older boys. But the little ones, they just break your heart. There's one out here named Jimmy—you'll meet him—he's my favorite. I feel like adopting him and taking him home every time I come out here and see him.

"Jimmy's parents split when he was four. Dad just dropped out of sight. The court went after him for child support, but it was a cold trail. The mother started going to the bars and leaving the kid behind, locked in the house by himself, for two or three days at a time. He learned how to open the peanut butter and flush the toilet by himself. Finally, his mother turned Jimmy over to *her* mother. The old lady had enough sense to know she couldn't handle it, so she turned Jimmy over to John. He's been there a year now."

"Where's the mother?"

"She's around. Gets drunk every now and then and calls up asking to talk to her baby boy. John won't let her talk to him, and she threatens to come take the boy back. He says the biggest favor she could do for Jimmy would be to go ahead and die."

"The kid still misses her, doesn't he?"

"How did you know?"

"A lot of kids like Jimmy grow up and go to jail. They still miss their mamas even when they're thirty years old, doing life, and it's Mama who made them what they are."

"That's what John's fighting."

"Good luck to him."

"He's an unusual man, Morgan."

"He'd have to be."

Semmes nodded and accelerated through a sweeping half-mile curve past a vast, green pecan orchard.

Chapter Two

It was midafternoon when we arrived at the ranch. Big John had his shirt off and was playing basketball with a bunch of his boys. Semmes pulled the Porsche into the shade of a live oak, where we stood and watched for a minute.

It was like no basketball game I had ever seen. The smallest player was four feet six and weighed ninety pounds. The biggest was John Fearson himself, who went six eight and somewhere around two sixty. There were players of every size in between, both black and white. Just about the only thing all the players had in common was a glistening film of sweat on their bare upper bodies.

They were playing some kind of local rules. Only the little guys could shoot from inside or go up for rebounds. While we watched, one lithe black boy who looked to be about ten or twelve made a nice head fake on John, dribbled around him, pumped once, and got a white eight-year-old up in the air, waited until he came down, and then went up himself, very smoothly, to sink a six-foot jumper.

"Out of my *jock*," Big John yelled. "Faked me right out of my jock, you did. Nice play, Roddy."

John brought the ball down the concrete court for his team. "All right," he shouted, "let's set 'em up and work 'em. Set 'em up and work 'em. Work for the good shot now. Pass and move, pass and move."

"Come on and *pass* it, then," a very small white boy said, dancing around the top of the key.

"That's Jimmy," Semmes said, sounding proud enough to be the kid's father.

"Get open and I'll pass it," Big John said, whipping a pass into a pimply-faced boy on the baseline. The boy fumbled the pass and quickly put his hands to his face.

"My fault," John said. "Threw it too hard. No touch."

They came back downcourt, and I saw John wink to the boy who had dropped the pass. "It's all right," he said. "We'll show 'em some D."

John stood to one side of the foul line, making himself a large obstacle to anyone who wanted to drive that side of the court. The biggest boy on the other team, a red-haired six-footer with suspicious, pea-sized country eyes, challenged him. Charged him, in fact, and John stumbled backward for a step or two. The redhead saw his chance and started up for the jump shot. But he was just a little slow. John recovered and went up with him. He had a look of thorough determination when he slapped the boy's shot right back at him.

"You can't get 'em that way, Rick," he said grimly. "No short cuts and no little cheating moves. You got to *earn* it."

The pimply-faced boy had recovered the blocked shot and was bringing it downcourt.

"Next basket wins," John said, nodding to Semmes and me.

"Ah, come on. No fair. Play to fifty." All the boys were protesting the ruling.

"Next point wins," John said and the boys shut up.

John worked to Jimmy, whose route to the basket was blocked by a quick black boy who kept his hands out just like he saw them do on TV. Jimmy whipped the ball back to John, who held it above his head and studied the flow. Boys moved around the court looking for position, and for a few seconds, the only sound that traveled across the still summer air was the slap of rubber soles on the flat concrete. Suddenly, without even looking that way, John flicked the ball to the pimply-faced boy, who was open under the basket for an easy lay-up. He jumped, put the ball against the backboard, and then watched, not quite believing as it hit the iron, rolled once, and then went through.

"Attaway, Joe Lee. Attaway to work 'em. Looked like the Bird himself on that one." John shook the boy's hand, then gave him a high five, and then slapped him on the butt.

"All right, boys, all right," he said, "now listen up." The afternoon turned quiet again, and the boys all looked at him. "Tonight, we've got our big cookout. I want this place looking *right* before we get started. Now, everybody is on a chore list, and everybody should know where to go. Housefathers will be in charge. So let's get going. I'll be around to check on you."

The boys left the court, mumbling, to pick up their

T-shirts, which were scattered across the grass next to the concrete.

"Shit," the red-haired boy said, just loud enough.

"Hey," John said. "What did you say?"

"Nothing."

"No," John said, walking in the boy's direction. "It wasn't *'nothing.'* It was worse than nothing."

The red-haired boy looked sullenly back at John but didn't say anything.

"Now, if you've got something to say, Rick, say it loud and make yourself understood. And whatever it is you have to say, make sure that you're not ashamed to repeat it. You understand me?"

"Yes."

"Yes, *sir.*"

"Yes, sir."

"Now do you have something to say to me?"

"No."

"No, *sir.*"

"No, sir," the boy said, slurring the words.

He tried to hold Big John's eyes with his, but he didn't have the nerve for it. Not many grown men would.

The boy gave up and looked at the ground.

"All right, Hoss," Big John said, "you and I are going to have a little private talk later. Right now, go get your shirt and get to work."

When the boy had picked up his shirt, John turned and walked our way. He was smiling.

"Greetings, Counselor," he said. "You got here a little late for the game."

"Too hot to play basketball."

"Nah," John said. "Just right. Run and sweat, run and sweat. Feels good. People play golf in this kind of weather, don't they?"

"I'm no golfer." Semmes sounded insulted.

"But a lot of lawyers are," Big John said. "How long does it take to play a round?"

"Four hours, from what I hear."

"Four *hours*. Man, I couldn't take *that*. Walking around with a heavy bag for four hours, wearing a lot of clothes. Sounds to me like what the mailman does." He shook his head and then abruptly stuck his hand out in my direction.

"I'm John Fearson, welcome to Sweetwater Ranch."

"Morgan Hunt," I said. "Glad to be here."

"Well, it's nothing fancy, but we're proud of it. You want to take a look around?"

"Sure."

"OK, but first I need something to drink. How about you men? Soda, tea, or water? I've got the world's best-tasting water. Comes straight out of the spring. Absolutely pure and so cold it will shrink your fillings."

"That sounds good."

"Absolutely," Semmes said.

We followed John to an old cast-iron pump. It was rusty, and so was the short length of pipe it stood on. There was a mason jar full of clear water on the ground next to it. John used the water in the jar to prime the pump. His muscles rippled with each stroke on the pump handle.

When the water was running steadily, I cupped my hands and drank. It was very cold, and like he said, tasted entirely pure. Just the faintest trace of limestone. It was perfect for a hot afternoon in July.

Semmes drank and then he pumped for John, who drank a pint or two and then stuck his head under the stream of clear water.

"Whooowhooo," he shouted. "Oh my, oh my."

He came out from under the water and looked at

us, smiling and dripping. "Man, that feels great. Just great. Cooled me right down." He worked the pump handle one last time to refill the mason jar.

"All right, now," he said. "Let's go get in my jeep and take the fifty-cent tour."

It was an old jeep without a roll bar. He started it, and we took off across a large pasture on a dirt road.

"You've already seen the basketball court," John said, shouting over the engine noise. "A contractor donated that. Sent a crew out one weekend to build it. He said he saw me play in the Sugar Bowl and that he wanted to repay me for all the thrills I'd given him. That's not necessarily why I want people to contribute, but I don't turn *anything* down."

He accelerated and the jeep went over a small rise. Below it were nine small brick buildings. They looked almost like those hastily built apartment houses marketed for transient singles or young marrieds.

"Those are my dormitories. I thought about building log cabins, you know, like a summer camp, but then I decided that wasn't right. These boys are different. They'll *always* be different. So at least I can give 'em something close to a suburb, like all the other kids live in. That's what they want—to be like the other kids.

"I built the first four houses myself. I didn't do it with my own hands, but I paid for them. With football money. Signing bonus. Playoff and Super Bowl share. All that payed for the land and the first four houses. Since then, it's been donations and what I could raise. I've been very fortunate. And the Lord has looked out for us."

He dropped the jeep into a lower gear and accelerated along the road, past one of the houses and on through some small pines planted near a ten-acre pond. When he turned off the road, there was a slight wash in our path, but he didn't brake for it. The jeep cleared the ground coming out of the wash and came down hard on a set of worn-out shocks. John yelled happily.

"All *right*. A man who never leaves the safety of the road is a man who has never lived."

He drove through the pines, dodging trees and bouncing through other washes until we were out in the open pasture, where a hundred or so Angus steers grazed lazily in the heat. John slowed the jeep, then brought it to a complete stop.

"We're a real farm. We raise beef cattle. What we don't eat ourselves—and Hoss, let me tell you how much hamburger forty-five boys will eat—we take to an auction and we sell. We grow our own hay and some corn. We have chickens because we eat eggs near about like we eat hamburger. We grow vegetables. And I've got some horses for the boys to ride. All the chores are divided up, and the boys do 'em. The housefathers and I supervise and check up on them. But the boys do the work. We want 'em to take pride in where they live and what they do. That's something most of them have never experienced before."

He dropped the jeep back into gear and drove off across the pasture. He shouted happily every time we took a bump. He stopped the jeep on the other side of the pasture.

"Come on," he said, "let's walk a minute so I can show you something."

We followed him down a little dirt patch through the pine trees. The ground fell off slightly and opened to a wide view of a big river bottom. You could see for miles, and in every direction there was only deep woods. We came to a small clearing. There were stakes driven into the ground, and strings ran between the stakes.

"Beautiful, isn't it?" John said.

"Great view," Semmes agreed.

"This is where I'm going to build my chapel. That's what the strings are for. It's going to be my little chapel in the pines. I'm going to build it with lumber that I've saw-milled myself, right off the property. It's going to be beautiful." Big John was looking off at the river bottom and the horizon beyond.

"When do you plan to start, John?" Semmes said solemnly, respecting the mood.

John turned to him with a wide, half-manic grin and said, "Just as soon as I get my gymnasium. I've got my priorities, just like everyone else. We can pray and sing hymns anywhere, but when it's been raining for three days I got to have some place where forty-five restless boys can burn some energy. I'm sure the Lord would understand."

"How you coming on the funding?"

"Coming along. It takes time."

We were silent for a moment. Down over the bottomland, a couple of buzzards circled lazily above the trees. Insects whined around my face.

"The gym is what I'm working on right now," John said, breaking the silence. "But my chapel here, that's what I dream about. That's something I *would* like to build with my own hands."

He turned and led the way to the jeep. We drove back across the pasture and through the trees to the little circle of brick buildings where John and his boys lived. Fearson parked the jeep next to a small weathered building that had probably been a stable at one time. He pushed open a screen door and led

the way past a secretary's desk, which was equipped
with a phone, a Rolodex, and a big IBM Selectric. It
looked out of place in a stable.

"This is my secretary's office," Fearson said. "She
took the day off, and on what I pay her I couldn't
argue."

He opened a door to another room. "This here is
my office. Excuse the mess. It's always like this. I do
a lot of things good, but administering isn't one of
them."

The office wasn't that bad. There were letters and
bills and the usual papers spread over the desk in
loose piles. There were pictures on the wall—Fearson back in his playing days when he was an All-
American. One of the pictures showed him ac-
cepting an award as most valuable player in the
Sugar Bowl. Unusual for a defensive lineman. The
shelves on one wall were lined with trophies.

Fearson sat down behind the big old partner's
desk, leaned back in his chair, and began talking.
He dropped the broad country locutions for something more businesslike.

"Luther Jordan is eleven years old. He's been
with me for six months. Parents got a divorce when
he was little. Mom got custody and remarried. Stepfather used to beat Luther. Mom couldn't stop it.
Luther still sees blurred out of one eye, the old man
hit him so hard one day." John's eyes narrowed.

"You know, sometimes I think I'd like to get my
hands on one of these big bad men who like to beat
up on kids. I'd want about ten minutes with Luther's stepfather. I'd even settle for five. Just five
minutes, me and him."

He paused, took a sip from his water glass, then
went on in his surprisingly soft voice. "But that's a

side issue. The real issue is that Luther has disappeared."

"Run away?"

"I suppose so. Some of the boys don't like the rules. Or the work. They run away. Once a year, one of them steals my car."

"What do you do?"

"Usually, I just wait for the phone to ring. Takes a day or two. Sometimes the law picks them up, and sometimes they just run out of money. Sometimes they go looking for their parents, and they find them, and then the parents call, saying 'Hey, *I* don't want him. *You* come take him back.'"

"What's different about Luther?"

"He's been gone almost a month. He didn't steal my car, by the way. He took his clothes and he took his radio. Luther likes music. I was always catching him listening to the radio when he was supposed to be doing his homework. I took the radio away from him a couple of times."

"Why did he run away?"

"No special reason. Far as I know, nothing had happened to make him any unhappier than he already was."

"Phone calls? Letters?"

"You mean from his mama, right?"

"I imagine that's a problem."

"Yes, sir, that's a problem. You wouldn't believe how much damage one phone call from a parent can do to one of these boys. These boys won't hear anything for weeks and weeks, and they'll be getting adjusted to it, learning to accept it, and then one night here will come a telephone call. All of a sudden, Mom or Dad reaches out to some little old boy who's been discarded, tossed on the scrap pile by the people who brought him into the world, and that little boy thinks to himself, Maybe now, this time, I can make them love me like they didn't love me before.

"I don't let a lot of these parents talk to their kids. Some, I won't even let 'em write. A few I can't do anything about. It's amazing, none of them seem to understand that they're the reason that their own sons are here."

"What about Luther's parents?" I said. "Did they ever try to get in touch?"

"Not once. Not even a card at Christmas. I'd feel better, in a way, if I thought that's what it was. But I don't think so. I think he just left. He's an unhappy, troubled, lonely boy, and nobody's really gotten through to him yet. I'm worried about him, and I want to find him and make sure he's safe. Here or someplace else, if that's the way it works out. Just as long as he's safe. I hate the idea of him out there by himself."

Big John Fearson plainly thought the outside world was no place for a small boy and maybe not for a grown man, either. It was hard to argue with that. I told him I'd do my best to find Luther. That's why Nat Semmes had brought me along.

"I really appreciate it," Fearson said.

"I can't promise anything."

"Well, from what the counselor here told me," he said, "if you can't do it, then the thing can't be done."

Chapter Three

I'd written a few things in my notebook, and Fearson had given me a folder containing all the information he had. Semmes and I were leaving when Fearson said, "Listen, we're having a cookout tonight. Why don't you men stick around? I'll feed you the finest grilled hamburger you've ever put in your mouth."

So Semmes and I helped him lay a charcoal fire and bring several boxes of ground beef from a walk-in meat locker out to a picnic table. John put out restaurant-sized jars of mustard and catsup and relish. Boxes of hamburger rolls. Cases of soft drinks, which we cooled in tubs of ice. As we worked, a couple of boys who looked about ten—one white and one black—joined us.

"Hello, men," John said. "You finished your chores?"

"Yes, sir," the boys said in unison.

"That's fine. Now you can give us a hand here."

"OK," they said. They made it sound like that was exactly what they had in mind.

"First, run over to the pantry, and bring out about four of those buckets of potato chips."

"OK," they said. They turned and took off, running for a small wooden building a hundred yards away.

"That's the age for boys," John said. "Right there. In another couple of years, the body will start to change, and they'll get interested in girls, and there won't be much you can say to 'em. Not me or anyone else.

"Those older boys give me so much trouble. But they're the ones who need love and discipline the most. Boy of sixteen, all full of juice, with no one to answer to, he'll do just about anything. He's a hazard to himself and everybody else. If I hadn't had football and good parents when I was that age, no telling how I might have turned out."

The two young boys came running across the yard, each of them holding a large tin bucket of potato chips wrapped in their little arms. The black boy beat the white boy by five strides.

"I win. I win," he said.

John took the bucket from him and smiled. "You about the fastest dude at Sweetwater Ranch, ain't you, Jackson?"

"That's right. I'm going to be a wide out when I grow up. Just like Mark Duper."

"Oh yeah," the white boy said, handing over his bucket, "well, I'm going to pump iron and get big and be a linebacker like Big John. Then I'm going to ring your bell."

"Big John wasn't no *linebacker*," the black boy said.

"He was too," the white boy said. "Weren't you, Big John?"

"Yeah," John said. "I was a linebacker in the pros. But I played end in college."

"Well, it's the pros that count, ain't that right, Big John?"

"It *all* counts, Jackson."

"But which one did you like best?" the white boy said.

"I liked it all. Long as it was football."

"How come you ain't still playing?" the white boy said.

"Because I decided I'd rather do this."

"Ah, come on."

"It's true."

"Why you want to do this instead of playing football?"

"Cause I get to hang around with a great bunch of guys like you."

"Ahhh, man."

"It's the truth. I liked football, but this is the best job I ever had."

"You know what, man?" the black boy said.

"What's that?"

"You *crazy*, that's what." When he said it, he reached out and gave John a hug around the waist, which was just about as high as he could reach on that massive body. John hugged him back. The boy turned and shouted to the other boy, "Race you back."

They were gone.

"That little sucker," John said as he watched them, "is about to wear a callus on my waist from hugging me. He's only been here a couple of months now. Came from Miami. Mama is a prostitute there."

"Tough way to grow up," Semmes said.

"Yeah. It is. He knows all about the things people do to each other, but I'll tell you something. At least he learned from *watching*. I've got some here who weren't that lucky. They learned from having it done to them. You see an eight-year-old boy who's been raped by his mother's ex-con boyfriend . . ."

He left the thought unfinished as the two boys came racing back with more potato chips.

When the cookout started, Big John put on an apron and worked the grill for two hours without a break, turning hamburgers in a cloud of smoke. The boys wandered around the grounds, eating and playing the spontaneous games that boys like to play: stealing each other's hats for keep-away, leg wrestling, slap boxing.

The smoke from John's grill drifted over the grounds, carrying with it the smell of cooking meat. The other adults, housemothers and housefathers who worked for John for low wages and the satisfactions of the job, sat around tables talking in low voices. Fireflies came out in the early gloom. Somebody turned a radio on. Merle Haggard sang about prison, whiskey, and the road.

"You get enough to eat?" John said to Semmes and me.

"Too much," Semmes said.

"How about you?"

"Just right."

"I know you'd have probably liked a beer to go with it," he said. "But I just can't allow it here. You understand how it is."

"Sure."

"Nice evening, though, isn't it?"

"Beautiful."

"This is how I remember growing up. Cooking

out like this. Playing in the yard until it got too dark, then coming in all itchy from the grass and the sweat and feeling like I was too tired to take my clothes off. But my folks would make me climb in a hot bath and get all clean and then say my prayers. Man, by the time I finally got into the bed, those sheets felt so *good*. And I'd be asleep in a New York minute. I'd like for these boys to remember that part of growing up and not just all the evil that's been done to them."

There was a loud cry followed by angry shouting. John turned and ran toward the sound. The rest of us followed. "Is somebody hurt?" one of the house-mothers said.

"Sounds like they're fighting," a housefather answered.

When we reached the spot, we found the tall red-haired boy with the suspicious eyes standing over a smaller boy, who was on his hands and knees, spitting blood.

"Come on and get up," the red-haired boy said.

"What's going on here?" John said.

The red-haired boy turned to face him. "He started it. All I did was finish it."

"You know the rule about fighting, Rick," John said quietly.

"Yeah, well, what am I supposed to do when he starts getting up in my face?"

"You know the rule," John repeated. "Now, who's that on the ground? Get up and let me look at you."

It was the pimply-faced boy from the basket-ball court. Joe Lee. He was probably three years younger and fifty pounds lighter than Rick. His nose was bleeding and tears streamed from his eyes, running into the smeared blood around his mouth.

"Looks like you showed him, Rick," John said softly.

"Yeah, I guess."

"Now you want to show me, Big Man." Fearson bit each word off cleanly.

Rick glared at him.

"Some of the boys tell me you think I'm not so tough."

"Who told you that?"

"Doesn't make any difference who told me. Question is, Did you say it? Do you *believe* it?"

Rick smirked.

"Because if you do believe it, you've got a chance, right now, to make your case."

Rick smiled a weak, sick smile.

"You like to fight, don't you? And you say you think I'm not so tough, don't you? So let's go, Bad Man. You and me."

Rick stood still, as though he were screwed into the ground.

"But you ought to know that I walked over men your size looking for a big man to whip."

Rick shook his head from side to side.

John stepped up closer to him. "Well *come on*, Bad Man. Fight me." His arms came up from his side in a blur, and he drove the heels of his hands hard into Rick's chest. Rick staggered back a step or two, and a bewildered look came over his face.

"Come on, Rick. I'm giving you your chance." John took another step toward him. He dropped his shoulder, and Rick flinched and tried to cover himself. It was a fake. John's arms stayed at his side.

"Don't want to get hit, huh, Rick? Well, you'll never be tough until you learn how to take a hit. Want me to teach you?"

Rick shook his head.

"I'd be doing you a favor. Teaching you something that's real valuable. You don't learn anything whipping up on men smaller than you, Rick. When you learn something—learn about yourself—is when you take a whipping from somebody bigger than you. You ready to learn that lesson?"

The boy's lips quivered, and he shook his head from side to side.

"Speak up, Rick. Don't make faces like a baby. Speak up like a man. Are you ready to learn that lesson?"

"No," Rick murmured.

"No, *sir.*"

"No, sir."

"Too bad," John said. "You're going to learn sometime, might as well be here, now, from someone who loves you instead of down the road from some guy who just wants a piece of your hide."

The boy didn't say anything.

"It's going to happen, Rick. You can't escape it."

The boy still didn't say anything.

"All right, then. You go to your room. You know what the punishment is going to be."

"Yes."

"Yes, *sir.*"

"Yes, sir."

"I'll be around later, then. Now get out of here."

The boy slipped away into the darkness, leaving a painful, awkward silence where he'd been.

After the boys had drifted away to their various games, John turned to Semmes and me and said, "That one there is on a dead-end road. I'd throw him out except he'd be in jail in a week. Here at least he's got a small chance. Real small."

He shook his head and offered us more to eat. We

passed and stayed just a few minutes longer. When we shook hands, Fearson looked me close in the eye and said, "Good luck with Luther. And God bless you for trying."

Chapter Four

I was on the road before dawn. Luther Jordan's mother was going to school in Tallahassee, about four hours away, and I hoped to knock on her front door before she left for class.

The highway was almost deserted. Only me and a few trucks. We all drove seventy, seventy-five. I sipped coffee and listened to one of the clear, fifty-thousand-watt stations that played the old songs. There's nothing like music for bringing back your youth. The only thing that comes close is seeing a woman you loved back then.

I drummed the wheel with my free hand, keeping time with Fats Domino, Chuck Berry, and Hank Ballard while I ate up the miles. By dawn I was driving through Eglin Air Force Base, where I'd trained for my last job in Vietnam. That was the one where we went in to get some of our prisoners in the north. The raid went off about as smoothly as any military operation ever has. The only problem was that the North Vietnamese had moved the prisoners. We liberated an empty camp.

Eglin is among the biggest military reservations in the country, and I wondered, as I studied the woods and swamps, if there were any secret operations being rehearsed out there. When we were planning our job, the mock prisoner compound we'd built had to be disassembled twice a day when the Russian spy satellite passed overhead. You can't be too careful.

For a few moments, while the sun was coming up and it was still so dim and cool that you could look straight into it, I thought about those days and I actually missed them. But the feeling passed when the sun rose above the tree line and the morning turned hot.

You move into Eastern time when you cross the Apalachicola River, so I was in the outskirts of Tallahassee by eight. I had an address for Bonnie Perkins—she was using the name of her second husband—from the file John Fearson had given me. The Luther Jordan file was a slim document, sad to read. It hadn't taken me fifteen minutes to read it, but it kept me awake for a long time after that.

When Luther was born, his mother was fifteen. His father was a soldier at Fort Benning. A PFC. He and the mother were married two months before Luther was born and divorced before he was a year old. There was another marriage, to a contractor who beat both mother and son. He'd hit Luther hard enough to detach a retina.

So there had been another divorce, and after that one Luther spent some time with his mother's mother. But for reasons that were not clearly stated in the file, that didn't work out either. So, at age ten and a half Luther was taken to a place he'd never seen or heard of before and left with a man he did not know and four dozen boys like himself. And now, he had run away from that place. Most likely he was trying to find the people who had jettisoned him. At his age, he would be hoping that they would take him back. In a few more years, he would be looking to make them pay.

I found the road where Bonnie Perkins lived, then the apartment building. It was one of those hastily built places with a French name, The Maison de something or other, that was nearing the end of its ten-year life expectancy. But it was close to the campus of Florida State, and that had to count for something with the people who lived there. Mostly students, I suspected, trying to live cheaply. I found 4A and knocked on the door. It was not quite nine thirty. I wondered if she might have already left for class.

"Who is it?"

"It's about your son, Miss Perkins."

"Luther?" The note of alarm in her voice was plain, even through the door.

"Yes."

"Who are you?"

"If you'll open the door a little, I'll show you my papers."

There was a sound of metal moving against tooled metal, almost without friction, as she freed the locks. At least three of them. The door came open a couple of inches. The night chain was still in place, and I could not see Bonnie Perkins's face. I put the letters from Nat Semmes and John Fearson through the crack and saw a hand take them. The door closed firmly.

"Show me some identification," the voice demanded after another minute or two.

I passed my driver's license through the door when it opened again.

"Stand in front of the peephole so I can see your face."

I did.

I heard fingers working with the night chain, the last restraint on the door. Then it came open all the way.

"Come on in. What's happened to Luther?"

She was short, wearing cotton pants and a short-sleeved cotton blouse. Blue tennis shoes. Her hair was cut close, as though for efficiency, and she didn't wear any conspicuous makeup. Her face was firm, and beneath the expression of concern for her child you could see a look of permanent melancholy that made her seem older than she was. Not used up or wasted, though. Simply older. The way anyone who has grieved looks older.

"Luther is missing," I said.

"*Missing?*"

"He seems to have run away."

"From that camp?"

"Yes."

"How long has he been gone?"

"Almost a month now."

She'd been standing, with one hand pressing the other to her left breast. Now she sat in a chair, and one hand went to her face.

"And nobody knows where he is?"

"We're kind of wondering if he's *here*, Miss Perkins."

She shook her head. "I haven't seen him since I left him with my mother."

"Have you talked to him since he's been living at Sweetwater Ranch?"

"No."

"Do you write him?"

She looked at me bleakly and shook her head slowly. There was something in the way she did it that said, You could never understand. Not in a million years.

"Miss Perkins, do you have any idea where he might have gone?"

"*No,*" she said impatiently. "Has anyone called the police?"

"Not yet."

"But what if he's in trouble?"

"Well, if you don't know where he is, then maybe it is time to call the law."

She stood abruptly and turned away from me. "Just when everything was going right for a change," she said helplessly.

You could read those words two ways. Either as concern for her child or irritation over the inconvenience of his disappearance. My impulse was to give her a break, though I wasn't sure why. Maybe I am just naturally sympathetic to anyone rebuilding a life.

"You probably blame me, don't you?" she said, turning to face me.

"No."

"Yes, you do. Everyone does. They all think, Well, if she'd been a better mama, none of this would have happened to that poor child."

I didn't say anything.

"I was trying to do the best thing for both of us," she said, with a note of permanent woe in her voice. "It wasn't a good thing, I know that. But I didn't have no other choices."

Like most people, she showed her roots in a crunch. Up until now, if you went by the way she talked, she could have been from any of the fast-growth cities that had latched onto the South like tumors: Jacksonville, Atlanta, Orlando, Birmingham—there were a dozen or more. But now, trying to defend herself, you could hear red clay and weathered board and a chinaberry tree in her voice. And that was a partial explanation for a lot of what had happened to her. Real country people have a hard time with the bright lights and the kind of life that doesn't start until after the sun has gone down.

"I didn't come here to judge you, Miss Perkins. I've got no standing to do that. I'm just trying to help John Fearson find the boy."

"That boy and me would both be dead now if I hadn't of taken him to my mama's. I couldn't know that she wouldn't want him neither."

"I understand."

"I came here to study for being a nurse."

I nodded.

"At the end of the summer, I'll have done everything for a high school certificate. Then I can start studying nursing. I always had it in my mind that when I was done, and working, I was going to do something to try to make it up to Luther. But maybe it just ain't meant to turn out all right."

Fatalism comes in the genes of those people. Or maybe it's in the dirt, like the hookworm.

"It might still work out, Miss Perkins."

She looked at me like I was raving.

"John Fearson said Luther was doing well at the camp, and at school. He's doing all right, and it looks like you are, too. Right now, we've got to find Luther. That'll put things back on track."

"I don't know where he's gone," she said. "I just

don't. There's nobody he could go to, and he's just a little thing. He can't get by on his own."

"Could he have gone back to your mother's?"

She gave me an angry, disbelieving look. "She sent him away, remember? Same as I did."

"Was he happy there? Before she sent him away."

"I don't believe Luther knows how to be happy. He hasn't had any practice at it."

"Where does your mother live?"

She told me, and I wrote it down in my notebook.

"How about your former husband?" I said.

"Which one?"

"Start with the last one."

"After what he done to Luther, I don't think that boy would go looking for him except to kill him. There was times when I thought about doing it myself." She looked at me and her eyes were hot. "You heard what he done to Luther's eye?"

"Yes," I said. "But just the same, tell me where I can find him."

She told me and I wrote it down.

"How about your first husband? Luther's father?"

She hesitated, then spoke quickly, so it came out sounding like a lie. "I haven't seen him since we got divorced. He was in the army."

"Is he still in the army?"

"I ain't seen him. I can't say."

"What was his name?"

"Jordan. William Luther Jordan. He was from West Virginia."

I wrote that down.

"Anyone else you can think of? Anyone at all?"

She shook her head.

"Do you have a phone?"

"Yes."

"Would you give me the number?"

She did.

"All right. Here's my number. Also the number of the man I work for. Call one of us, please, if you think of anything or hear anything. All right?" I tore a sheet out of my notebook and handed it to her.

She nodded.

"Try not to worry."

"I'm way behind on worrying about that boy. I worried about other things too long."

"Don't blame yourself."

She shook her head. "You don't know. None of you goddamned men know." That was her final word on the subject.

After I'd left, I could hear her turning the locks behind me.

Chapter Five

Jubal Early was waiting for me when I pulled up at the River House. Jubal was a two-year-old liver and white English pointer. I found him at the vet, where his owner had dropped him off to be put down. "I'm tired of spending more time hunting for this dumb son of a bitch than hunting for birds," his owner said. "I've tried check cords and shock collars and everything I can think of, and nothing works. I'm through chasing him *and* feeding him."

I paid the vet what he would have charged for giving the dog a lethal shot and brought him back to the River House. There was plenty of room, and I needed some kind of company.

The River House was a sagging old structure that had been built by a man who made his living going to sea. It had started out small and then grown. It seemed like every time he came home from a long cruise, the sailor found a new baby and the need for another room. So he added to the house as he added to the family, and by the time he'd finished there were a dozen children and twenty rooms.

The children grew up and left home, but there was no way to shrink the old house. Finally, all the kids were gone, their mother was dead, and the sailor was too crippled with arthritis to go back to sea. He went to live in the retirement home for merchant seamen in North Carolina, and the house was left unoccupied and derelict for several years. He and his children couldn't agree on what to do with it.

Vandals—probably kids looking for a place to party—had broken into it repeatedly, breaking furniture, spray-painting the walls. By the time the old man died, the house was not fit for much more than the bulldozer or a spectacular late-night fire. I got it cheap at auction.

I'd spent so much of my life packed into small spaces with other men that the idea of all those rooms was irresistible, no matter what shape they were in. I'd had enough, forever, of concrete and steel, bunk beds and latrines. More than enough of the pressure that builds when you fill those spaces with men who are as dangerous and unstable as old dynamite. I'd spent years where *crowding* was the uppermost thing on my mind. Don't crowd another man. Don't let him crowd you. With twenty rooms, a man could bounce around.

Also, I figured to make some money on the place. I'm a pretty good carpenter, and I planned to spend a couple of years making the old house into a thing of beauty, with oiled wood floors, paneled walls, intricately molded windows. All the little touches. When it's finished, I'll sell it as a bed and breakfast or an inn and see a pretty good profit, if you don't count the cost of my labor, and I never do. It would break my heart.

Jubal had been sleeping when I pulled up. The sound of my tires on the oyster-shell drive woke him. He stretched and then trotted over and waited for me to open the door. He didn't bark or whimper. He wanted to be stroked and patted, but he has his dignity.

"How you making it, Jube?" I said, rubbing his ears and stroking his neck. He leaned easily against my leg.

"You getting plenty of rest? That's important on a hot day like this. You start moving around and over-exerting yourself, then you'll fall down and die with heat stroke."

Jubal followed me into the kitchen, which was just about finished, and waited while I filled his water bowl and got a cold can of beer for myself. It had been a long drive back from Tallahassee.

We walked out to the side porch that looks over the Perdido River, a dark, sluggish stream that is lined with saw-grass marshes and abrupt little ridges grown up with juniper and long leaf. A couple of miles downstream, the Perdido opens into a wide bay that eventually empties into the Gulf of Mexico. It is a tame, insignificant river, and there is something restful about sitting and watching it flow.

I sat on the porch step and put Jubal's bowl between my feet. He lapped at the water and then lay down on the grass. I took a long drink of beer to wash the taste of the road from my mouth. The surface of the river was as slick and dark as a pool of oil.

I had been watching the river for probably a quarter of an hour when the phone rang. "That'll be

Semmes," I explained to Jubal, "calling to see how I made out."

He barely opened his eyes. I went back to the kitchen to answer the phone.

"You've been gone all day," Jessie Beaudraux said when I answered. "I've called five or four times now."

"Drove to Tallahassee," I said, "doing a job for Semmes. How are you?"

"Drove and came back already?"

"I left early."

"I'm fine. What kind of job? Why don't you tell me all about it at dinner? I'll cook if you'll catch."

"I'll try. What did you have in mind?"

"I've got a taste," she said, "for some green trout. How does that sound to you?"

Green trout is what some Cajuns call largemouth bass. I'm told that in the old days, only the Cajuns would eat bass because bass live in fresh water and will eat anything, including frogs. People who were not Cajun thought that the only thing worse than eating frogs was eating something that ate frogs. Cajuns ate both.

"Green trout sounds good," I said. "Real good. But I can't promise anything. They'll be hard to catch in this heat."

"You can do it, Morgan," she said. "I got a lot of the confidence in you. I'll fall by your house about eight o'clock."

"See you then."

I whistled to Jubal, who came trotting around to the kitchen. "Come on, Jube," I said. "Let's go fishing."

He followed me down the path behind the house to the bank of a small slough that curled off the river like a section of gut. I kept a canoe and a juniper skiff there. Jubal stayed back, like I'd taught him, while I rolled the canoe over. Moccasins will curl up under it for shade, but there weren't any today. I slid the bow through the saw grass and picked up the old fiberglass fly rod that I had left in the skiff.

"OK, Jubal, mount up."

He splashed through the water and climbed into the canoe while I stood on the bank and held the stern. Then I climbed in and pushed off. I made a few strokes with the paddle, enough to carry us out of the slough and into the current, which eased us, almost imperceptibly, downstream.

"OK, Jube," I said. "What I need to do now is catch us a couple of those green trout."

I guided the canoe down into a little bayou where a deep, cold spring undercut the bank. There were usually some fish in there, drawn by the cooler water. I grabbed a handful of cattails and sat on them to anchor the canoe. Then I checked the hook on the popping bug. It was sharp enough to draw a bead of blood from the fat part of my thumb. I stripped off some line and made a cast in tight against the bank. Jubal tensed when the bug dropped onto the water. When a fish struck, Jubal barked. He had decided somewhere along the line—probably after seeing me miss some strikes—that it was his job to keep me alert. I set the hook, and the little bass quickly jumped, shaking his head and showing his creamy white belly and dark red gills. I got him into the canoe and onto the stringer quickly. Jubal moaned approvingly.

I made another dozen casts, and Jubal tensed each time, but there were no strikes, and I began to wonder just how far Jessie could stretch one small bass. Then Jubal barked, which was a good thing because I had taken my eyes off the bug to watch a small water snake slip into the river and swim in its eerie, undulating fashion across the current. I snatched back and set the hook and put another bass on the stringer.

"Good job, Jube. I appreciate you covering for me that way."

I turned the canoe back upstream and paddled to the slough. It felt good working against the slight resistance of the current, and I was actually sorry when it was over. I was stiff from spending the day behind the wheel.

I rolled the canoe over, stored the rod and paddle in the skiff, then stopped on the way back to the house to cut a magnolia blossom from a low branch on a tree in the backyard. The old sea captain's wife had spent much of her time, between children, working in the yard, planting trees and shrubs. Most of them were pretty far gone, but the magnolia still produced.

I cleaned the fish in a wooden trough, under a hand pump, then took the fillets inside and soaked them in milk. I fussed around for a few minutes, making sure that the kitchen was in order for Jessie, and I put the magnolia blossom in a bowl of water and then put the bowl in the middle of the kitchen table along with a hurricane lamp. When everything was in shape for our little candlelight supper, I left the kitchen to shower and change. Jubal and I were sitting on the porch, watching the river and the beginnings of the sunset, when I heard Jessie's car turn into the driveway. I felt a little surge of something at the sound, like a kid expecting a present.

She wore white shorts and a loose cotton jersey that was somewhere between orange and pink and suggested citrus. She was richly tanned, and her hair was dark as a raven's back. She smiled when I came out to meet her. Her teeth were strikingly white and not quite perfectly symmetrical, so her smile was just crooked enough that you noticed. She was beautiful without being flawless, not like one of those mass-produced models who look like they could have been milled, by the thousands, on some kind of computer-controlled machine.

"What about this evening, Morgan," she said, happily, "ain't it just *beautiful*?"

"Just about perfect, I'd say."

"Help me with these groceries," she said, "and then make me a strong one. Quick, so we don't miss too much of this sunset."

I went back to the kitchen and made Jessie her drink: bourbon and bitters with a couple of ice cubes. She had the Cajun taste for whiskey but as far as I knew always stopped in time. I got another beer for myself and went back to the porch, where she was watching the sun as it dropped toward the line of pines on the far bank of the river.

"Thank you, sir," she said when I handed her the drink. She put the glass to her lips and took a cautious sip. "Mmmmm," she said, smiling. "Now, that tastes just right. Tastes exactly like evening to me, you know what I mean?"

"Tastes more like corn whiskey and charcoal to me," I said.

"That's because you've got no imagination, Morgan. That's the only way you'll find what's hiding inside most things. You've got to use your imagination. Take it off the leash and let it roam."

"I'll try."

"Good. Now, did you catch me some fish like I told you to?"

"I did."

"Good for you, then. I like a man who goes out and does what I tell him to do. Now, why don't you sit here beside me while I enjoy this drink and this sunset. You can tell me about going to Tallahassee and what Nat Semmes has you working on."

I told her the whole thing, from the trip up to Sweetwater to Luther Jordan's mother, who had finished our conversation by saying that I was just like all the other goddamned men in the world and would never understand what she was trying to tell me.

"She's right about that," Jessie said. "You might think you understand how she's feeling, but you never will. Because it just ain't possible."

"OK," I said. "I'll buy that. But I was never interested in understanding how she feels in the first place."

Jessie smiled. "You just want to find her kid, am I right?"

"That's right."

"All this business about the feelings, that just confuses you, right?"

"I suppose so."

"But sometimes, you know, if you understand how a woman *feels*, then you can guess how she's going to act."

I shook my head. "I tried that one. Bonnie Jordan got so choked up talking about the boy that I thought maybe she had him with her and was hiding him. I waited for her to go to class. I was going to break into the apartment—if I could get past all the locks—but I decided that was too risky."

Jessie's face darkened. "Don't do anything like that, Morgan. *Please*. There's no job you can do for Nat Semmes that is important enough for you to go back to jail." Jessie had been one of my strongest supporters. No telling how many letters she'd written or how much time she had spent helping Semmes on my case. She did not approve of my work for Semmes, thought I was capable of "something better." I knew, but did not try to tell her, that the work for Semmes was not merely something I did. It was a part of who I am.

"Exactly what I thought," I said. "So when I left her place, I drove down the block and parked behind a gas station that had gone broke and watched her building. She came out after a while carrying a bag of schoolbooks, but all alone. So I waited a couple of hours, thinking maybe the kid would come out if she had him stashed in her apartment."

"Must have been some kind of hot, just sitting in that truck," she said.

"I'm here to tell you."

"And you didn't see the child?"

"Nope."

"So you thought some more about breaking in?"

"Right. But what I did, instead, was knock on doors in that apartment building and up and down the block and show anyone who answered a picture of Luther that John Fearson gave me. Nobody had seen him. I'm sure of that."

"And that surprised you?"

"I don't know if it surprised me, exactly," I said. "But that woman confuses me."

"How?"

"Well, she says she loves her child—and I believe her—but she gives the boy away. First to her mother and then, when that doesn't work out, to John Fearson. She even signs away custody."

Jessie smiled sadly. "And that confuses you?"

"Absolutely."

"That's because you are a man, and men think

simply. Men don't understand complexity and para-
dox. That's what accounts for most of the trouble in
this world."

"If you say so."

She laughed. "I do say so. I do, indeed. Now you
want to go inside and watch me fix supper, or do
you want to stay out here a little longer?"

The sun had gone down, and for a few minutes
the surface of the river glowed like a bed of cooling
coals and the sky turned deep, pure purple just before it went black. The martins had come out to feed
on the mosquitoes, which were beginning to swarm.
It was time to go inside.

Jessie cooked, and I set the table and did what I
could to help her. She rolled the fillets in some meal
and half a dozen different spices, with a heavy hand
on the cayenne pepper, then dropped them in a
cast-iron skillet full of hot oil. They sizzled and
turned yellow and curled slightly at the edges. She
turned them once, then took them out of the grease
and put them on a brown paper bag to drain. She
made some hush puppies that were about two thirds
Vidalia onion. On her way over, she had picked up
some sweet corn and big, red tomatoes. She boiled
the corn, sliced the tomatoes, and served it all up at
the little kitchen table that I had covered with a red
cloth.

I opened a bottle of wine that she'd brought with
her, poured two glasses, and we sat down to dinner.

"It's great," I said. "I didn't know you could
make a bass taste this good."

"Well, I'm proud you like it."

She looked serene in the candlelight, with her
hair brushed out so that it framed her face. She had
good features. Big eyes, a wide mouth, and razor-
thin creases in her cheeks from laughing. Some-

times when she came over to cook dinner like this, Jessie would stay the night. I never knew when that would be, and so far I had never tried to persuade her to stay when she wanted to leave.

After we'd finished, we cleaned the dishes and made coffee. She kept French market coffee in the kitchen. It was the only thing of hers in the house. She used my toothbrush and things in the morning after she'd stayed over. One of my old shirts if she wanted something to sleep in.

We drank the coffee on the porch, looking out at the gleaming black slick that was the surface of the river.

"It troubles me to think of a child like that," she said, sounding melancholy in a way I didn't recognize, "out there on his own, with all the things that could happen to him. They used to come to New Orleans. Every big city has them, I guess. Probably Los Angeles and New York are the worst, but New Orleans was bad enough. You'd see them on the street. Ten or twelve years old. They looked so used up, Morgan, like the pictures you see of those kids who've been bombed in some stupid war. All dead in the eyes."

"What can you do, though?" I asked.

"Find the boy," she answered.

She laughed. It was like a song on the night air. We stopped talking and listened to the whippoorwill that sang every night from a spot on the opposite bank of the river. His voice was the purest in a chorus of night sounds that included frogs, crickets, mockingbirds, blue herons, and an occasional bull alligator.

She finished her coffee and said she had to leave. She didn't say why. Maybe talking about the missing child had turned her blue. She had never yet stayed because she was feeling down and wanted company to bring her up.

I walked her out to her car and held the door for her. We said good night. She smiled without much conviction. "I'll call you in a couple of days. Maybe I'll cook some shrimp."

"Sounds good."

"I hope you find that boy, Morgan."

"I do too."

Chapter Six

I was up early, before the sun came over the tree line and while the air was still dry and cool. I pulled on some shorts and a pair of nylon shoes and went out to run.

I never knew which way I would go when I hit the highway or which way I would turn when I came to a road junction. This was just a way of asserting my bottomless freedom. There was a running track in prison, and the choice came down to clockwise or counterclockwise. For some reason, almost everyone ran clockwise.

I went out the driveway, crunching oyster shells under my feet, then turned onto the blacktop and headed east. The weak, gray light of dawn had gathered into a broad arc of orange that grew hotter and brighter as I ran. After a mile or so, the sun appeared, clean and distinct and perfectly geometric. I ran east as long as I could look into the sun and then turned off on another country road and jogged up a gentle incline for a mile or so.

There was a lush bean field on one side of the road; horse pastures surrounded by white fences on the other. A dozen quarter horses grazed behind the fences. The early morning light seemed to accentuate the separations between their hard muscles and give their coat an additional oiled luster.

Fine-looking animals, I thought, looked after by someone who takes his responsibilities seriously. He feeds these horses correctly, calls the farrier when he's needed, and keeps the fences up to make sure some horse doesn't get out on the highway to be run down by a speeding semi. Beautiful as they were, those horses were too dumb to comprehend any meaning in a sunrise except that it was time to eat and maybe move around a little to let the warmth of the sun play across those well-muscled bodies.

Inevitably, it occurred to me that the owner of this farm treated his horses better than a lot of people treat their children, who might, with a little help and some luck, look at a sunrise and see something new and grand instead of just another beginning of one more fearful day. It seemed like the Luther Jordans of the world ought to have at least a chance of that. Ought to be treated as well as some horse. But like the philosopher said, "Don't hold your breath."

I stirred up some crows that were roosting late in a stand of planted pines. They circled over me for a while, giving me a lot of indignant hell, like the crowd at a ballpark heckling the visiting team's star. I stopped running and made a few owl hoots. That got the crows even more excited. They hate owls for some reason. It was as though that star ball player had turned around and given the crowd the finger.

I turned off on another farm road and ran into a swampy bottom. I'd been out for about thirty minutes now and was sweating heavily. I made one more turn and cranked it up a notch for the last half-mile. Jubal was waiting for me when I came sprinting into the yard.

He looked at me like I was a goddamned fool.

"Jube, I promise you that I don't do it for my health."

I stripped and showered under a nozzle I'd rigged to a corner of the house. The water was cold, straight from the well, and it tightened my skin and took my breath away.

I went into the kitchen, dripping wet and naked, and peeled four peaches. They were as orange as the sunrise. I toasted and buttered some bread, brewed a small pot of coffee in one of those rigs that looks like an hourglass, and then, as a finishing touch, poured fresh farm cream over the peaches. I sat at the kitchen table and ate. The peaches were so good that it felt right, in a way, to be sitting there naked while I ate them. What I really needed, I thought, was an Abyssinian queen to feed them to me. I had a second cup of coffee and talked to Jubal, who lay on the kitchen floor watching me.

"Jube, I believe I'm going to have to leave you here alone again today."

I took a sip of coffee.

"I hate to do it but I know you'll cope."

Most days, I never left the River House unless it was to go to the hardware store or the lumberyard, and then I'd let Jube ride with me, up front. He liked to put his nose outside the window to feast on the scents.

"If I'm going to be late or gone overnight, I'll call

the Dahlgren kid and get him to come look in on you and put something in your dish."

I actually felt a flutter of guilt about leaving the dog alone all day.

"I'll make it up to you, Jube."

I finished the coffee, cleaned the dishes, and dressed.

It was a little after eight when I got in my pickup. It had been a good morning so far. I spent the rest of it driving out to Sweetwater Ranch to talk to Big John.

"Poor Luther," he said after we shook hands. "Poor little guy."

"Unless you can think of some other likely place he might have gone," I said, "I think you ought to talk to the police."

"Man, I should've been paying closer attention. I had my mind in the *wrong* place. Worrying about building gymnasiums instead of thinking about the boys."

Men like Fearson seem to believe that they have it in their power to control events, and when something goes wrong it is always because they blew it. I suppose some of it comes from football, where the other guy never makes a great run behind a great block. What happened is you missed the tackle.

"Nothing you could have done," I said. "Kids run away, even from happy homes. In my opinion, you should report it to the law."

"Man, I hate to do that."

"I know. But they have the manpower and the equipment. If the boy gets picked up or hurt, then his name might come up on one of their computers."

Fearson studied my face. I could see that his rational side was winning.

"I think you've got to report it, John," I said. "For the boy's sake."

He nodded.

"If you want, I'll keep looking for him too. There may be something else I can do."

"I can't pay you."

"Not your concern," I said. "I work for Semmes."

"He pays you?"

"That's right." I didn't try to explain the whole situation to him. I'd told Semmes, again and again, that I didn't want to be paid. That I owed *him*. But he wouldn't have it. So he wrote checks and deposited them in a tax-free account that drew some pretty robust interest according to the reports I saw. I never touched the account, and when Semmes asked me, one day, what I planned to do with the money, I said, "Nothing." Then he asked me if I had a will. I said I didn't, and no heirs, either, as far as I knew.

That meant the government would get the money when I died, Semmes said, and he knew I didn't want *that*. So we drew up a will that left everything to Ducks Unlimited, the Nature Conservancy, and a little outfit that tries to feed war orphans. Whatever I earned looking for Luther Jordan would go—eventually, and I hoped not too soon—to those good causes.

Fearson called the sheriff's office and was told a cruiser would be around. He could make his report to the deputy. While he waited, we talked.

"School was still in session when Luther left, right?" I asked.

"Yes," Fearson said. "But only for a few more days."

"Did you talk to his teacher?"

"No, I didn't think of it. I probably should have."

"Not necessarily."

"Yes. I should have done that. I get so busy sometimes, trying to keep everything going, that I don't think like I should."

"Don't worry about it."

"I should have gone up there, should have thought of it first thing."

"I'll do it," I said. "Today, if I can find her."

Fearson called the school for me. The faculty was in for a summer workshop. I left and followed Fearson's directions to a red-brick school building that was low and long the way they all are now. I liked the old two-and three-story buildings with the tall windows and the high peaked roofs. Just looking at those buildings made you think that learning was something magisterial. The new school buildings look grim and furtive. The only thing big and assertive on the school grounds was the football stadium. It made its intentions plain.

I gave my name to a secretary at the front desk and asked when the faculty meetings would break. She looked at the clock and said it would be another ten or fifteen minutes.

I waited in the corridor, between the banks of steel lockers. Without kids, a school is a pretty lifeless place. It brought back memories of barracks and cell blocks. Institutions I have known—a good title for my memoirs.

When the clock marked the hour, a bell rang, just as though the classes were full. But the corridor was not instantly teeming with students. Instead, one door swung open slowly, and two dozen adults stepped out of what must have been a conference room. I stopped a young woman and asked if she was Ruth Nolan.

"No," she said, "that's Ruth."

The woman she pointed to wore a navy-blue cotton skirt and a knit shirt. Her hair was short and dark, just over her ears. She had a sweet face that was just a little prim.

"Are you Ruth Nolan?" I said.

"Yes, I am," she answered nervously and looked around, as though to make sure we were not alone.

I introduced myself and said I was helping John Fearson look for Luther Jordan. Would she mind talking to me for a minute?

"No," she said, "not a bit. Why don't we go into my classroom."

There were posters and maps on the walls. Some of the posters encouraged the kids to try reading instead of watching television. Others warned them about drugs.

"Has anyone heard from Luther?" the teacher asked. She sat on the corner of her desk.

"Not yet."

She shook her head. "I couldn't believe it when he ran away. He didn't seem at all like that type of boy."

"When did you find out about it?"

"The principal sent a note down one morning. It said John Fearson had called to say Luther wouldn't be coming to school and that it looked like he'd run away."

"Did Luther seem any different just before then?"

She thought for a minute. "No. I don't think so. He was such a quiet boy. He kept to himself and was very polite. It would be hard to know if anything was bothering him."

"Did he ever get called out of class, for doctors' appointments or anything like that?"

She tapped a fingernail on the surface of her desk and thought. "You know," she said, "I do think there was something, just a few days before he left."

"What was that?"

"I'm not sure. He got called to the principal's office one morning and was gone for about fifteen minutes. Nobody ever said anything to me about it."

"That sort of thing happen often?"

"Yes. The students need to talk to their parents, or to the doctor, or meet with the guidance counselor. Sometimes they have to go to court," her voice went into a different register, one of disapproval. "They have to answer questions about drugs and that sort of thing."

"And you never know what it is?"

"The principal doesn't want us to know. He wants the teachers to look at their students as students, not as people who are being investigated for drugs or something like that. He wants the administration to take care of those things and for us to worry about the teaching." She plainly didn't agree with the program.

"Usually," she went on, "you find out anyway. The kids themselves will come back talking about whatever it was they were called out for. Of course, Luther wasn't that way. He hardly ever talked about anything. The poor child just never opened up."

"Was he a good student?"

"Yes. I think Luther was"—she corrected herself quickly—"*is* very bright. I think he could do better, but he's so shy and withdrawn that most of the time he won't ask questions, even when he doesn't understand the instructions. With most kids like that, I get on them. I tell them they'll never learn unless they ask questions. But I couldn't do that with Luther. I felt like it might make him draw up even tighter. I feel so *sorry* for that little boy."

She said nothing for a few moments, and it seemed awfully still in that empty room.

"Who would know why Luther was called out of class that day?"

"Marion. She's the receptionist."

"Well, thank you for talking to me."

"I'm happy to help," she said, looking out at the vacant desks, lined up perfectly for now. "I just pray you find that little boy."

Both Marion, the receptionist, and the principal remembered the day Luther had been called out of class. It was for a phone call from a man who had identified himself as one of John's assistants at the ranch. "We don't know them all," the principal said. "But we've had excellent relations with Mr. Fearson and the rest of his people. I had no reason to doubt he was who he said he was. I called the boy out of class."

"Did he talk privately?"

"No, but he might as well have. He said 'Yes, sir' and 'No, sir' several times and that was about it. When he hung up, I asked him if there was any trouble, and he said, 'No, sir.' I didn't press him and he went back to class. That boy had never given us a minute's trouble until then."

The implication was plain enough. Luther had caused trouble by disappearing. I was tempted to say something. The principal was like a prison warden in his way: he hated disruptions above all things, and for those who were at the center of them, no matter how innocently, he had no pity at all. But I didn't say anything. My indignation wasn't going to move him or anyone else. And I wasn't the one with the problem.

I thanked him, asked him to get in touch if he heard anything, and drove back to Sweetwater, where Big John asked all his volunteer help if they knew anything about a call to Luther at school. None did.

"I should have asked that teacher," he said. "We lost a *whole month* because I was too dumb to call her."

"It might not have helped," I said.

"We'd have known about that call."

"That call is probably a dead end," I said. "We don't know who made it. There's no way of tracing it. All we know now is that if Luther had a reason to run away, it might be connected to that call. I'll keep looking for him and I'll be in touch."

"You're right," he said. "Thank you and God bless you." He was in torment, and it was a confusing thing to see in a big, confident man. He was like a bear with an abscess. You wanted to help on the one hand, but you didn't want to get too close on the other. I was glad to leave the ranch, and I hoped that when I saw Fearson next I could bring him some relief.

Chapter Seven

It was two hours back to Nat Semmes's office. Pensacola had been a vital city until the businesses left for the big new malls on the perimeter of town. A few bars remained, where a merchant sailor could get drunk, cut, and rolled all in the same evening. Places where you could pawn a watch, sell a pint of blood, buy "adult" magazines, or eat a greasy grilled-cheese sandwich. There were also dozens of offices that belonged to lawyers. They hadn't moved because their business was in the courtroom, and the county courthouse had stayed put.

Semmes's office was on the top floor of a ten-story building that was about one-third abandoned. The people who remained enjoyed cheap rent, and so far as I could tell, had no interest in gentrifying the neighborhood. Semmes said he stayed because he liked the view. From his window, you could see all of the bay, the barrier island, and beyond that, the vast green surface of the Gulf stretching to the horizon. I suspect that a lot of Semmes's clients looked out the window while he talked to them about their troubles, and dreamed of sailing away to some new, clean, uncomplicated place. I'd had those exact thoughts when I first sat in that office.

I took the old, slow elevator, with its intricately carved-oak paneling, to the tenth floor, walked down the hall past the door with Semmes's name on it, and knocked at the private door to his office. It was after four, and Semmes usually let his secretary go early, then stayed around for an hour or so to catch up on his reading. I was fairly sure he'd be in.

"It's open," he shouted.

He sat behind an old partner's desk. He had taken his coat off, loosened his tie, and rolled up the sleeves of his blue cotton shirt. He was working his way through the three or four newspapers he read every day. Semmes studied the current world the way I ignored it—diligently. But he read his newspapers in the afternoon, which seemed unusual to me. He said that the morning was too good to waste on the news and that by late in the afternoon he knew, somehow, which stories he could afford to ignore. In the morning, everything seemed worth his serious consideration.

"Hello, Morgan," he said. "Be with you in just a minute."

"No hurry."

I sat in one of the chairs that faced his desk and looked over his shoulder at the view. The Gulf was calm; a single oil barge made its way down the bay, and I watched it while I waited for Semmes to finish the article he was reading. The paper spread out in front of him was *The Wall Street Journal*. This meant that he had finished *The New York Times* and the local *Astonisher*. He had either *The Miami Herald* or *The Atlanta Constitution* to go.

He did not appear to be concentrating very hard on what he read, but then, he never did. You could look at Semmes as he read his newspaper and think that he would not be especially smart, quick, or subtle. But he was all three and also exceedingly determined. This did show in his face. He is a sweet man, in the best sense of that word, with very little vanity in his makeup. His determination does not come from a need to assert himself through winning but from a few fiercely held beliefs. One of them, I think, is that the world is losing its hold on civilization. I'd heard him say once that when he thought about the world his children would live in he felt "like you do when you touch a snake." I don't understand him completely but I admire him entirely.

He finished the article and walked over to a little bar in the corner of the room. It was a sturdy, comfortable room. One wall was built-in bookshelves, floor to ceiling. The others were paneled in persimmon wood the color of ripe grain. Semmes's framed law degree hung on one wall.

He put a glass in my hand. It was filled with quinine water. He was having the same, with a little gin.

"Cheers."

I raised my glass and took a sip.

"So, how did it go?"

I told him about my trip to Tallahassee. He listened with his eyes half-closed and his face turned toward the window.

"You think she's telling the truth?" he said when I'd finished.

"Yes, I do." I wondered about the first husband but not enough to bring it up.

"Then where's the boy?"

"I don't know, Nat. But I don't like the possibilities."

"You talk to Big John?"

"Yes," I said, and told him about my trip that morning to Sweetwater Ranch.

"So the sheriff's department has it by now?"

"Right."

"Well, we can't count on much there."

"No?"

Semmes tasted his drink and looked out the window. "The modern world runs on incentives, Morgan."

I gave him a look to tell him I didn't understand what the hell he was talking about. He is comfortable with abstractions and enjoys making intricate distinctions. In a lot of ways, Semmes is a thinker. You could even call him an intellectual, though he would deny it.

"Yep," he said, "a couple of years ago, they even gave the Nobel Prize to an economist for discovering what everyone with a brain has known for the last fifty years. What he won the prize for is a theory that says people don't do things anymore because it is their duty or because it is God's will or even because it is the law. They do something because there is a payoff."

"Can't argue with that," I said. "But what does it have to do with the price of fish?"

"Everything," he said. "The police don't have any incentive to find a lost kid. There aren't enough rewards. It's not like one of those drug busts, where you get your picture in the paper. And it's not like bringing in some citizen who has been holding up banks or raping college girls. Those are high-profile cases. They bring rewards. You get a promotion and a raise. If the case is big enough, you might get on television. They could even write a book about you and turn it into a movie or a series. Now *those* are incentives.

"On the other hand," Semmes went on, "if you spend three months looking for a lost kid and find him on the streets of Jacksonville, nobody cares except the parents. You can't take that to the bank. Furthermore, it's depressing work. There is no adrenaline excitement in it. Nothing but grief and frustration. Those are *negative* incentives, according to the economics jargon."

"I see."

"That's all the long way of saying that you are probably not going to get much from the law."

Semmes turned my way and put his elbow on the desktop.

"Morgan, I'd consider it a favor if you'd stay with this thing."

"I already told Fearson I would."

"What did he say?"

"That he couldn't pay me."

"I'll take care of that," Semmes said firmly.

"Blow it out your barracks bag, Nat."

He grinned. "Something wrong with my money?"

"Not my kind of incentive."

Semmes laughed. "I'll drink to that," he said and emptied his glass.

I told Semmes I planned to see Luther's grandmother and his former stepfather.

"Why bother?" he said. "Neither of them ever gave that kid a reason to miss them."

"They gave him a reason to want to kill them, though," I said. "Especially the stepdaddy."

"Yeah, but the kid is only eleven years old."

"They start early these days, Nat. You, of all people, ought to know that."

"I do," he sighed. "Lawyer friend of mine has a sixteen-year-old right now that the prosecutor wants to try as an adult. Stabbed his girlfriend fifty-six times with one of those big goddamned slab-sided survival knives. You almost wonder why he decided to quit after fifty-six, you know what I mean?"

I nodded.

"He was probably cranked up about nine miles. Well, let me know if there's anything I can do."

"Sure."

"You're a gentleman to take this on, Morgan."

That was high praise from Nathaniel P. Semmes. I don't think he believed there had been more than seven or eight real gentlemen born since the end of the nineteenth century.

"Good luck."

"Thanks."

I went home, fed Jubal and myself, got to bed early, and was on the road to Pineville, Georgia, before dawn. I listened to the farm reports on the radio: beans were going down. We'd had plenty of rain when we needed it, and now we were getting lots of sunshine when we needed that. But I was betting that the heat would hold and bake the beans in the fields. My contracts were all for October and I was buying.

I crossed the Georgia line a little after seven and was in Pineville by seven thirty. I parked on the main street of town and ate breakfast at the Pineville Café. Eggs, sausage, grits, and coffee. The café was full of men wearing jeans and work shirts and nylon gimme caps with decals from the tractor

and tobacco companies. They all knew each other
and they talked about fishing. It was that time of
year. In a couple of months, they would talk about
football or hunting.

I finished my breakfast and drove around town
for a while, looking at street names and trying to get
a feeling for the place. It turned out that Bonnie
Perkins's mother lived in the old part of town. Not
the good part of old Pineville but not the bad part,
either. Just the old part. She lived in an in-between
neighborhood of clapboard houses with small yards
with camellia bushes and maybe some azaleas along
the walk. The neighborhood was a few blocks from
the slow-dying main street and closer than that to
the railroad track and the long-dead cotton gin. Cotton hadn't grown in the fields around Pineville for
more than a generation, and the trains hadn't run
for almost that long. But Bonnie Perkins had probably grown up hearing train whistles from her bed-
room window and feeling all the longings that
sound produces. I could remember the feeling myself, and the way it made leaving seem like the most
important goal in life.

The house looked all right. It could have done
with a coat of paint, but the yard was neat, and
there were curtains on the windows. In front of the
door was a mat that said WELCOME.

I knocked twice.

"Who is it?" The voice was strong and suspicious.

"My name is Hunt. I'm with an attorney, trying to
find your daughter."

"I have no daughter any longer," the voice came
back.

"It's her son I'm looking for, actually."

"Luther?" There was a change in the voice.

"Yes, ma'am."

"Just a minute."

The woman who came to the door was between forty-five and fifty. That caught me by surprise, even though it shouldn't have. If you start breeding at sixteen and your kid does, too, then you can be a grandparent before you hit thirty-five. Nothing to it.

This woman didn't try to hide her age. Or, for that matter, accentuate what was left of her youth. What had probably once been a pretty face had been made angular and severe, most likely by pain.

I introduced myself and showed her a copy of my To-Whom-It-May-Concern. She read it slowly and then studied my face as though she were trying to match it to a photograph.

"I don't know how I can help you, Mr. Hunt," she said bleakly, "but please come in."

"Thank you, Mrs.——"

"Wilson. I never remarried."

"Thank you, Mrs. Wilson."

"Can I get you a glass of tea? I have a pitcher made. And some fresh mint."

"Tea would be fine."

"Sugar?"

"No, thank you."

"Make yourself comfortable. I'll just be a minute."

I studied the living room while I waited. It was small and tidy and sterile. The old furniture was covered with gingham. There were cut flowers in a small vase on the coffee table, and the Lord's Prayer in needlepoint hung on one wall. No books or magazines anywhere in view.

"Here you are." She handed me a tall glass of iced tea with a sprig of mint and gestured toward an old wing chair. I waited until she was on the couch before I sat down.

"Has something happened to Luther?"

"He's run away. It's been more than a month now, and nobody has seen or heard from him."

She shook her head helplessly. The movement put creases into her neck.

"Has he been in contact with you?"

"No," she said and touched the corner of her eye. "No, he hasn't."

She looked at the floor and then at me and then sighed deeply. "I wanted to do what was best for that child. That is all I wanted to do. I messed up my own life before I was sixteen, and my daughter did the same thing. When she came to me with that boy, I knew it would be more than I could handle. But it would be worse if he stayed with her.

"My husband died just two years after we were married. I got a little insurance, but I had a baby, and I hadn't even graduated high school. I didn't know how to do anything. I never could get a good job, so I never had enough money. I work all day on my feet, clerking, just to make enough for me—this is my day off. How was I going to raise a young boy? Where was he going to get the raising and the discipline he needed? A boy needs a daddy. He needs a man to look up to and to discipline him.

"So when I saw a newspaper story about that man and his ranch, where he takes those boys in, I wrote to him and asked him if he'd take Luther and look after him. I thought Mr. Fearson would be like a daddy to him."

She shook her head again and took another little sip from her glass. "Now you say he's run away from Mr. Fearson's ranch."

"Yes, ma'am."

"Poor little thing."

"Have you been in touch with him since he went off?"

"He wrote me a postcard every now and then. I think they must make the boys write home, if they have anyone to write to. They were nice cards."

"He never said anything about leaving?"

"No. He always wrote about how he was happy and how he remembered me in his prayers."

"Mrs. Wilson, did you get any calls about Luther in the last month or so?"

"Calls?"

"Anyone who wanted to know about Luther for any reason? Because an insurance policy had come due, or maybe because the school district needed some information."

She thought for a moment.

"Yes, sir. I do remember there was one call. It was from a man. He said he was with the County Health and they were checking up to see what kids had been vaccinated for smallpox. I thought they were getting rid of things like that, but he said it was for a study and they really did need to know."

"What did you tell him?"

"I told him Luther wasn't with me anymore."

"Did he ask you where Luther was?"

"Yes, he did."

"What did you tell him?"

"I told him about Mr. Fearson's ranch. It seemed all right. He was with the county and all. Or maybe it was the state."

"Do you remember when this was?"

"I think I have it written down. I got a calendar next to the phone, and I write things down. I'm so tired at night when I come home, I just can't remember unless I write things down."

"Would you mind checking the calendar?"

"No. Wait here just a minute."

She left the room and returned carrying a little engagement book. It was the kind with a picture of flowers and an inspirational quote on every left-hand page.

The date she gave me was two days before the call Luther got at school, the week before he ran away.

The probability that these two calls were linked was high enough to matter.

"Do you think that call had something to do with Luther running away?"

"I don't know, Mrs. Wilson. It might."

"I don't see how it could. That man was with the county."

"You're probably right."

"I think they must have done something to Luther at that place."

"What?"

"I don't know," she said grimly, "and I hate to even think about it. But sometimes in the morning before I go to work I watch the television, and they'll have these children on who have been treated so bad in these day-care places that it just breaks your heart. You can't believe anyone could do that to a child. There was one in California where they made those children do all sorts of horrible things, and then they would have a devil worship where they would lie down in coffins and things like that."

"You think Luther might have been mistreated at Fearson's ranch?"

"Why else would he run away?"

"I thought you said his postcards were happy."

"They could have made him write them that way. Nobody really knows what goes on at those places until something bad happens and they decide to investigate. By then, it's too late. They ought to do something about it before there's trouble."

I nodded, wrote down Nat Semmes's office number, and got up to leave.

"I pray you find that child," she said. "And I pray that the people who made him suffer will be punished. Even though it isn't Christian to pray for that, I hope that the people who hurt him will suffer like he did."

I thanked her again and left without mentioning just how risky that prayer sounded to me.

Chapter Eight

I came up on Columbus in the late afternoon, hoping to find Luther Jordan's stepfather. I'd seen Columbus before, years ago when I'd come to Fort Benning to learn how to jump out of airplanes. A new city of shopping malls and franchise restaurants had grown up around the old grubby town that lived off soldiers and seemed to consist mainly of used-car lots, pawnshops, and bucket-of-blood bars.

The old part of town still existed. It looked sad and run-down, just like I remembered it.

For fifty miles, I'd been telling myself, over and over, to stay calm. There were all sorts of good reasons for keeping cool around Luther's stepfather. In the first place, it wouldn't do any good to slip out of control. I was here to find Luther, not avenge him.

So I breathed deeply and concentrated on a small spot of light the size of a half-dollar located at a point about an inch behind my eyes. It was a trick I'd learned from a weapons sergeant named Roosevelt Jackson who studied the disciplines for fifteen years on Okinawa. He had all the belts and said things like, "Keep the mind cold, Old Son. Recall that a hot fire quickly consumes itself."

So I felt remote when I pulled into the lot of a small steel building with no landscaping and a sign that said PERKINS' CONSTRUCTION. I told myself I wasn't going to get excited and lose control. I was going to talk to a man, and then I was going go find a barbecue place where I could eat supper.

The secretary took my name and said that Mr. Perkins was in. What was the nature of my call?

I told her it concerned a legal matter.

The secretary picked up the phone and whispered something into it. Then she looked back at me and said, "Just a moment."

It didn't take long. A man came through a door and looked at me and said, "I'm Johnny Perkins. You looking for me?"

I introduced myself and showed him my letter from Semmes. He read it carefully. His hands trembled slightly. He had curly red hair and his eyes were red, too, but that looked like a temporary condition—an ordinary, noncontagious hangover.

He handed the letter back without a word.

"Is there someplace we can talk?" I said.

"My office." He turned and led the way.

It was a plain office with a metal desk, telephone, and Rolodex. There were a couple of nice-sized bass mounted on the wall.

"Pretty fish," I said.

"What the hell you mean, coming in here, talking to my secretary about a 'legal matter'?"

"She asked me a question," I said, trying to focus on the light behind my skull. My voice was calm.

"Yeah, well, now she thinks I'm in trouble with the cops."

"I'd be happy to explain to her."

"Why don't you explain to *me* first?" he said, sitting behind the desk and reaching for his cigarettes. "Am I being sued or some such shit?"

"Not that I know of."

"Well, just what the fuck is it, then?" He lit his cigarette and tossed the pack onto the desk. He sucked so deeply on the smoke that I felt a pain in my own chest.

"It's about Luther Jordan."

Perkins rubbed at a spot just above his ear. "What's the matter? Kid get himself in some kind of trouble?"

"Not exactly."

"Well, whatever it is, it's not my problem. Go talk to the kid's mother."

"I tried that. She's missing." I lied to see where it would lead.

"Missing on about three cylinders, I'd say." He took another greedy drag on his cigarette and spoke as he exhaled. "She'll turn up. She always does."

"Have you heard from her?"

He shook his head slowly. "Nope. I've been lucky that way."

"What about the boy, have you heard from him?"

"Him neither."

"He's missing too."

He put the cigarette out in an ashtray already full of butts.

"That's not my problem. The kid has a mother. I was married to her but now we're divorced. I've got

enough on my plate without having to worry about
a kid I haven't seen in three or four years.''

"You gave him something to remember you by,
though. Didn't you?'' I couldn't help myself. My
voice sounded remote to me, but I was boiling, and
my body suddenly felt much too small to contain
what was inside.

"What's that supposed to mean?''

"He's half-blind, thanks to you.''

"*That* was an accident,'' he said quickly. How
many men could admit to beating children?

"Is that what you tell yourself?'' I said.

He glared at me. I think I was supposed to melt
under the heat of his evil eye, but I didn't feel anything. If he had to use his fists on a kid, he was
nothing at intimidation.

"Gonna whip my ass like you did Luther's, huh?''

"Listen you—''

"Shut up,'' I said. "If you've got to do something
with your mouth, stick a cigarette in it. Or your
thumb. You keep talking to me, and I'll knock your
goddamned eye out and make you eat it. I expect
you'd give me about as much trouble as Luther gave
you. Except you'd probably cry more.''

I stepped over to his desk, and when he tried to
stand up I popped him in the chest with the heel of
my hand. Hard enough to force the air from his
lungs and to knock him back down into the chair.
Then I leaned over the desk and got my fingers on
his neck in a spot where the nerves were clustered
against bone. I gave the spot a squeeze in the old
Oriental way, and he screamed.

I assumed that the secretary had heard the
scream and would call for the law or at least for
some help from around the office. So I got to the
point.

"Just tell me if you know anything at all about Luther Jordan. If you know where he is or where he might be or if you've heard from him or his mother in the last few weeks."

"No," he croaked.

"You call up anybody saying you were doing a survey on smallpox vaccinations?"

"No."

"You ever write the kid? Call him?"

"No."

"Probably didn't send him any money, either, did you, Perkins?"

He didn't say anything, so just for fun I gave him another little squeeze. He screamed again.

"In a better world, he'd come for you in a couple of years. I might go find him and start training him to do just that. Send him after you with a sharp knife and a pair of rusty pliers."

Perkins nodded. It was probably all that he could think to do to keep me from squeezing that nerve cluster again and sending the pain into the core of his body. There were tears coming down his cheeks.

I let go of his shoulder.

"Keep your eyes open," I said. "Because Luther will be around. You owe him an eye, Perkins, and he'll be coming to collect."

I left just as the secretary came into the office with another man.

"What's going on here?" the man said.

"I'm not sure," I said. "I was talking to Mr. Perkins about a legal matter, and all of a sudden he started complaining about a pinched nerve. Probably stress."

They went in to check on the boss, and I walked out to the truck and drove away feeling like a goddamned idiot.

* * *

It was nearly midnight when I got home. Even so,
I was up early the next morning so that I could
work out in the old mule barn behind River House
that I had converted into a gym. The smell of mule
sweat and mule shit had soaked deep into the dirt
floor and the untreated wood walls until there was
no way to get rid of it. Which was all right since I
liked the smell. I went right to work and lifted
weights for an hour and a half.

I wasn't doing it for my health or out of vanity.
Exercise had kept me from losing my mind while I
was in prison. I believe that if it hadn't been for
lifting weights and running laps, I would have killed
somebody: a guard, another inmate, the prison doctor, or maybe even myself. Mixed in with the sweat
and the fat and the lactic acid I burned off every day
as I went around the track or did my bench presses
there was a portion of rage and frustration. I never
got rid of all of it—you can't lift anything that heavy
or run that far. But I got rid of the surplus, the part
that makes you do crazy things.

By the time I got out, it was habit and I was comfortable with it. I didn't need any surplus rage outside, either. There was always something to make
the rage rise like a blister where you'd burned your
skin.

You could, for instance, run across someone like
Perkins. But that was yesterday. Now, this morning,
I was back home, at the River House. I'd had my
exercise and I felt fine.

After I had showered and dressed, I drank a cup
of coffee, read some, and then watched the river for
a while. Jubal Early sat next to me. I rubbed his ears
and he moaned with pleasure. Jube would have

been happy to pass the whole day that way, but I had things to do.

"You take it easy," I said to Jube before I left.

He stretched and looked at me with sorrowful eyes.

"I'll try to get back early," I said, "but don't wait up if I'm late."

Jube looked at me in a funny way, then walked over to a nice shady spot next to the front porch, lay down, and went immediately to sleep.

I drove into town and found Tom Pine at his desk.

"How you, Morgan?" he said when he saw me. "Come on in and sit."

Pine sat back in his chair, which he filled. He is six four and weights two fifty, more or less, depending on how hard his wife has been after him about his weight. His skin is as black and smooth as poured tar. His teeth are white as raw cotton, and his voice falls somewhere between a growl and a purr.

"I'm good, Tom, how about you?"

"I could get insurance," he said. "What brings you around?"

"I'd like to talk to you about a missing kid."

"Yours?"

"No. I don't have any."

"Is this official?"

"I don't see how."

He thought for a minute. "I'll talk to you," he said. "But not here." We were in the offices of the county sheriff. Pine is a lieutenant, nonuniformed. People used to say he'd gotten his job because of his color, but nobody said that anymore. He'd been with the department since he got home from Vietnam, where we had walked some of the same hills at different times. In his mind, the A-Shau Valley was a bond between us.

"Let's go somewhere for a coffee," he said. "I'm due for a break."

So I followed his unmarked cruiser half a mile to a little place that sold diner food: pork chops, turkey with dressing, and high-starch breakfasts. I had coffee. Pine had coffee and a piece of pecan pie. Pine loves to eat and he can put enough away to make *you* feel full. I'd seen him eat a bucket of Popeye's fried chicken for lunch, the spicy kind, and then ask about dessert. His wife told me once that she never baked just one cake. Always two, because Tom will routinely sit down and eat a whole chocolate cake.

"You ought to try some of this pie," he said. "It's special."

"Too early in the morning for me."

He took a bite and chewed. "Man," he said, "that there is *right*. They didn't make no mistakes."

I sipped my coffee.

"So what can I do for you, Morgan?" he said when he'd finished his pie.

I told him about Luther, only that he was missing. I left out what I'd done so far to find him.

"And you're going to try to find the kid?"

"Yes."

He shook his head in a slow, sad rhythm. "Don't do it, Hoss. Spare yourself the grief."

"Why?"

"Because you've got a better chance of finding out who really killed Kennedy *and* who the Tylenol killer is."

I didn't say anything.

"The lost-kid thing will break your heart, Morgan. That's a promise. I saw it happen to a cop I thought was so tough you couldn't drive nails into his hide. He spent six months looking for a kid, getting worse and worse, until the boss just pulled him off the case. Few weeks later, he turned in his badge. Month or two after that, he woke up one morning and killed himself."

He took a sip of coffee, then said, "At the end of a really bad day, the worst I feel is frustrated. I want to drop off at some kick-ass supper club and break somebody's ribs. But usually what I do is go home, and if my wife is through with work we have a beer together. We play with the kids for a while, eat some supper, and then I'm OK. It's just another day at the office. With missing kids, it's different. If you have a heart any bigger than your fist, you can't drink beer knowing that kid is still out there on the street somewhere. You feel guilty knocking back a Bud while the kid is getting it in the ass from some animal. Until you find that kid, you don't have any good days, the way I sometimes do when I come down out of the trees on some creep who has been holding up hardware stores with a sawed-off pump gun." He looked into his empty coffee cup and asked for a refill.

When the waitress brought it, he smiled at her and said, "That was some world-class pie."

"Proud you liked it, Lieutenant," the waitress said and moved on to refill other cups.

Pine shook his head, then turned his attention back to me.

"I appreciate the warning, Tom," I said. Then I told him about what I'd been doing, including the part about Perkins and the scene in his office. I knew Pine would sympathize. He'd been reprimanded once for jumping some prisoner's bones.

Pine and half the sheriff's department had been looking for this one for weeks. He seemed to like young mothers, and he carried a knife that he always used before he was finished. Pine had to be pulled off him. He told me later that he would have been suspended, "except I was the only tame nigger they had." He'd kept it on a short leash since then. But it was always there.

He nodded while I told my story. Then I said, "Can I ask you a favor?"

Pine looked at me for a while without saying a word.

"I knew I could count on you," I said.

"All right," he said cautiously. "What is it?"

"John Fearson reported the kid missing. Somebody in your outfit went out and took everything down. So I suppose that means it's an active investigation even if nobody is looking very hard or expecting very much."

Pine nodded in a sleepy, passive way.

"So I was wondering if you could just make a run at locating the boy's real father. Check with the army, maybe. It would take me forever, and I still wouldn't get anywhere without official status."

"You're talking about the GI who knocked up his mom?"

"Right."

He nodded.

"You see where I'm going."

"Oh, yeah," he said. "Indeed, I do."

"Could you check, then?"

"All right. I don't see how that could hurt. I'll call you in a day or two."

"I appreciate it, Tom."

"I'm not doing you any big favors. You'll probably

wear yourself out looking for that kid and never find him. Goddamned shame."

"Well, I appreciate it just the same."

"All right, then," he said, "if you're so grateful, what I'll do is let you get the check."

Chapter Nine

I spent the rest of the day building a new wall. I'd
found some tongue-and-groove black walnut and
had bought a couple of pickup loads of it. It was the
most beautiful wood I had ever seen. The color was
dark and rich and the weave of the growth rings so
graceful that it made you think of a woman's hair
moved by the breeze.

It was the kind of hot July day when the air
doesn't move and you can work up a quick sweat
standing still. I had taken my shirt off, and I kept a
large glass of ice water within arm's reach and
sipped it almost constantly. I was shedding the water like a saturated sponge. The radio was on, but I
couldn't seem to listen to it. My mind was on the
boy.

I worked through the morning, getting the wall
up without being on top of it. I measured each
board and checked the width of the studs and then

put the boards over the sawhorses and made my cuts carefully with a hand saw. And I still made one or two mistakes and had to put one of my beautiful walnut boards on the scrap pile, where I might find a use for it later on, maybe for framing.

I just couldn't stop thinking about that boy, trying to figure what I was missing. The idea that he was too insignificant even to leave a trail was insupportable.

In the afternoon, when the sun was down enough that the River House was in the shade, a car came up the drive, slowly, crushing oyster shells under its tires. It was Nat Semmes's Porsche. I put on my shirt and went out to meet him.

"Tell me some good news," he said. His face was tight as a fist, the way it looked just before he went into court.

"No good news," I said.

"Well, give me something to drink, and I'll tell you some bad news."

I went inside and mixed a gin and tonic for him and opened a beer for myself. When I got back, he was sitting in the wicker rocker looking out at the river. His expression hadn't changed.

"Health and all that other bullshit," he said and raised his glass.

We drank.

"You remember the pig-eyed kid out at Fearson's, the one who was in such a hurry to kick some ass?"

"Sure," I said. I remembered seeing the boy standing over the gentle, awkward kid whose face he'd bloodied. I also remembered thinking that he was on his way to jail somewhere.

"Well, guess what he has gone and done?" Semmes's tone was like a saw blade cutting a nail.

"Run away?"

"Oh, no. Much better than that. Guess again."

"I'm not much good at guessing games, Nat. I give up."

"OK." Semmes sighed, and tasted his drink. "And anyway, you were right. He *has* run away. That is the good part. The bad part is that he has gone out and found himself a lawyer. He is suing John Fearson and Sweetwater Ranch."

"For what?"

Semmes shrugged. "Lots of things. It's all in the usual mumbo jumbo. Repeated humiliation, intimidation, and excessive use of force causing prolonged and extreme emotional suffering and so on and so forth."

"How much?"

"Chicken feed by today's standards. Kid wants a mere three and a half million."

"Can he get it?"

Semmes shook his head. "Not from Big John, even if a jury finds for the kid. John doesn't have three *hundred* lying around loose. Every dollar that touches his fingers goes right back into the ranch."

"So they'll take the ranch if he loses?"

"I suppose they could," Semmes sighed. "But marginal farmland and cheap apartment buildings aren't exactly scarce around here. The kid and his lawyer have bigger fish to fry."

"I don't get it."

"Well, the papers, which were served last night so I could miss my supper to stay at the office and read them—those papers name Sweetwater and John Fearson, of course. But that's just for openers. They go on to mention the sponsors of Sweetwater, the people who make the big donations and sit on the board. Those are the people with deep pockets, and that's who the kid and his lawyer are after."

"They'll be on trial too?" I asked.

"Oh, sure, they've got some *exposure*, as we say in the trade. But it doesn't have to go to trial. A trial is probably the last thing that kid's lawyer wants. He'll be looking for a settlement."

"John doesn't strike me as the sort of man who'd go for a settlement."

"No. And neither am I." Semmes's blood was up. He was ready for a fight, half-afraid he wouldn't get one.

"So?"

"The board of directors at Sweetwater—those men are all good citizens, prominent men. Been here forever. I know them all, and I'd go partners with any of them. But this isn't their fight. The only thing at stake here, for them, is money. A trial would be expensive and inconvenient. And they'll be insured against this kind of thing. The insurance company has *nothing* at stake except money. The kid's lawyer could make a settlement look just too good to pass up. Happens all the time."

"Sounds like a shakedown to me," I said.

Semmes grinned. "Those are fighting words, Morgan. Especially around a trial lawyer."

"Well, say it does go to trial. Can you win?"

"Depends on the jury. And the lawyer."

"What about him, then? He any good?"

Semmes sighed heavily. "I don't know. Never heard of him before last night. His name is Edward Straylow, and he comes from Panama City. Used to be I knew every lawyer in this part of the state, but now I can't even keep up with those in town. Phone book is full of them. The law schools turn them out like factories stamping steel. There are more lawyers than there is work for them to do, so they circle these personal-injury cases like buzzards over a road kill. All of them hoping for the big score, like these folks who line up at the minimart buying tickets when the lottery gets up to fifty million.

"Anyway, I'll find out soon enough if he's any good or not. I'll tell you what, though. It doesn't make any difference how good he is, he'd better buckle his chin strap."

Semmes looked out at the river. It was ink black and smooth as polished steel. There was no breeze yet to ripple it.

"You said two things—the lawyer and the jury." I couldn't imagine anyone would believe the punk I'd seen out at Sweetwater over John Fearson, especially with Nat Semmes asking the questions and making the arguments.

Semmes turned away from the river. "Morgan, when I first got started in this business, I thought the jury was the last stronghold. I *knew* about lawyers and judges. I'd been around them all my life, been to law school with them. I knew they could make the law jump through all kinds of flaming hoops. But I still believed that twelve good and true citizens would use their common sense and come to the truth."

"What happened?"

He shook his head. "Well, I saw a couple of juries come back with rulings that were incomprehensible. It was like they had retired to their little room and started throwing goat bones and studying chicken guts to decide on a verdict.

"But"—Semmes smiled darkly—"I hung in. Kept the faith. Figured it was my fault. I wasn't *reaching* those juries, for some reason."

He took a sip of his drink. The last. He reached into the glass with his finger, probed around among the ice cubes, and fished out the wedge of lime. He ate it, made a face, and then went on.

"Then it all came to me one day. I was in the grocery store picking up some things, and I got in line with my cart. It was one of those days when they've got one register out of eight working, and the girl who's running it can't chew gum and count at the same time. I was about tenth in line.

"I watched, Morgan, and half of the people ahead of me picked up a copy of *The National Enquirer* and bought it, along with the frozen pizza and the Diet Coke. *Half* of 'em.

"That's when it came to me. When you pick a jury, the short odds are one of your people is going to believe that Raquel Welch is a space alien and that eating peach pits will cure cancer. Forget standards of proof and precedents of law and all of the rest of that high-sounding stuff. You can sell a jury *anything.*"

Semmes sighed again, then tilted his glass and let an ice cube fall into his mouth. He chewed it angrily. It sounded like grinding glass.

"Man, but I feel for John Fearson," he said. The words were thick, probably because his tongue was cold. But it could have been from feeling. For a lawyer, Semmes was an awful sentimentalist. "That ranch is his life."

"Is he innocent, Nat?"

Semmes smiled the dark smile again. "Details, details," he said.

"Do you know?"

He sighed. "John Fearson disciplines those boys. He puts up with no lying, back talk, stealing, fighting, or shirking. He's hard on them. A lot harder than most parents have the guts to be with their own kids. But I'm convinced he doesn't hurt them. They get punished when they do wrong. He'll spank them with a big leather belt, and that's something I've never done to my own kids. But there are a lot of parents, probably, who wish they had done that to their kids while there was still time. In a way, the discipline, even if it is hard, is the biggest favor John does for most of these boys.

"What most of them had before they came to Fearson's ranch was different. There weren't any rules. Either they got the hell beat out of them for nothing at all, or no matter what they did nothing ever happened to them."

"OK," I said.

"Let me put it this way," Semmes went on. "When I started out, I was a prosecutor. A pretty good one, too, if I do say so. Probably because I believed I was doing something that needed to be done, doing my duty, which is a quaint notion, but I couldn't help myself. After a couple of years, though, I quit. You know why?"

"No."

"I quit because of an *attitude*. I'm kind of fussy that way; the other prosecutors thought I was a wimp. The attitude that poisoned it for me was really easy to put in words. You heard people articulate it all the time. 'Any good lawyer,' they'd say, 'can convict a guilty man, but it takes a real stud to convict an *innocent* man.' I just couldn't take that. Didn't have the stuff, I suppose. And," he said, looking at me emphatically, "I haven't changed because I'm working for the other side. I don't try to get guilty men off."

"Then I'm in," I said. "What do you want me to do?"

"Well," he said, beginning to pace with purpose and rhythm, "the first thing is to nail the kid. I mean, put his hide on the wall."

Chapter Ten

Jessie wore a white cotton dress that buttoned up the front, with the top three buttons open so you could see where the line of her tan changed to pale white skin. She looked cool and desirable.

We sat in her big, bright kitchen among a number of hanging plants and copper pots, pans, and utensils. It is the kind of kitchen where you look around and know right away that you are in the home of someone who likes to cook and is good at it.

She had boiled some shrimp, with the heads still on, in a pot of salt water and spices. The shells were scalded pink, and the cayenne and other spices clung to them like dark red scales. She had made a sauce from some of the same dark, earthy spices. She also had cold beer in chilled mugs.

"I want to tell you," I said, chewing on one shrimp and peeling another.

"Good?"

"Better than that."

"The boy who sold them to me said these shrimp were still swimming when the sun rose this morning."

"And the sauce," I said. "Can't forget that."

"You like it?"

"Never had anything like it."

"I'll show you how to make it sometime. Nothing to it. Take you four or five minutes." She peeled a shrimp with the long, pointed nail of her index finger, then held it up and examined it like a jeweler studying a stone. Then she dipped it in the sauce, popped it in her mouth, and chewed. A little bead of sauce clung to the corner of her mouth, and she flicked it away with her knuckle.

I poured more beer for both of us and looked at my watch.

"Time yet?" she said.

"Pretty close. Maybe we ought to move this into the other room."

I'd come to Jessie's house to watch the news since I don't have a television. There had been at least one set going constantly in prison, until it seemed like the metallic signal bounced directly from the ionosphere into your skull. After months and months of it, suddenly not hearing that sound was the sweetest possible relief.

But Nat Semmes had said that there was something on Sweetwater and John Fearson scheduled for the evening news and that I might want to see it. I called Jessie and she said to come over. When I got there, she was putting the shrimp on the table.

Watching the news makes me feel like I've become one of those people who wait around the site of a car wreck until the ambulance has gone. The first segment on the local news was about a fire in a housing project. A welfare mother and her two kids had burned to death. After the shots of the gutted building, there was an interview with a weary, wet fireman, who said it looked to him like the fire had started where some wires had been stripped of their insulation.

"Might have been rats," he said.

When the reporter finished with the fireman, he interviewed the mother of the dead woman—grandmother of the two dead children.

"All I could hear," she said, "was them babies screaming."

I concentrated on the beer and shrimp for the rest of the broadcast, an entire half hour of car wrecks, drug busts, plant openings, golf tournaments, and weather.

There was not a word about Sweetwater.

"I guess Nat got it wrong," I said. I stood up to turn the set off.

"I wonder if he meant the national news," Jessie said.

"Seems like they'd have better things to report."

"Let's just watch for a few minutes and see."

"All right," I said and got myself another beer and sat back down to watch. My eyes were on Jessie more than the screen. The dress had billowed a little around her shoulder, and I could see where her body went from the sharp ridge of her collarbone to the soft roundness of her breast. I felt something catch inside me, like a nerve had been touched so delicately that at first you didn't know if the sensation you felt was pleasure or pain.

The network news came on with a few somber notes from some classical tune. The anchorman appeared and he delivered his lines with gravity. Five people had been blown away in Paris when some creep left a bomb in a café.

A senator with a forty-dollar haircut charged that another senator with a forty-dollar haircut was insensitive to the plight of the poor. The second senator denied the charge. Both haircuts had their eyes on the White House.

Twenty minutes into the broadcast, immediately after an aspirin ad, the anchorman went into a new register of gravity.

"There are reports tonight," he began, "that a former football star has been abusing children at a camp he established using his fame and reputation to raise money and win government approval. We have the details from . . ."

He was replaced on the screen by some footage of Sweetwater Ranch, shot from the highway, the way you would film a prison or a high-security base—someplace where you were a little nervous about getting too close. The reporter's voice supplied some stuff about how long Sweetwater had been in existence and how many boys lived there and how they came tó be there in the first place. This was followed by some old clips of John Fearson playing football, including the famous game that he played with a broken leg.

Then the narrator's face appeared, and he said, in a hushed voice, "But today, John Fearson may be up against the toughest opponent he has ever faced. And the stakes will be higher than any he has ever played for. More than a championship is on the line. More than individual honors like those he won in both college and the pros. More than money. For John Fearson, what is on the line this time is—his reputation.

"What is also on the line," the reporter con-
cluded, "is the fate of fifty young boys."

This was followed by an interview with the lawyer
for the kid who was suing Fearson. Edward
Straylow sat in his office with a wall of books behind him. He looked and talked like the forty-dollar
haircuts who were running for president.

He had small, suspicious eyes set deep in a long
face with conspicuous bones, and his mouth was
tight and humorless, though he had a way of forcing
it to smile when he was asked a question. There was
something slightly predatory about the smile. His
expression, when he listened to questions, was intent and intelligent, but he was plainly the sort of
man who considered thinking a contact sport and
did not stop looking for some kind of advantage, a
small edge, until he went to sleep at night. His eyes
never relaxed.

He wore a suit and tie, and you could see that he
paid some attention to his clothes. The tropical
khaki suit jacket fit him perfectly and was no more
wrinkled than a windowpane. His tie was knotted so
that it covered his collar button, and the base angles
just touched the collar flaps. A precise half-inch of
shirt cuff showed at the end of each jacket sleeve.
But he didn't look comfortable in the suit; he looked
like he was working at wearing it.

His hands were restless and moved almost constantly. First one hand would pick at the thumbnail
on the other, then reach up to tug at the thick lobe
of an ear, then rub the beveled edge of his chin as
though he were checking to see if he'd missed a
place shaving. He radiated impatience.

"We're talking here about a pattern," he was saying urgently. "A pattern of force, abuse, and excess
that should not be tolerated in the marines, much

less at a camp for disadvantaged youngsters licensed by the state and funded by some of the most influential people in this part of the country. We're asking for damages for my client, for pain and suffering, and also for punitive damages. But there is more to this case than justice for one boy who has been injured, physically and psychologically, at this camp by this man. There are literally dozens of other boys out there. No doubt some of them have been mistreated but were afraid to come forward.

"We're hoping that by making this case we will force the responsible authorities into appropriate action. There should be an investigation, and there should be steps taken to make sure that this sort of thing does not happen again."

Several questions were shouted at Straylow. He smiled like a fox showing its teeth in warning and nodded to someone who repeated the question "What form did the abuse take? Was it sexual?"

"We don't have any reports of that, so far," Straylow said, leaving that door open and giving Big John no slack, which they called presumption of innocence in the trade.

Then, what *specifically* did he have reports of? a reporter insisted.

"Physical punishment," Straylow said, touching the back of his neck. "Frequent and very severe physical punishment."

Spankings, in other words, I thought. Lawyers could make simple trespass sound like an armed invasion.

Had it been going on for a long time? another reporter wanted to know.

"Yes" Straylow sighed. "I'm afraid so."

Did he think there had been a cover-up?

"Well, you're talking about a very popular figure

here, in this part of the world. He has a lot of friends, and some of them have quite a bit of influence."

The camera cut from Straylow's face to the correspondent's. He looked concerned, as any good citizen would.

"Just after that press conference," he said, "in an exclusive interview, we asked John Fearson to respond to those charges."

Now Big John's face came on the screen. He looked puzzled, the way someone would after hearing for the first time that he had cancer. When the reporter asked him if he'd ever abused any of the boys at Sweetwater, he shook his big head and said, "No, sir. We love them boys. That's why we're here. That's why *they're* here."

"And you've never used physical force on them?" the reporter said.

"I've never tried to hurt the first one of these boys. Everything I've done has been to help them."

"But have you ever punished them physically?" the reporter insisted.

"Yes," Fearson said uncomfortably. "Boys get spanked, sometimes, when they break the rules. But we've never tried to physically hurt anyone."

"You're saying that spankings don't cause physical pain?"

"It hurts their pride mostly," Fearson mumbled.

"And how do you explain these charges, then? What motive does this young man have for bringing suit?"

"I don't know."

"Are you saying that he's lying?"

Fearson glared into the camera. You could tell that he would have enjoyed shivering the reporter's skull, but that was against the rules of this game.

"I think he's confused."

"Then, you think you will be exonerated?"

"For sure."

The camera left Fearson and came in close on the reporter's face. "For now," he said, "it is merely an allegation. But it could turn out to be much more than that. It could be one act in a tragedy in which a self-styled defender of the weak and the innocent turns out to have been their tormentor."

Jessie turned the set off. For a moment or two, we sat in the silence.

"Well," she said finally, in a soft voice, "what do you think?"

"I don't think he helped himself," I said. "But there probably wasn't any way he could have."

"Do you think he's guilty?"

"Of what?"

"Hurting those boys."

"No."

"Are you sure about that, Morgan?"

"I saw him get a little rough with the kid who went to the lawyer. And he might have gotten even rougher later on. But he wasn't *abusing* the kid."

"Funny they didn't show the kid," she said, after a long silence.

"His lawyer probably wouldn't let him go on the air," I replied. "He's the boss. I'm sure the kid would have loved it."

"What happens next?"

"Nat Semmes is going to help Fearson keep his ranch."

"And you're going to help him?"

"Yes."

She stood and stepped away from the couch where we'd been sitting.

"Maybe he should lose it," she said.

I looked at her.

"Old methods, Morgan. And old values. Maybe John Fearson isn't right for these times. Maybe you're backing a losing cause."

"It wouldn't be the first time."

She shook her head and narrowed her eyes. "I mean it."

"OK," I said. "But if Fearson isn't right for these times, then who is?"

"Trained people," she said. "Educated people. People who work under some kind of supervision. John Fearson is a football player, and maybe that's not the right background."

"You believe in the experts?" I asked quietly.

"I suppose *you* don't."

"Nope." I'd seen the experts up close. They came to work in the morning, and they went home at night. They typed up their reports at the end of every week. They met their projections and they filled their quotas. Meanwhile, the war was being lost, the men in jail died one more dismal death, and the world at large slid a little further down the pole. But I wasn't going to get into that with Jessie.

She was looking away from me now, through one of the big double-pane windows in her living room and out at the yard, which was full of camellias, azaleas, dogwood, and gardenias. Only the gardenias bloomed now, in the summer heat. Gardening was Jessie's passion. She had moved here to grow things after she got rich during the oil boom. She had the sense to get out early, and now she had this house and the yard of flowers. She dedicated herself to causes—I had been one of them—and to growing beautiful things.

"It just seems like you're taking his side awfully quick, Morgan. Just because he's a big man with a strong handshake and a football career behind him.''

I shook my head. "I've been out there. I've met him. And I talked to Nat Semmes. I asked the same question you're asking."

"Well, he's going to be a certain way around you. That isn't the way he is going to be around me, necessarily, or with kids. You know what I mean, Morgan?"

"Yes," I said.

"Just go careful, please. On my account. Don't back something on a hunch and then stay on it because of your pride. That's how men do."

I nodded.

"Study things and be sure. Leave it alone if it doesn't look just right."

"All right," I said. "I can promise that." I wondered what had set off her alarms. "Thanks for having me over," I said.."And for the shrimp."

She smiled. "Sure."

"I ought to get back."

She nodded. She looked fragile, standing there in her white cotton dress. I hated to leave.

"But maybe," I said, "you would like to go for a moonlit cruise."

She smiled with more conviction this time. "Now, that sounds like a fine idea."

"I'll be back in about an hour."

"I'll be right here."

I drove home and fed Jubal Early. He was happy to see me but even happier to see something go into his bowl. While he ate, I called Nat Semmes at home.

"Hello," his wife said.

"Hello, Bobbie, this is Morgan."

"Well, Morgan Hunt. How the hell are you? Why don't you ever come around?"

"I don't know," I said. "I sure miss seeing you and your kids."

"Well, get yourself over here, then."

"I'll do it. How's Nat?"

"He's been better. Want to talk to him?"

A few seconds later, Semmes was on the line. He spoke with the kind of tight anger he used on a lying witness. "You see it?"

"Yes, I did. What happens now?"

"I'm going to defend John Fearson in a court of law."

"What are your chances?"

"Too early to tell. But I'll promise you this: when it's over, they'll know they've been in a fight."

"What can I do?"

"Find out what you can about the little creep, for starters. His name is Rick Hewes, and before he went to Sweetwater he lived in Columbus."

Semmes gave me an address, the last one John Fearson had for the boy's mother. I wrote it in my notebook.

"I'll get on it tomorrow."

"Fine. Now Bobbie is signaling me to tell you that you'd better drag yourself over here soon."

"Tell her I'll do it."

"See you."

I hung up. Jubal was finished with his supper and ready for some affection. So I rubbed his ears and scratched his brisket for a while. He moaned, in a satisfied way, and I felt momentarily bad for leaving him alone. But that passed. Dogs do fine, with or without company.

Jubal followed me outside and watched while I rolled the canoe over. I got a grip on the thwart and dragged it across the already wet grass and slid it into the water. I loaded a paddle, two old kapok cushions, a flashlight, and a cooler with some ice and a few bottles of beer.

Jubal moaned loudly when I pushed off and started paddling upstream against the negligible current. I could still hear him barking when I was half a mile upriver. I was making easy strokes that seemed to follow on each other without my even thinking about them. It was a sweet rhythm.

The moon came up on schedule, and Jessie and I watched it wordlessly from the middle of the river. For the first minute or two, the moon seemed improbably close and brilliant.

"You know," Jessie said when the moon was fully above the tree line and the sense of its rising had passed, "if you could take that show on the road, I believe it would purely go." Her voice was throaty and Cajun now. She could give it another texture for business, but when she was off duty this was the way she talked. I loved the sound.

We stayed on the river for an hour or two. She told me about nights like this that she could remember from when she was a little girl growing up in a wet, sparsely populated parish west of New Orleans.

"Those were some good times, Morgan. Even if I was too stupid to know it back then. We had everything a body needs. Plenty for the soul, too. Seeing that moon puts me in a mind of those days. Sure does. You know what's funny?"

"What's that?" I took a stroke with the paddle, just to keep the canoe lined up with the current. I didn't care where we went.

"What's funny is we thought we were poor. You know, like *po'*."

"Were you?"

"I suppose maybe we were, if you measured it in the ordinary way. We sure weren't rich. We ate some muskrats and coots. We ate alligator tail, and we ate a lot of crawfish before rich people found out about them. But we were never *suffering* poor. You know what I mean?"

"Sure."

"But everybody was convinced that we had to get rich. And some of us did. Oil, mostly. And when I was rich, I used to sit in my office in New Orleans missing the days when I was poor. I still miss those days some, Morgan. I come from a big family. Five brothers and sisters and so many cousins I've lost count. And even with all those mouths, we always had plenty to eat. That's what I remember about our house: there was always some good smell coming out of the kitchen—"

She stopped abruptly and looked at me. "Morgan, I hope you understand why I worry about you."

"I do."

"Then I can understand why you want to keep looking for that boy."

"I just hope we find him," I said.

"I do too. I feel it especially tonight."

We drifted for a while. Jessie hummed a tune softly. I didn't recognize the song, but it was simple and a little sorrowful.

I could have stayed out on that river all night. It was the kind of thing I had dreamed of, through many agitated nights behind the wire. But after a while, Jessie stopped humming and said, "Morgan, why don't you crank up the engine? Let's get on downstream to your house and get into bed."

Chapter Eleven

"We got something here on your man," Pine said. "Got it from the army, and that is like pulling teeth. I hope it's worth it."

It was nine o'clock. I had just gotten back from taking Jessie home.

"Tell me about it," I said.

"He was in the army until a year ago. Kept reenlisting, but all of a sudden he decided not to go for his twenty and took a discharge. Twelve years in and an SFC."

"Uh-huh."

"I don't understand that. Seems like if you are going to live the green life for twelve years, you might as well stay for twenty and get the retirement. This way, all he gets is an 'attaboy' from a grateful government."

"And VA college benefits," I said. "Don't forget that."

"Oh, absolutely not."

"Where was he when he got out?"

"Fort Benning. You remember the place?"

"Believe I do."

"He was assigned to the Ranger School. I called there and talked to the colonel in charge. Turned out he'd been a lieutenant in the Hundred and Worst. We talked a little about old times in the central highlands.

"Anyway, I finally got around to asking him about Sergeant William Luther Jordan, and he told me some interesting things.

"Jordan was the senior NCO on the Survival Committee. He'd come to Benning after that little Grenada thing, where he got a bad one in the leg. The school assignment was supposed to be light duty while he convalesced, but according to the colonel he jumped on it like a dog on the meat wagon. Turned himself into an expert on survival.

"The colonel said that Jordan literally rewrote the manual. And he wasn't just a classroom guy. He could flat *do*. They used to put him out in the bushes somewhere, and he'd have nothing but the clothes he was wearing. He'd tell the troops to come find him in a week. They'd do it, and he'd ambush them just to show them he could keep security while he was staying alive. Then he'd take them into his camp. He'd have a low-smoke fire going for cooking, plenty of water that he'd purified, some kind of animal that he'd killed and turned into a stew that would be simmering in a pot he'd made out of a turtle shell. He'd have the hide stretched out and brain-tanned. He'd show them a knife and a hatchet that he'd made out of stone. A dugout canoe. Bones made into fishhooks. Medicines that he'd made out of roots. Dude was red-hot, according to the colonel."

"So why did he quit?"

"Hey Morgan, this *is* the army we are talking about."

"Uh-oh."

"Right. Jordan had been doing the survival job for about five years when one day a message comes down from the Pentagon. They wanted to transfer him. The colonel wrote letters saying it would be a waste of Jordan's talents to put him in any other job. Army sent back tough-shit forms with all the official signatures. So the colonel flew to Washington to make his case. The army gave him a little slack: said he could have a civilian billet as a survival instructor, and if Jordan wanted to get out of the army but keep on with what he was doing he could have the job. But if he wanted to stay in uniform, he was going to have to transport his ass, bag and baggage, out to Kansas, where he would be platoon sergeant in a leg division."

"And Jordan told them where to put that, right?" I said.

"Sure. Colonel said Jordan cried when he filled out his separation papers."

"Did he know what Jordan was going to do on the outside?"

"No. He said he could talk to some of the guys Jordan worked with and find out if they had any ideas. Maybe one of them would have even stayed in touch. I told him I'd get back to him. I thought maybe you'd like to ask those questions yourself."

"I think so."

"Well, say hello to Benning for me."

"I will. And thanks for all this information."

"Glad to do it," Pine said. "Give me a call when you get back, let me know how you made out."

I packed a bag and called the Dahlgren kid, who lived up the road and did some work for me now and then. I asked him to look in on Jubal for me, told him I'd pay him, and he said he'd take care of it. I pulled out of the driveway and started for Columbus, a place I had never expected to see again after jump school and that I was now visiting for the second time in less than a week.

The drive took most of the morning. A little after noon, I was driving down a rutted dirt road to the trailer park where Rick Hewes's mother lived.

There were about thirty trailers laid out randomly along a lopsided grid. I turned the corners looking for the correct number and studied the place as I went. Most of the trailers were the long, narrow kind—this neighborhood was too poor to support double-wides—and you could read the character of the occupants by the landscaping and the things left lying around the yard. The yards were mostly bare earth or a patch of weeds. They looked like they had been left over after a distress sale.

It was hot. There were a few cars parked on the street, but no people in sight. The trailers were buttoned up tight with their air conditioners straining to keep them cool. There was a steady background noise in the air: the hum of thirty compressors.

I found the number I was looking for. Even for this neighborhood, the trailer and the yard looked bleak. It was a yard that would have been improved by an old Buick resting on blocks.

I walked to the door, stood on the cinder block that served as the front step, and knocked, loudly, since I assumed that both the air conditioner and the television would be turned on. Those would be the only comforts in a place like this, and both would be in operation almost constantly.

There was no answer. Before I knocked again, I realized that there were no sounds coming from the trailer. No thin, metallic television sounds, no throb from an air conditioner. No voices. Nothing. The shades, I noticed, were drawn.

I checked the street. No car or truck parked in the space that would go with this trailer. Pretty plain, I thought, that nobody was at home.

I checked the address against the one I had written in my notebook. I had the right place. I stepped off the cinder block and started to walk around the trailer looking for something that would tell me that she had moved out or was only gone for the day and would be back. I wouldn't have minded a window with the shades up, so I could get a look inside.

But before I got all the way around back, a man walked into the yard. He had short, black hair and a belly like the bow on a pusher tugboat. He put his hands on his hips and pointed his gut my way.

"You looking for something, fella?" he said. He had narrow eyes and a hostile voice.

"Waiting for someone."

"Who?"

"Who's asking?"

"The man who owns the property, friend. That's who's asking. And if you don't pay rent here, then you don't belong."

"I'm waiting for Rita Hewes."

"Then you're wasting your time. Whatever she owes you, write it off and get out of the sun."

"She's left this address?"

"And stiffed me for three months' rent," the man said. "Whatever she's into you for, you can forget it.

There's a long line and not enough time left in the universe for that worthless bitch to make the money to pay her debts.''

"I'm not looking for money," I said. "I'm looking for her kid, and I suppose I shouldn't have started snooping around without checking in first. Sorry."

That pacified him, slightly. His hands came off his hips and hung at his sides in a helpless way.

"Well, this goddamned heat," he said in a way that made it seem like an explanation.

"Have you seen her kid?" I said.

"No, mister, I haven't. And I've got a feeling that you are going to ask me a lot of questions about Rita Hewes and her sorry son, Rick. I don't mind answering them as long as I don't have to stand out in the sun to do it. How about coming in my place and we'll talk there, where it's cool."

His place was a trailer. Small, tidy, and well air-conditioned. I took the chair that he offered but passed on the beer. I didn't want to be his drinking buddy.

I asked him how long Rita Hewes had been in his trailer park.

"Ever since I started," he said, making that sound like a long time. "That's almost three years now. I retired from the army and bought this place. I took anyone who could pay the deposit, that was my mistake. I didn't know that once you had 'em, you couldn't get rid of 'em. I wouldn't take her again if they put a gun to my head."

"That bad?"

"Oh, man," he said, and shook his head. "And I couldn't evict her. Welfare Department would have come down on me with both feet if I'd tried that. Once you take 'em in, buddy, they're yours. They

have got to *die* before you can get that trailer back.
And her kind doesn't ever die, you know."

"When did you last see her?"

He touched a finger to his gut, like he might do
his thinking there. "Been a couple of months. Last
time I saw her, we had a screaming match. The rent
was overdue, as usual. But she still called me in the
middle of the night because her toilet was running
over. She was drunk. Raising hell and telling me she
was going to report me to the county lawyers.

"So I had to go over there. Tried a plumber's
friend and then a router. She was yelling and bitching the whole time about how it was my job to keep
things working and she was going to get the lawyers
on my ass. I wanted to stuff her head down the toilet.

"I finally had to drain the toilet and take it off the
bolts to get at what was clogging it. You know what
it was? A pair of panty hose. She'd gotten ham-
mered on wine and pills and flushed her goddamned panty hose down the toilet. And it could
have been a bed sheet for all she knew. Could have
been a cat, if she'd had a cat.

"I remember telling her that if she wanted to stay
here, she'd better learn how to take care of things.
She just laughed. She knew she had me by the balls.
If I tried to evict her, the county lawyers would have
me in court. I'd have to hire a lawyer of my own.
I'm already paying for *her* lawyer with my taxes.

"You know," he said, "if I don't pay the bank on
time, I'm in a crack. But if you're Mexico and owe
money or if you're a welfare witch and owe money,
then you don't have to pay on time. You have the
right not to pay on time.

"I'm hoping for two things. First, I'm hoping that
your friend Rita crawls in a hole someplace and

dies. And then I'm hoping that the real estate agent
I've listed this place with can find someone stupid
enough to buy it for what I've got in it. I want to sell
this son of a bitch and go west. I get enough from
Sam every month that I won't starve. Piss on being
a businessman."

I told him I understood the way he felt, and that
made him happy. Then I asked him about Rita
Hewes's son, Rick.

"Just a little badass, you know. He was here, with
his worthless mother, a lot of the time. He'd play his
music too loud, and I'd go over there and tell him to
turn it down. He'd turn it down just a fraction, you
know, so it was still loud enough to blow the doors
off a barn. I'd go back over and tell him again. It
would take three or four trips, and by then I'd be
ready to break his goddamned arms. I think he was
just bad, like he had a goddamned snake inside of
him."

"How so?" I said.

He rose slowly to get himself another beer and
then massaged his big gut tenderly before he sat
back down in what was plainly his special chair.

"Two things made me think he was real trouble,
not just an ordinary screwed-up kid who needed his
ass kicked. First, there was the time when he got in
a fight with a kid who lived in one of the other trailers. They did the usual pushing and shoving, and
then, when he got the other kid down, he wouldn't
let him up. He kept hitting him until the other kid
was out cold. I saw it from my window. While I was
on my way out there, he stopped hitting the other
kid, got up, and started looking around for something. Before I got there, I saw him come up out of
the grass with an old rusty reinforcing rod. He
wrapped both his hands around it like it was a base-

ball bat and was headed for the other kid, who was still out cold on the ground. I got there just in time, running as fast as my old fat ass would let me. I believe he would have beaten that other kid's brains out with that goddamned steel rod if I hadn't stopped him."

He took a long sip of beer.

"What was the other thing?" I said.

"Well, one night there was screaming from his mother's trailer. If I had a hundred problems a year, then you could bet your paycheck that eighty of them would come from her trailer. Anyway, there was screaming and yelling and banging on the walls, so I went over to put a lid on it. Just about the time I start to knock on the door, it blows open and out comes the witch screaming, her darling son right behind her, holding a knife big enough to jack up a truck. I guess he had it in mind to chop his sweet old mother into stew meat."

"What did you do?"

"Broke his fucking nose." The old sarge shrugged, like there was nothing else for it.

"He went down on his knees and put his hands over his face. But a couple of seconds later, he took 'em away and looked up at me. His eyes were flat *burning*. When he told me he was going to kill me, I believed he'd really try. And I've heard my share of young punks talking about all the bad shit they're going to do. Rolls off me, you know, like fine rain off hot steel. But not with this one.

"I can still remember the way he was looking at me. The top half of his head was covered with hair, and the bottom half was covered with blood. All I could see, in the light coming out of that trailer, was those eyes. And I'll tell you something, they were enough to shake me up.

"He got on his motorcycle and left, still bleeding, and his mother went back into her trailer to find her bourbon bottle. Me, I came back here and checked out an M16 I keep around for emergencies. I made sure the magazine was full, and I kept that thing close by. If that kid had come in here looking for me with his knife, I was going to light him up."

I asked the sarge how long it had been since he'd seen the kid. He said it had been several weeks at least. Rick had moved out after the night he'd gone for his mother with a knife.

I told him that I appreciated his help. I figured that he'd make a good witness, but I didn't tell him that.

"Anytime," he said. "Now is there any chance you could tell me what this is about?"

"It's a lawsuit," I said. "The kid is a witness, and the lawyer I work for wants to get a reading on him before the trial starts."

Sarge rubbed his chin this time, instead of his belly. "Like that, huh. Well, tell your boss to watch out for anything the kid says. He's the kind who would rather climb a tree and lie than stay on the ground and tell the truth."

From the trailer park on Sidney Lanier Lane, I drove to the high school out on Calloway Street. I talked with the guidance counselor there, who said that Rick Hewes had a good mind and a sociopathic personality.

"You know what that is, don't you?" she said.

"I'm afraid so."

"He charmed me. Told me stories about how bad it was at home and how he was going to go to college and make something of himself. He was very convincing. Then he"—She hesitated and her face, which was plump and pretty, darkened—"Well, he tried to put his hands on me. He was very strong. I was lucky that one of the janitors was out in the hall."

I thanked her. Another good witness. Before I left, she said, "He's dangerous, you know. He'll hurt someone."

The social worker at the county office felt the same way. "He'll kill someone," she said. "If he doesn't kill himself first."

She had believed in him too. Then, a couple of months after she had started with him, he had gone in late to his after-school job at a bakery. The boss had said something that set him off.

"He grabbed that man," the social worker said, shuddering and making a face, "and put his hands into the hot grease they used for frying doughnuts. That poor man had to go to the hospital for skin grafts. Rick felt absolutely no remorse. He said it was the man's fault for 'getting in his face.'"

She stopped for a moment and drummed her long fingers on the desk. Slowly.

"I'm a professional bleeding heart," she said. "The kind who thinks everyone is a victim. But after that, I wanted that little monster put in jail."

I nodded. Her expression softened. There was an honesty in her face that made her pretty, even striking.

"He didn't go to jail, of course; he went to that boys' camp, down across the line, in Florida. The man who runs it was a football star, and he thinks he can do anything. We call it a messianic personality. But he'll find out."

I thanked her, and she shook her head to pass it off as unnecessary.

It was late afternoon and I felt like I'd gotten enough evidence on Rick Hewes for one day. I was tired of talking about him and thinking about him. But I still had time to go out to Benning and see what I could find out about Luther Jordan's real father. I felt I owed that to John Fearson.

Chapter Twelve

They were blowing retreat when I got to Harmony Church. A formation of troops halted in the middle of the road; guards were posted to stop traffic. The soldiers snapped to attention, faced the flag, and presented arms as the notes from a recorded bugle call went out across the evening. Back at main post, a cannon sounded.

The bugle notes were clean and firm, and as I sat in the truck listening to them I was reminded of the days when I still wore green. This time of day was especially sweet. After retreat, you would head for the barracks and a shower and some clean clothes. Later, wearing your cheap civvies, you would go out into the cool evening to drink beer and look for women. The nights never turned out to be as good as the possibilities seemed in those few moments after the last note of retreat died on the air.

"Ohdah ahhms."

The road guards were called in, and the formation of Ranger candidates marched down the road. I parked and walked to one of the old World War II barracks that was still in service as the office and supply room of the Ranger School Survival Committee.

"Yes, sir, can I help you?"

"I'm looking for Sergeant Hollibird."

"Just a minute, sir. He's around. I'll find him."

The man who called me sir was not that much younger than I. An inch of bristling hair covered his scalp and the contours of his skull showed through his tightly stretched skin. He was lean but well muscled. He wore a green T-shirt, fatigue pants, and mirror-polished jump boots.

When he came back, there was another just like him at his side. Same clothes, same haircut.

"Mr. Hunt?" the new man said.

"Yes."

"I'm Sergeant Hollibird."

"Good to meet you," I said. "Appreciate your taking the time."

"I hope I can help."

The other man left, so Hollibird and I were alone in an office with waxed linoleum floors, clean metal desks, and posters listing the code of conduct and the elements of a five-paragraph order. It was standard military space.

"You knew Sergeant Jordan?" I said.

"Yes, sir, real well."

"Do me a favor, will you," I said. "Don't call me sir."

"All right." Hollibird smiled.

"I was an NCO myself. Makes me nervous to be in a room where somebody is saying a lot of 'sir's."

"When did you get out?"

I told him. And then I told him how long I'd been in, and after he'd asked I told him where I'd been. The Vietnam part interested him.

"Not many of you guys still around," he said. "Most of the guys around here with combat experience got it in Panama or Grenada."

"I understand Jordan was there."

"And goddamned lucky to still be able to talk about it," Hollibird said. "Got one in the leg from one of our own gunships. King-sized fuckup. Most of us thought Jordan was one of the really righteous dudes around here. It's hard to believe he got out."

"Did he talk to you about it?"

Hollibird sat on one of the metal desks with his arms folded. His eyes were mildly curious and hostile. He smiled in a slightly sinister fashion and said, "Listen, Sarge, I've had a long day and I am thirsty. You drink a cold beer?"

"I will."

"Let's go, then."

An hour later, we sat at a table in one of the places just off the post. A cinder-block building with a cement floor, a jukebox, and a pool table. The place had a stuffy, dead smell that was a blend of stale beer and cigarette smoke. We ordered beer from a barmaid who chewed gum like it was the sure cure for her acne.

"Jordan was into religion, if you can believe that," Hollibird said. "But not in the usual way. He called God the Big Ranger. Used to say that the Big Ranger had made the world as a testing ground, a place to suffer. He said the secret was to know it and look it in the face, and then you'd be all right. He said if you walked with him and handled the tests, then you got your reward in the next world.

Jordan believed the world was always going to be a tough son of a bitch because that's the way God *wanted* it.

"Now, let me ask *you* a question," he said to me, after he had a beer. "What's your interest in Jordan, anyway?"

"I'm trying to find him."

"Well, no shit. I thought maybe you were writing a book about him."

Hollibird looked across the table at me. His eyes narrowed into slits, and his smile shifted into a sneer. You could see he liked to fight and that before this night was over he'd find the fight he needed. I planned to be somewhere else when it happened.

"Actually," I said, in the mildest voice I could manage, "I'm looking for a kid. Jordan's kid."

"Kid?"

"From a long time ago. More than ten years."

"*Jordan's* kid? You *sure* Jordan had a kid?"

"Absolutely."

"One of those deals where the woman got pregnant but he never knew about it?"

"No. He was actually married to the mother for a little while."

"She run away or something?"

"They got a divorce. He shipped overseas. Never saw the kid again as far as I know."

"Ten years ago?"

"Yes."

"Well, I'll be damned."

"He never said anything about it, then?"

"Not a single goddamned word. Not to me, anyway. And I knew him as well as anyone."

"Did you talk to Jordan about what he was going to do when he got out?" I said.

Hollibird shook his head. "We didn't talk a lot

after he got told he was going to have to move on or get out of the army. He felt like he'd given the army his best and gotten kicked in the nuts for thanks."

"Heard from him since?"

"Nope."

"Expect to?"

He shrugged again. "Guys always make a big deal about copying down addresses. But most of them never write."

"Well," I said, putting some money on the table, "I appreciate your taking this much time."

"And I appreciate the beer."

I wrote my name and phone number across a sheet in my notebook, tore it out, and handed it to him.

"If you hear from Jordan," I said, "ask him to get in touch with me, would you?"

"Wilco," Hollibird said, and folded the paper before slipping it into his pocket. It would be there in the morning, I thought, with the wet bills and the loose change, and he would have trouble remembering where he got it.

"Listen," he said, "you don't have to hurry off. How about we hit another couple of places? Maybe you could tell me a war story I haven't heard."

"Can't do it," I said. "Thanks, anyway."

"OK," he said. "But you might be missing something."

Not likely, I thought. I shook my head and left him to whatever action he could find. I liked Hollibird and even sympathized with him. But I didn't want to get drunk and go bar fighting with him. Not on a bet.

Chapter Thirteen

The police stopped me less than ten minutes later. When I saw the blinking light, I assumed I'd been speeding, and I pulled over and got out of the car. I was reaching for my wallet when one of the patrolmen put his hand on his holster and shouted, "Freeze!"

I did what he told me.

"Face the car, spread your hands, and put them on your head."

He patted me down nervously and then said, "Now put your hands behind you."

While he put the cuffs on me, he read me my constitutional rights.

"What's the charge?" I said.

"Attempted murder. You're going back to the joint, friend."

"Who did I try to kill?"

"Just get in the car, asshole."

They took me in, fingerprinted me, and shot my picture. I noticed a facsimile of my record on the desk where the shift sergeant worked.

"Call your lawyer," he said, and pushed the phone across the desk to me. "You're allowed to do that."

"Long distance?"

"Least we can do."

I called Semmes at home and was relieved when he answered.

"*Who* are you supposed to have attempted?" Semmes asked after he'd listened to my story.

"I don't know."

"Uh-huh. And how close are you supposed to have come to getting it done?"

"I don't know that, either."

"Ask somebody."

"Could you tell me who the victim is and what kind of shape he is in?" I said to the sergeant.

"Name of Perkins. Contractor. We found him in his office with a fractured skull and a busted jaw. He's in the intensive ward."

I repeated this into the mouthpiece.

"Let me talk to the sergeant," Semmes said.

I pushed the phone across the desk. The sergeant's end of the conversation amounted to the occasional yes or no or seems reasonable.

He hung up without giving the phone back to me and said, "Wait right there. I'm going to take your picture with the Polaroid."

He left and came back a few seconds later carrying the camera.

"I wonder," he said, "can I make this sumbitch work?" He was a big man with a wide face and long ears. There was a patch of scar tissue the size of a matchbook at the corner of his left eye. He was a country boy in the city, doing a job of work. He was willing to be reasonable, and that was a break for me.

"OK. Look up at me, and let's see what we can do."

The strobe popped, reminding me, briefly, of an illumination round.

"Sixty seconds," the sergeant said, fiddling with his cheap digital watch.

We waited. There was a high-pitched beep.

"OK," he said, and pulled the film from the camera and separated the papers to inspect his work.

"Not bad," he said, and handed it to me. The picture showed me looking about as unhappy as I felt, but it was a reasonable likeness.

"We're going to take this down to the hospital and see if the victim will say that this is a picture of the man that done him upside the head. Save everyone time. Your lawyer says he'll bet me a month's pay you ain't the one and that if you are you ain't his client anymore. I didn't take his bet because I don't think you did it either."

"I appreciate your confidence," I said. "But why am I here?"

"We've got a witness. I can't tell you any more than that right now. Let's wait until we get word from the hospital, and if it's good I'll tell you all about it. You want a cup of coffee?"

"Sounds good."

"How do you like it?"

"Black."

"Sit over there." He pointed to some chairs. "I'll bring it to you."

He did. Right after, he sent the patrolman to the hospital with the Polaroid.

I drank my coffee and read a two-day-old newspaper. I didn't allow myself to think about where I was or why. Or about the man in intensive down at the hospital. I concentrated, instead, on a story about an airplane crash. Officers came and went. They talked to each other. The radio crackled to life now and again. I ignored it, both the broken, static-infested voices of the men calling in and the bored, uninflected answers of the dispatcher.

While I waited, two men in civilian clothes walked up to the sergeant's desk. One was black, the other white.

"Where is he?" the white one said to the desk sergeant.

"Who you got in mind?" the sergeant asked.

The white man made a show of being exasperated, for his partner and anyone else who might be watching.

The black one rolled his eyes in return.

"The suspect in the construction-company thing. Victim was named Perkins. Right now it's attempted murder. By daylight, it'll be just plain murder. *That* is who I've got in mind." It was said loudly, for the whole room to hear.

"You mean Mr. Hunt, then," the sergeant said in an offhand way. "That's him, sitting over there in that chair."

He pointed in my direction, and they turned and looked at me. Then the white one's face turned a kind of dirty red color, and he showed his teeth to the sergeant. "Why is he out here reading the goddamned newspaper? Why the fuck isn't he back in the tank where he belongs?"

The sergeant shrugged and started to say something, but the black one interrupted. "No, baby, just save your wind. Don't say nothing, don't think nothing, just sit back and write up your reports. We'll take it from here."

They walked across the room and stopped three feet from me.

"On your feet, scumbag," the white one said.

"You best get up, bro," said the black one. "Make it easy on yourself."

I carefully folded the newspaper I'd been reading, making sure of each crease, then stood. I kept my eyes on the white one's face the whole time. He didn't like that.

"What are you looking at, shit bird?"

I didn't say anything.

He grabbed me by the elbow and said, "Let's go."

I went in the direction I was pushed. But if I yielded physically, I was resisting with every other part of myself. I hate it when anyone puts his hands on me, and I especially hate anyone who does it just to demonstrate that he can. I clamped down on my back teeth and tried to focus on a point of light inside my skull. My feet moved on their own, carrying me along a corridor and into a small, bright room with a table and three chairs.

I was pushed into a chair. "Sit down," the white one said. "Make your fucking self comfortable."

A weak transformer in the overhead fluorescent hummed and popped. The only other sound was a soft whistling as the white one sucked air through his teeth.

The black one sat in a chair directly across the table from me. He looked at the floor when he talked. "What about it, bro? You feel like making a statement? Either way you tell it, you'll be helping yourself."

The white one put his face very close to mine but to the side, so he was just out of my field of vision and I could only feel him there, just a few inches away, breathing on my cheek and neck. His breath was heavy and wet.

"Come on, shit bird," he said. "Start out simple. Tell us where you were and what you were doing at five o'clock this afternoon, and just go on from there. Don't stop to think about it. Just tell it."

Tiny drops of his saliva splattered on my skin.

"Do yourself a favor, babe," the black one said.

"Talk, motherfucker," the white one said directly into my ear.

They waited a few seconds, and when I didn't say anything they started again. The white one got red in the face and pointed his finger at me. He hit the wall once or twice with his fist, and each time he snuck a quick look to see if I'd gone to pieces over the possibility that he might lose control and hit me that way. I don't know what he saw, but my face felt like stone.

The white one took off his jacket so I could see his shoulder holster and his nickel-plated nine millimeter. He wore a short-sleeved shirt and one of those big plastic digital watches that have functions for keeping track of everything except the price on feeder cattle. A high-tech watch for today's man of action.

The watch and the pistol were for adornment. You were supposed to look at them and get the message that this man was a *designer* cop, not some common production model.

I let my concentration slip, just for a moment, away from the small spot of light inside my skull, and I wondered if he had ever killed a man. Ever been shot at. He hadn't, I decided, and it plainly bothered him.

"Keep wasting my time, asshole," he said. "See if

you can get me even more pissed off at you than I already am. I'll make sure you die in a Georgia jail cell.''

"You running out of time now, bro," the black one said. "Try to do the smart thing just once."

I concentrated, again, on the cool, blue light behind my eyes. It seemed like we'd been in the interrogation room for an hour. I was just getting started. I regulated my breathing. Six to the minute, slow and deep. It felt like the slow roll of waves before they break against a beach, that same soothing rhythm, and I began to imagine the sound of pounding surf in my ears. I breathed deeply, watched the blue light with my inner eye, and listened to the sound of those breaking waves. The words of the cops were nothing more than noise. I could feel them when the white cop put his mouth next to my ear and sprayed me with saliva. Otherwise, it was no different from the sound of a television in a crowded room, a kind of pointless, white noise.

I barely noticed when someone knocked on the door and the black cop pulled it open.

The desk sergeant stood on the other side looking smug.

"What do you want?" the white cop said.

"I thought you detectives might be interested to know that this man didn't do it," the sergeant said.

"Well, no shit, now," the black one said. "And who says so?"

"Only the victim," the sergeant said. "We showed him a Polaroid and told him it was the same guy who visited him a couple of days ago. He said he remembered and that he wasn't the one who squashed him."

"Guy could have been out of it," the white cop

said. "Busted up so bad and doped for the pain so he wouldn't know what he was saying. He might change his story."

"That's going to be tough," the sergeant said, "now that he's went and died."

"Perkins *died*?"

"About fifteen minutes ago," the sergeant said.

"Shit."

"I knew you'd be all broken up to hear it."

"Whose idea was it to show him the picture?"

"Mine," the sergeant said.

"Jesus." The white cop shook his head, then glared at me for a few seconds. "Why don't you take this one here with you when you leave, Sergeant. Tell him he's free to go."

The sergeant nodded in my direction and I stood. The white cop put his face close to mine. "I'll find out what it was between you and Perkins, my friend. And we'll meet again."

"I'd like that," I said.

He grinned and said, "You want a piece of me."

"No," I said, "I'd actually like a little more than that."

He smiled. I could see it was shaky. "Maybe you'll get your chance."

"Nothing I'd like better."

He turned away and said, over his shoulder, "Get him out of here, Sergeant. I've got more important things to do than screw around with him."

"Why sure, Detective. Anything you say."

I followed the sergeant down the corridor to his desk.

"You got a head I could use?" I said.

He nodded and told me how to find it. I stood at the urinal and felt like I was getting rid of some poisonous fluid. I ran some hot water and washed my face and hands thoroughly with soap. Then I rinsed carefully with cold water. I was drying my hands when the door swung open and the white detective walked in.

"Well, well," he said.

I finished drying my hands while he stood in front of the urinal. My hand was on the door when he said, "Wait a minute, I want to ask you something."

I waited but did not turn around.

"If you didn't do it, you shouldn't mind helping the law find out who did, right? I mean, that's what a good citizen does, isn't it, help us out?"

I turned around and looked at him. "Friend," I said, "I wouldn't piss on you if you were on fire."

He tried to smile, to show it just rolled off him, but he couldn't make it work. "Hey, that's personal. You don't like me. That's OK, because I don't like you. But we're talking something bigger. Something that isn't personal."

"Maybe I should stand at attention. Put my hand over my heart."

"Just think past the personal."

"Maybe one day, when you grow up, you'll understand that it's all personal," I said. "All the rest is bullshit." I pushed the door open and said, "I'm still looking forward to meeting you again sometime. My turf and no badges."

"Fuck you, yardbird," he said as the door swung closed behind me.

The sergeant waited for me by the front door of the station house. "They'll have a wheel lock on your truck," he said. "I got the key. I'll walk out with you."

It was still hot outside. But damp as it was, the air felt clean on my skin.

"I'm sorry about those children," the sergeant said. "They ought to teach 'em to behave before they give 'em the badge."

"Why don't you spank them?"

"Supreme Court won't allow it."

"Either one of them any good?"

"The black one shows signs, every now and then. The other got a terminal dose of television when he was growing up. It ain't a satisfactory day for him until he gets to call somebody scumbag. After that, he's happy."

My truck was parked next to a cyclone fence, with a big locking wedge of metal hanging off the rear tire. The sergeant went through a ring of keys, looking for the one that would unlock it.

He went down on one knee and spoke to me over his shoulder. "You don't have to tell me if you don't want to, but I got to ask. What was it between you and Perkins?"

"You want me to tell you about the other night?"

"I sure would. No reason you should, except it *might* help us out. But I could see how that wouldn't be real important to you right now."

"I don't mind," I said. "As long as you tell me what went on tonight."

The wheel lock came free. He removed it and put it on the ground. Then he stood up and dusted off his hands.

"We got a call around six thirty from his secretary. Seems she had gone home and then remembered something and returned to the office. We think she might have gone back because she was giving something sweet to the boss. She's married. Anyway, when she unlocked the office, she found Perkins stretched out on the floor with his head all scrambled. She dialed nine-one-one, and when the cruiser got there she told the patrolmen that you two had had some words a couple of days ago and when you were leaving she wrote down your license plate, just in case. We put it out over the radio, and that's how we nailed you."

"Any chance it was the secretary who did him?"

"Not much. She can account for her movements, and besides, there was a lot of blood. None of it on her."

"Any suspects other than me?"

"Nothing formal. But we already know enough about this Perkins to know he makes enemies. He drinks hard, and he comes down strong on his help. Slow-pays his suppliers and double-bills his customers. A model citizen and businessman."

The sergeant put his hands on his hips and raised his face to the sky. He took a deep breath, then looked at me and said, "Now you show me yours."

I told him about Luther and why I was talking to Perkins.

"You thought he might have seen the kid?"

"I was hoping Luther had gone to someone he knew."

"Doesn't sound like Perkins is someone the boy would want to see again."

"No," I said and told him about the beatings Luther took from Perkins.

The sergeant shook his head and spat. "Man, I hate that. Had Perkins seen the kid?"

"Nope."

"And you two had hard words. Probably because you were brought up the way he used to treat the kid."

"Why do you say that?"

"I saw you with those detectives. You're that way. Buys you a lot of grief too."

"You don't know the half of it, Sarge."

"Yeah, I do," he said. "I saw the fax on you, remember. Anyway, that's your problem. My problem is Perkins. When you made him scream, in his office, that afternoon . . . that was the last time you ever saw him, right?"

"That's right."

He nodded and slapped his hands together a couple of times, like a man trying to stay warm. It looked out of place on a ninety-degree night.

"So explain one thing to me," he said.

"What's that?"

"What are you doing in town two days later?"

I looked at him. "You know," I said, "you should be a detective."

"Obvious question," he said and shrugged. "You don't have to answer."

I told him about the lawsuit, and he said he'd seen something about it on the television. When I said I'd been talking to people about Rick Hewes, he let out a breath. "That creep is the one who's suing?"

"Yes."

"You find out the kind of stuff you need?"

"I think so."

"Well, if you come up on your trial date and you feel you're light, give me a call. I know a few stories about that one. I figured we'd hear from him one of these days, but I thought it would be for making it to death row. But he's young yet. You got to give a man time."

He shook his head, and I thought that was the end of it. I was about to reach for the door handle when he said, "You give any thought to the possibility that Perkins might have been killed by the kid you're looking for?"

"A little. But he's still young for that kind of work."

"Uh-huh. And you talked to the boy's mama?"

"Right."

"Is she a possible?"

"I don't think so."

"What about the real father?"

The man was wasted on the desk, I thought.

"I haven't been able to find the real father," I said. "But he hasn't seen the kid for nine or ten years."

"Still a possibility, though?"

"Sure. And you've got the resources and the manpower to run it down. Those ace detectives of yours ought to make short work of it."

"Pair of polished pistols, aren't they?" the sergeant said. "They just plain *look* dangerous, don't they?"

"Good night, Sergeant," I said. "Enjoyed talking to you."

"Name is Val. Tom Valentine, but only my wife calls me Tom."

"OK, Val. Nice talking to you."

"Stay in touch, if you want," he said. "We might be able to help each other. Come straight to me. You don't want to waste time with Batman and Robin. Life is way too short for that."

I thanked him again. We shook hands. I got in the truck, pulled out of the parking lot, and went looking for a quiet, cheap place to spend the night. I wanted to put my head down and close my eyes and think about nothing at all.

Chapter Fourteen

I woke in a small room in a motel operated by one of the chains. The only window had been sealed shut around a six-thousand-BTU General Electric air conditioner. You could not open that window with anything less than a crowbar and a ten-pound maul. If you wanted air, it had to come through that machine.

I'd have given a lot for a window that opened, but when I asked the clerk he looked at me like it was the first time anyone had requested *that*. Then he shook his head.

So I spent a bad night. Before dawn, I was up and out. I ran for an hour through the still streets of a subdivision. Dew was beaded on the grass and the windshields of the parked cars. A few dogs, let out to do their morning business, barked at me as I ran along the blacktop. When I finished, I did some cal-isthenics, showered, and checked out.

* * *

I wanted to be at Harmony Church early, before Hollibird arrived at work, so I skipped breakfast and stopped for a cup of carry-out coffee at a convenience store. It was scalding hot, and I sipped carefully as I eased along toward Fort Benning with the morning's first wave of traffic. There was something strange about all those cars, bumper to bumper, driven mostly by men wearing clean camouflage fatigues. Were they warriors or were they commuters? Didn't seem like they could be both.

I was at the Survival Committee offices ten minutes before Hollibird. His boots were shined, and he had the early-morning confidence in his step. He also wore a line of stitches under one eye.

"Morning," he said happily.

"Trouble?"

"Nothing I couldn't handle," he answered.

"Glad to hear it."

"You should've stuck around. It was pretty interesting."

"Sorry I missed it."

"Well, you never can tell," he said, touching the puffy red flesh around his eye. "What brings you out here this morning?"

"I wanted to ask you about a couple of things."

"OK."

"First, did Jordan leave a civilian address when he got his discharge?"

Hollibird frowned. "I don't know. But I suppose I could find out. What's the other thing?"

"Where is Jordan's gear?"

"There wasn't much."

I nodded. One of the seductions of being a lifer is the way you can put all your goods in a couple of duffle bags and a plywood footlocker.

"But there had to be something," I said. "You know anyone who helped him move his things out?"

"No. But I'll ask around. What else can I help you with?"

"That's all," I said. "Can I get back to you in an hour?"

"Yeah. Do that. I'll have something for you."

He touched his sutures again, grinned happily, and walked into the building, taking the steps two at a time.

I left Harmony Church and drove until I found a newspaper rack. I bought the local paper and read the story that appeared under the headline LOCAL CONTRACTOR MURDERED IN OFFICE. My name was not in it.

Next, I found a phone booth and called Semmes. I told him I was out and clear.

"That must have been a hard night," he said quietly.

"It wasn't so bad."

"I feel badly about putting you in that position."

"Not your fault, Nat."

"If I hadn't asked you to help me on this thing . . ."

"I'm a volunteer, Nat. Volunteers don't have any legitimate complaints. Anyway, I've spent a whole lot of nights that were a whole lot worse. The toughest part was trying to sleep in that motel room."

"You want to drop this thing? Take some time off?"

"I'm fine, Nat. Swear it. And I've dredged up some good stuff."

I told him about Rick Hewes. He listened and said, "That's good work, Morgan. Damned good work. Four good witnesses. When I finish with Mr.

Hewes, he'll be lucky if he still has an ass in his
pants. You going to wait around up there for the
police to come after you again, or you coming back
here?"

"One more thing," I said. "Then I'll head back."

"Would you be careful, then? Scares Bobbie to
death when the phone rings in the middle of the
night."

I went back to Harmony Church. Hollibird was
waiting for me outside his office.

"I got what you wanted," he said. "But I don't
know if it's going to do you any good."

"Let's hear it."

Jordan had left the address of a mail-forwarding
service. Anything that went to him went through the
service first. It was a good way to avoid process
servers, collection agencies, and ex-wives looking
for alimony.

"Wonder why he had to deal with one of them,"
Hollibird said.

"Maybe he thought he'd be moving around," I offered. "They'll hold your things until you get settled."

"That goes along with what he did with his gear,"
Hollibird said.

"What's that?"

"Stored it in a miniwarehouse where you can rent
space. One of the guys here helped him move it."

"Which place was it?"

Hollibird gave me the name and the address.

"You going out there?"

"I thought I would."

"Think you can get in to see what he's got?"

"I don't know."

"Need help?"

"I might."

"Want me to meet you there?"

I thought for a minute, and when I had the ragged outline of a plan I explained it to him.

"I've got to go sign out on the duty roster," he said. "I'll be back most soonest."

Fifteen minutes later, we walked into the place where Jordan had stored his gear. We were not quite together but more like a couple of customers who happened to have arrived at the same time and just started talking.

It was called U-Store, and it occupied about five acres of red clay on the side of the highway. There was a cyclone fence around it, and inside, the small, steel sheds were lined up in a dozen rows separated by rutted drives. It looked like the sort of place that would do a lot of trade with people who had been evicted, divorced, or otherwise found themselves temporarily on the street.

A thin kid whose skin was pale as a mushroom sat at the desk listening to the radio.

"Can I help you?" the kid shouted over the music.

"I came to pay my buddy's rent for him," Hollibird said. "He's down in Honduras, doesn't know when he's going to get back."

"Yeah, what's his name?" the kid asked.

"Jordan, William L., Sergeant First Class."

The kid flipped through a small tin box full of alphabetized file cards. U-Store was slow getting into computers.

"Jordan. Let's see. Jordan," the kid mumbled as he flipped through the cards. "Here it is. William L. Jordan. He pulled the card and laid it flat on the desk, where he studied it carefully.

"Says here," the kid said, "that he is paid up. Paid

for six months in advance and hasn't used but one
of them so far."

"Let me see," Hollibird said.

The kid pushed the card over to him.

"He must have forgotten," Hollibird said. "You
get so busy when you ship out."

"Yeah, well." The kid reached for the card.
"Thanks, anyway."

Hollibird left and the kid looked up at me.

"Something I can do for you?" he said, like all
this hard work was truly getting him down.

"I need to store some things for a couple of
months," I replied.

Hollibird was waiting outside. "Number forty-
six," he said.

"Good. Thanks for your help."

"Man, wouldn't you just love to grab a little shit
like that by the throat, drag his ass off, give him a
haircut, bathe him, put him in some clothes, and
then run him into next month? Make something out
of him?"

"I know what you mean."

"Let me know how it goes," Hollibird said. "You
got me curious now."

"I'll call you."

He pulled out into traffic and I followed him. I
turned off at the first shopping center. In ten minutes I had my pickup loaded with empty boxes that
looked like the sort of containers a man going to
U-Store would use for protecting his valuables. I
closed them all with duct tape. That made them look
genuine and, I thought, a little pathetic.

I also picked up a padlock at the hardware store.
The kid had told me I'd need one.

"You get yourself a good lock," he'd said, "and

you keep the keys. Long as you pay, your stuff stays locked up. When you don't pay, the guy who owns this place gives you thirty days. Then he cuts the lock off with a pair of bolt cutters and sells anything that's worth money. The rest of it he takes to the Goodwill or the dump.''

I stopped by the office to tell the kid I was back. Then I drove down a dirt trail between the steel sheds until I found the one I'd rented. Number sixty-four. Same row as Jordan's and just a few down from it. I parked in front of mine and walked back to his. The lock was a bonus. I had expected something that would take a set of picks. What I found was one of those padlocks the size of a soup can, the kind that you open with two keys. These locks are very expensive and would deter any non-professional on looks alone. But among the professionals you run across in prison, it's a joke.

I had to get back in the truck and drive out to the highway to find the tool I needed. Once I had it, I returned and started moving empty cardboard boxes into my own rented locker. After a couple of loads, I eased down to Jordan's locker and slipped my lock-picking tool out of my pocket. The tool was the tab from a pop-top beer can.

I bent the flat aluminum until it was the right shape and slipped it into the thin gap between the hasp and the housing of the lock. I pushed the ring until I felt the tumblers begin to drop, and then I torqued the ring hard. The lock popped open.

I put the pick back in my pocket and eased into William L. Jordan's locker. If these were his worldly goods, then all he owned could have fit in a good-sized closet.

I pulled the steel door shut behind me. It was already hot in the locker, and it became hotter by the minute. I wanted to work quickly but without rushing things. It helped that there wasn't much to go through.

I traced the beam of a small flashlight over the contents of the locker without feeling entirely sure of what I was looking for. I started simply by peeling back the flap on the closest cardboard box. It held a small, out-of-date Japanese tape deck, the kind the PX had carried for years. No telling how many servicemen had bought them.

The next box held civilian clothes, the kind you can get made quickly and cheaply in Hong Kong. You went in and showed the tailor an ad you had clipped out of a magazine, and he made a close approximation from one of the few hundred bolts of material piled around the store.

The next box held camera gear, and the one after that was full of books. Martial arts, survival, Vietnam.

A wooden footlocker had been pushed into one corner. It wasn't locked. It seemed to hold mostly file folders and notebooks. Also some small envelopes with rubber bands wrapped around them. Written on each envelope, in careful script, was a description of the contents. "Insurance." "School records." "Birth certificate and passport." "Bank statements." "Car papers."

A bead of sweat dropped from my face to the surface of an envelope. It was blazing inside the steel room. Hot and airless and dark enough to take me back to other dark, hot, close places. I'd been in the hole in prison, and worse, in Vietnam I'd had to climb into a dark tunnel that wandered through a bunker complex that I had hoped was abandoned. If it has been abandoned, I said to myself before I went in, then I probably won't need the pistol. And if it hasn't been abandoned, the pistol probably won't do much good. But I carried it anyway and went in, wearing a miner's lamp and trailing a rope. The earth oozed fluid all around me, and the smell was a mingling of several kinds of rot. First I stood, then I stooped, and finally I crawled. I prayed, as the blood pounded heavier and heavier in my temples, that I would not have to get on my stomach and slither.

I went almost five hundred yards down that tunnel. It was dark like the night never is. My lungs couldn't get enough air, not underground. Not ever. I crawled ahead, down one side shaft, and at the end I found a small room where the earth walls had been bulkheaded with American ammunition boxes. There was a wooden table in the middle of the room. Bowls on the table. Rancid rice in the bowls. One dead Vietnamese soldier, sitting in a corner, a rat devouring his face.

I followed my rope out of that tunnel, swearing I would go to the Long Binh jail before I'd crawl down another.

I felt myself slipping back down that tunnel now. Easy, I told myself.

I tried to sing a little song I remembered from some nightclub. A song about rain. I tried to make my chest stop heaving and my lungs stop gulping for air. When I had my breathing under control again, the pounding behind my eyes seemed to slow and the screaming in my ears quieted, then died. My hands still quivered, but only slightly. The panic had passed.

I took out the notebook and pencil, put the flashlight in my mouth, and copied down anything I thought I might need. It took about half an hour. By then my clothes were soaked, but I had what I was looking for. So I slipped outside, and five minutes later I was on my way out of town.

I drove for twenty or thirty minutes, and though the air was hot and dusty it felt like spring water flowing over my face and neck. When it no longer felt that way, and was merely air again, I stopped at a roadside place and bought a cold beer. I drank it in two long swallows, and it did for the inside of me what the rushing air had done for the outside. Then I called Hollibird to tell him everything had gone fine and to thank him for his help.

He wanted to know if there was anything more he could do, and I told him I'd let him know. He wished me luck, and I did the same for him.

"Just pray for war, man," he said. "Pray for war."

I hung up and called Bonnie Perkins. No answer.

I decided to drive to Tallahassee. She had good, strong locks on her door, but for some reason I wasn't sure that was enough.

Chapter Fifteen

I made it to Bonnie Perkins's apartment a little after noon and was waiting out front when she came home for lunch. When she recognized me, her face seemed to draw in on itself, and her pace slowed. She approached me reluctantly, on guard, the way she had learned to approach all men, strangers or not.

"Miss Perkins."

"I hope you're here to tell me that you found Luther."

"No, I'm not."

Her shoulders slumped. "It must be something worse, then. You came to tell me he's in jail or dead, didn't you?"

"No. Nothing worse about Luther."

"Then what?"

"It's about your former husband," I said.

"Which one?"

Both of 'em, lady, I thought about saying, but she wasn't my enemy. I could afford to go light on her.

"Perkins died last night. He was murdered."

It could have been a weather report the way she took it. She kept her eyes on mine, and nothing showed in them. "I'm not surprised," she said.

"You wouldn't know who did it, would you?"

She shook her head. "No. Been years since I saw him. I didn't keep up. But if he didn't change—and I don't suppose he did—then there would have been plenty of people wanting to do it. He never had any trouble making enemies."

"What about your first husband?"

The look crossed her face again, the same one I'd seen when I mentioned her first husband the last time I talked to her.

"You keep asking about him," she said in a sullen, childlike way, "when it's been more than ten years since I've seen him. I don't know anything about him."

I knew she was lying.

"Could he have had a reason to kill Perkins?"

"Far as I know," she said, "they never laid eyes on each other."

It took me a minute or two to explain why I thought there might be a connection between Luther's disappearance, Perkins's murder, and William Jordan's leaving the army. It didn't sound especially convincing, even to me.

Nor to her, apparently. "That child was in diapers the last time Jordan saw him. He never even *tried* to see him since then. I don't see why he should start caring now about what Perkins or anyone else has done to the boy."

"Maybe not."

"And I don't believe he's got Luther, either." She was trying to convince herself.

I nodded.

"You going to keep looking for him?"

"Yes."

"Well, I'd appreciate hearing if you find anything. I thought it was bad before, just missing him and feeling all the time like I'd done the wrong thing. But this is much worse. Sometimes I feel like I just can't stand it."

"I'll call if there's any news. In the meantime, you should be careful, just in case I'm right. Careful about who you open the door to."

"I always am. Believe me, I know about the animals who live around here."

"I'm sorry about Perkins."

"No need," she said. "He was just one of them animals."

It was a long four hours back to the River House, even on the interstate. You forget how much of Florida runs east and west. After I pulled in the drive, I spent a few minutes with Jube, rubbing his ears and talking to him in a way that he seemed to appreciate, even if he didn't understand a word. Then I called Nat Semmes and told him I was back.

"Well, I'm glad to hear it," he said. "What you need now is some relief. A day off. You got any plans for tomorrow?"

I did. But I didn't want to discuss them with Semmes, since he is an officer of the court and I would be looking for someone who was, by now, probably an official felon. "There's an old floor here that needs tearing out," I said. "It's eaten up with dry rot. I've been wanting to get to it for a couple of weeks."

"Sounds like just the thing."

"I could check out Straylow."

"That can wait for a day or two. Busting up a floor sounds like just the thing after what you've been through."

I hung up and took a shower to get rid of the road and the sweat of that stifling storage locker. After I dried off, I felt much better, so I called Jessie and asked her if she'd like to go out to dinner.

"Give me half an hour," she said.

We went to a place on the water. I liked it because all the seafood was local and fresh, and the prices were fair. I'll never learn how to pay what some people charge for food you could go scoop out of the water yourself.

We ate steamed shrimp and rice and some crabmeat salad. We drank a bottle of wine. It was fine and so was the food.

"Next time, I'm taking you out," Jessie said.

"That's the way it's done?"

"That is the way it is done."

Her hair was brushed out somehow, so that it both touched her shoulders and framed her face, drawing your attention to her eyes. She had dark eyes, a kind of green that made you think of jewels and ice. But it wasn't the color, so much, that struck you as the way her eyes seemed always to be peeling back the layers of concealment and trying to look straight inside you. There was nothing bored, detached, weary, or remote about those eyes. They were unmistakably alive, taking in the here and now. Jessie was a here-and-now woman, for that matter, who liked beautiful things, interesting talk, food, wine, and pleasure. She wasn't coy about it, and she didn't learn it from a self-help book.

The top buttons of her blouse were open, so when she leaned across the table a little I could see where the line of her tan stopped and the soft white rise of her breast began. She was not lean enough to be a model. Not shockingly ample, either. Merely womanly in the most natural, mysterious, and provocative way. When you looked at her, you didn't think of diets, exercise, and a kind of abiding struggle with her own body but of a kind of easy accommodation. Of pleasure. It was a fine body, you'd think, and she was comfortable with it.

When we went out like this, she somehow made me believe that an evening with her man was one of life's payoffs. She listened when I talked, looking at me with those eyes, and talking to me with her wonderfully full but delicate mouth, smiling or laughing, reaching across the table to touch my hand, using the language of her body to say that these were good times and that before the night was over they were going to get a lot better. She had the trick of making you feel like more man than you were and you wanted to make her feel like she was all the woman in the world. Being with her, like this, brought out something in me that was otherwise cold and dormant. That alone was all the excuse I needed for being crazy about her.

When we'd finished our dinner, she said, "That was wonderful, Morgan. Just wonderful. You got something else in mind for this evening?"

"How about a little music?"

"I'd *love* it."

So we drove about ten miles out a backwoods two-lane with her sitting close, a hand resting on my knee and her hair touching my cheek, and parked

under a large live oak in the hard clay parking lot
outside Rusty's.

"How did you *find* this place?" she asked.

"Rusty's an old friend," I explained.

Rusty's was an old bare-boards farmhouse re-
modeled just enough to make it functional. In other
words, someone had knocked out all the walls and
built a bar and a small stage at one end of what was
now a single, large room. Rusty called the place a
nightclub, which seemed a little grand to me.

"You'd never call it pretentious, would you?" Jessie said on the way to the door.

"All they're selling here," I said, "is music and
whiskey, with an occasional card game and knife
fight thrown in."

"Are we safe?"

"We're friends of Rusty's. That's as safe as you
can get here."

We went through the door and into a dark room
that was thick with smoke. Our eyes were getting
adjusted when I heard a familiar voice shout, "My
man."

I greeted Rusty and we hugged. He was big and
strong, the way a working animal is big and strong.
You could look at Rusty and think mule. He had a
big black face, with the bone so close to the surface
that it looked like the skin had been painted over it
in one thin coat. His teeth were big and almost
shockingly white.

"This is Jessie Beaudraux," I said. "A friend of
mine."

"Better be more than just an old *friend*," Rusty
said. Then he turned to Jessie and made a kind of
half-bow that brought his head down to the level of
hers.

"It's a pleasure to meet you, Miss Jessie, and welcome to my little place. Is this cat behaving himself?"

Jessie smiled. "More or less."

"That's good. You got to keep a short leash on him, though, because he don't have good sense."

"Isn't *that* the truth," she said.

Rusty turned away and spoke to a thin, black woman wearing tight jeans. "Hey, Louise. Show my friends here to a front table."

She did. I ordered a beer. Jessie wanted a bourbon neat.

When the waitress had gone, Jessie asked, "Does it bother you that we are the only white people in this place?"

"Not a bit," I said. What I did not say was that I felt out of place pretty much everywhere.

Ten minutes later, Rusty came on stage with a bass man and a drummer. The three of them were the entire band. Sometimes, Rusty made them leave the stage and he played alone. Once in a while, he would put down his electric guitar and do a set on an old acoustic, just the way Lightnin' Hopkins had done it. He had wonderful fingers and a bone-deep feeling for the music.

Rusty could not tell you what the music meant any more than I could. People have written a lot about the blues, trying to get at what makes the music dig so deep and linger so long. But nobody really gets it because it can't be done. If you could explain it, then it wouldn't be good. It is music that makes feeling bad seem natural. The blues is about sorrow without self-pity. Just the sorrow itself.

The first set lasted a little more than an hour. We decided to stay for the second. By the end of it, the place had filled and it was getting loud. People talked over the music and Rusty paid less attention.

The music was still good but not as good as it had been.

"It was great," I said to Rusty on the way out.

"Thank you, my man. Don't be so long coming back."

"You are the best," Jessie said.

Rusty smiled. His big white teeth, the size of dominoes, glittered in his massive head. "Miss Jessie," he said, "come back any time. If the old fool here won't bring you, I'll send someone to fetch you."

"Be good," she said.

"Naw," Rusty said, still smiling. "I got better things to do."

Chapter Sixteen

The sun was well up when I turned off the interstate. A couple of F-4s made a pass almost over my
head, low enough that I could smell burned ker-
osene when they were gone. I'd almost forgotten
how it smelled.

I took a rutted dirt road through a mile or two of
low scrub until it ended at a cyclone fence. Big, red-
lettered signs said that the land beyond the fence
belonged to the U.S. government. No civilians allowed.

I locked the truck and slipped an Alice pack filled
with dry socks, extra water, a space blanket, and
first-aid gear over my shoulder. Then I walked along
the fence line toward a beaver swamp I'd seen on
the map.

The air force had not run its cyclone fence
through the standing black water of the swamp. I
took a compass line across the swamp and found a

distinctive snag on the azimuth I wanted. I cut a fairly straight branch from a hickory tree, trimmed it for a snake stick, then started across the swamp.

The water was unpleasantly warm and thick against my legs, and the bottom, which was soft with rotting leaves, seemed to pull at my boots and suck them down. Each step sent up a swarm of mosquitoes, and by the time I'd gone twenty yards they hung around my face like trapped smoke.

I stopped to put on some repellent. It was quiet and still in the swamp. Small yellow butterflies moved on the stationary air, and it seemed odd that they could move without making any sound at all.

The swamp was three hundred yards across. I moved the way a Cajun trapper had once taught me: slow and fast at the same time, so your feet don't get sucked into the bottom muck and cause you to fall. You tiptoe, almost, taking very short steps, and you keep your feet moving. You have to concentrate to do it, and just when you think you have the rhythm you inevitably trip on a sunken log or step into a hole.

I stopped when I saw a moccasin hanging from a branch about six feet in front of my face. It was heavy, and one coil of its midsection drooped from the branch the way a fat man's beer gut hangs over his belt. The snake's body was glistening black, its eye dead and unblinking.

The water looked deep on either side of me, and I didn't want to detour. So I took a couple of quick steps until I was close enough to lift the fat, dangling coil with the stick. The moccasin opened its mouth and hissed. The tissues inside its mouth were white, but not so much the white of cotton as the white of something dead. The white of pus or maggots. I flipped the snake aside and finished my mincing walk to the high ground beyond the beaver swamp.

I had dry land the rest of the way, most of it through old growth, where there was no underbrush to speak of. I was in shade but it was not cool.

I followed a compass line toward a stream I wanted to cross and kept a rough account of the distance I'd traveled. It was three miles to the stream, and I made it in about an hour and a half. By then it was midmorning and hot enough to stun you.

I soaked a bandanna in the soupy green water and wiped my face and arms. I took a drink from my canteen, shed my pack, and sat on an old blowdown for ten minutes, resting.

I could see the edge of another beaver swamp downstream. This put me about two hundred yards from a point of land that led into a narrow finger of high ground. When my sweat had dried and my breathing had settled, I slipped back into the pack and made a wide swing out from the creek, upstream. I moved slowly, listening and looking for man-sign as I went.

Where it was not covered with leaves, the earth was dark, rich, and wet. It held tracks and there were plenty of them. Mostly deer, along with a few from the feral pigs that roamed the bottomland, getting ranker with each generation. They competed with the deer for acorns but would eat anything. That was made about as plain as it could be a couple of years ago, when some of them chewed up the body of a hunter who'd died of a heart attack.

I took my pack off again and sat on the exposed root of a large oak. There were acorn caps scattered on the ground around the tree. This would be a busy spot during the fall.

I took a swallow of water from my plastic canteen
and wiped my face again with the damp rag. I
pulled off my boots and socks, which were still wet
from the beaver swamp, let my feet dry in the air,
then put on a pair of clean socks from my pack.

I was far enough from the sluggish creek that I
could not hear it. It hardly made any noise, anyway,
except where a blowdown backed up some water
and broke the flow. The only sound was a woodpecker driving holes into a tree trunk somewhere
close by. I saw him after a minute or two. A big bird
with a red head. What they call a pileated woodpecker. I had hoped it would be an ivorybill. They
are supposed to be extinct, but like a lot of people I
believe that some of those big, beautiful birds still
survive in the deep swamps. I don't have any logical
reason for believing this; I just don't want to admit
that they were shot into oblivion to dress up
women's hats.

I was still watching the woodpecker, somewhat
hypnotized by the ragged rhythm of its tapping,
when I caught some movement on the ground at the
edge of my vision. At first, I assumed it was a deer.
But as I eased my head in the direction of the movement, I saw that it was a man.

He moved slowly. Not sneaking, though. He was
just walking without haste. People who don't like
being in the woods always move through them
quickly, like they want to be somewhere else. This
man moved through the woods like he was comfortable there.

I sat perfectly still with my back against the big
oak, not blinking and taking air in small breaths
through my nose. Sometimes you hold your breath
without meaning to, and when you finally take air
you gulp it. The sound, or the movement, of your

chest rising can give you away. You have to remember to breathe.

The man looked right at me but did not see me. I was wearing jeans and an old fatigue shirt. My face was hidden by the bill of my boonie hat. But it was not the clothes that concealed me. All the camouflage in the world won't hide you if you move. Stillness is the best concealment.

I stayed still until the man had moved onto the high ground and was out of sight. Then I got up slowly, slipped into my pack, and followed him. I found his tracks in the leaves.

I moved as slowly as he had. And I kept my eyes moving, trying to pick out his shape in the shadows of the tall trees ahead. But I did not sneak. I wanted to look like a careful bird-watcher, or a hunter out scouting locations before opening day. I took a pair of armored binoculars out of my pack and hung them around my neck. I didn't have a gun. That alone ought to make me look harmless, I hoped.

I smelled smoke. The odor was faint but precise. It smelled warm and clean in the thick, wet air of the bottom. I made a show of studying things through the binoculars. Then took a sip of water. Wiped my face with a bandanna. Then began walking again, following the falling contour of the finger of land.

"Hey." The voice came from a little fold in the earth twenty yards off the line I was following.

I had guessed he would be there. But I was still startled enough to jump convincingly.

"Damn," I said, "you scared me."

William Jordan came up the bank of the little fold carrying a small sporting rifle, which was pointed at the ground, not at me. He wore camouflage fatigues. No pack or load-bearing gear. His face was shaved and he looked clean, which was surprising since he had been living in these woods—off and on —for more than a month now.

"I sure thought I had this place to myself," I said, trying for the false friendly tone of someone who wants to make it clear he has no hostile intent or capability. I was just a harmless guy out for a harmless walk in the woods.

Jordan studied me for a second. He squeezed his eyes close together in the middle of his long, thin face. He had a small jaw and thin lips. It was unmistakably a mountain face, and its normal expression was suspicion.

"What are you doing out here?" he said. There was an edge to his voice. He wasn't asking a question so much as issuing a challenge.

"Came out to do a little scouting."

"Scouting?"

I made myself sound apologetic. "Well, yeah, *scouting*. For bow season. I like to come out and see what kind of mast crop we've got. Look for trails. Places where I can build a tree stand. Nice to get out in the woods, too. You know what I mean?"

His suspicious eyes stayed locked on mine.

"How about it," I said, "you seen anything?" The woods felt very still and quiet. It seemed as though we were absolutely alone, if not in the entire world then certainly in the part of it that made any difference. Neither of us had allies or help. There were no referees. It made every word and every gesture very important.

He moved his head an inch or two. It was a nod of sorts.

"Deer?" I asked.

"Uh-huh."

"You scouting too?"

He gave me the same fractional nod.

"Well, I'll move on," I said brightly. "I don't want to crowd you."

When I started walking again, he spoke up. "I've got a camp up there."

I turned and looked at him. I tried to put some honest concern in my face. I wanted him to think I might just possibly report him and his campsite when I got out of the woods. I wanted him to think it was to his advantage to show me his camp so I could see that he wasn't doing anything illegal there, like killing alligators or picking up bundles of dope that somebody had kicked out the door of a low-flying airplane. The deep parts of Eglin had been used for those purposes. Jordan wouldn't want anyone coming out to see what he was up to because some suspicious hunter had reported him.

"Yeah, well, before you leave, why don't you come talk to my boy? He's been out here with me. Maybe we can tell you something that will help you come hunting season." He was trying to sound friendly, but it was an effort and it showed.

"Well, thanks," I said, like he had me fooled. "I appreciate that. Appreciate it a lot."

He led the way for the last hundred yards. The first sign of the camp was a clothesline made from five-fifty parachute cord and draped with jeans and fatigue shirts drying, after a fashion, in the wet heat of the swamp. Beyond the clothesline, a shelter fashioned from a nylon tarp and some skinned hickory poles covered several packs, cooking gear, another rifle, and a couple of waterproof bags tied carefully at the neck.

Across the clearing, there was a fire pit with a spit stretched across it and a small table built of lashed sticks to one side. A low and very hot bed of coals glowed in the bottom of the pit, giving off almost no visible smoke. But I could feel the heat as I passed.

There was a drying rack near the fire pit. It had been made from thin, green branches woven into a mesh and lashed at the corners. Some strips of meat and several fish fillets lay on the rack, covered with what looked like pepper. That would be to keep the flies away, I thought.

In a small, shady, open area, two jungle hammocks hung from sturdy trees. The mosquito nets had been rolled up to ventilate the hammocks. I could see the creek bank a few yards beyond.

"Luther, come on up here," Jordan said.

A boy appeared at the lip of the creek bank, which had concealed him. He held a small, square net in one hand and a stringer with four catfish in the other. He was not smiling, but he didn't look unhappy. More curious than anything else.

He held the catfish up for his father to admire.

"That's real good," Jordan said. "I'll help you clean 'em in a minute. Right now, come over here."

The boy left his stringer in the creek and joined us. He was not quite chest-high on his father, and he had one of those utterly calm faces you see on kids who are never sure what might happen next and are not about to commit themselves to anything. His left eye seemed to wander, as though it were not entirely under his control.

Still, Luther Jordan was a healthy-looking boy. Like his father, he was clean. He had good color, and he looked strong and well fed.

"Ran into a man doing some scouting for deer season," Jordan said.

The boy nodded, still noncommittal.

"Thought we might as well tell him what we've

seen since we'll be long gone by then." It sounded like a promise of some sort. The kind a man might make to a discouraged wife. *Honey, I swear, one day we're going to leave this rinky-dink town.*

The boy nodded again, like he'd heard it all before and was not going to hold his breath.

Jordan looked at the boy, and where I had expected impatience or disapproval or outright anger there was something else. A look of almost tender concern. The look of a father who would do almost anything to see a smile on his son's face.

"How about this?" Jordan said. "Let's clean your fish and we'll all have lunch. It's nearly that time of day, and that's what you ought to do when a stranger comes into your camp. You ought to invite him to break bread and share your bounty."

It sounded strange, but I remembered the stories about Jordan and the Big Ranger.

"Fine," Luther said in a voice full of indifference.

"Will you have some lunch?" Jordan said, looking at me now.

"I don't want to put you out."

"You won't," he said. "We've gone a while now without anyone to talk to. We'd like the company."

"All right, then. But let me help clean those fish."

"No," the boy said. "I'll do it."

"He likes doing it," Jordan said, giving me a proud look and a smile. "Catches 'em, cleans 'em, and cooks 'em. All by himself."

"That's good," I said. "Real good."

"He's a tiger in the woods," Jordan explained. "He can do it all."

The boy walked back to the creek without saying anything. We followed, a little behind.

"I brought him out here for the summer because I thought he could learn more doing this than he could watching television at home or playing the video games down at the mall," Jordan said. "He didn't like it at first. Hated the bugs and being dirty. Afraid of snakes. Missed the radio and the television. But then he started to come around. Lately, he's come around *strong*."

"How long have you been here?"

"Around a month now."

"Long time for a boy."

"For most men, too," he said. "One night of this is too much for a lot of people. My boy there already knows more, and can do more, than most grown men. Watch him with those fish."

We stood on the bank and watched while the boy worked. He used a small folding knife with a long, thin blade, which he tested with his thumb. He pulled a small stone from his pocket and worked the blade across it, ten strokes to the side. He tested the blade again, and this time it satisfied him. He cut open a fish, taking fillets with single strokes and then laying them skin-down on top of a smooth cedar log and working the blade between skin and flesh and separating them in one motion. He laid the fillets aside and threw the heads and offal into a small basket made from woven branches.

"He'll use the guts and stuff to bait snares," Jordan said. "Nothing in season right now, and the pelts ain't no good. I let him do it for the experience, you know." He looked at me to see if I disapproved and if I was the kind to report a kid for taking fur-bearing animals out of season with improvised snares.

"More boys ought to be learning how to do that," I said.

Luther rinsed the fillets in the creek. Then he put

them in another woven basket and climbed up the creek bank.

"All set?" his father asked.

The boy nodded.

"Then let's go fry 'em up."

Luther did the cooking in a large, black skillet. I wondered if the grease had been rendered from the fat of a wild hog or if it had come from a can. I saw some apples and some coffee, which certainly came from a grocery store.

"I brought a few things with us," Jordan said, answering my question in a general way. "The idea was to see if we could make do. I wanted it to be a challenge without us living like cavemen. But we could do *that* if we had to."

We talked while the fish was frying, about where they had seen game trails and actual deer. There was one big buck, in particular, that they wanted me to know about, and I made a point of looking interested. The fish smelled good, and the boy was careful to turn the fillets so they didn't burn. He served them on steel plates. Before we ate, Jordan said grace over the food.

"Lord, we thank you for providing and for teaching us to provide. Keep us strong for the battle. Amen."

I tasted the fish. It was crisp and sweet. Catfish has no status even though it has wonderful flavor. Someday, I suppose, that will change. If people can be sold on redfish, they will eat anything.

"This fish is special," I said.

The boy thanked me.

"He cooks it just right," Jordan said. "But after a month of it, we're about ready for something else."

"How much longer will you be out here?" I asked, looking at Luther.

"Rest of the summer," he said.

"Then back to school, right?"

"Yes, sir."

"Where's that?"

"Out West somewhere—" the boy started. But his father interrupted him.

"We ain't sure yet. Been in Columbus, Georgia, up to now, but we're thinking we might try something different. Who knows, we may go to California."

"Be different," I said.

"Sometimes that's not so bad. We're looking for something new, isn't that right, Luther?"

"Yes, sir," the boy said carefully.

"You ever been out West?" I said to the boy.

"No, sir." He shook his head. "But I would like to go."

"Why's that?"

"I don't know." He shrugged. "I guess because I'd like to have a horse. Place to ride."

"But I'll bet you'll miss this swamp," I said.

He made the same shy smile. "In a way."

The boy gathered the steel plates and carried them to the stream. He returned carrying a bucket of fresh water, which he hung over the fire pit. He dropped the plates into the bucket.

I stood and thanked them for the lunch. Shook both their hands. Jordan was plainly glad to see me go. Luther didn't seem to care much one way or the other.

I left the camp and took a compass line back to the road. It was a quiet walk, and I had time to think. I had told Semmes and Fearson I would try to find Luther, and now that I'd done it, it didn't seem as important as it once had. But I was still pleased. I felt the boy was safe even though I was sure, now, that William Jordan had killed Perkins.

Right now, I thought, the best place for both of them was right in this swamp. I knew where they were, and if I needed them I could go in and get them. Otherwise, they could stay right there and get to know each other a little better.

Chapter Seventeen

"Very impressive, Morgan," Semmes said. "Very impressive. You wouldn't want to tell me how you did it, would you?"

"One of Jordan's Ranger School buddies told me where he stored his stuff. There were some maps, along with the insurance papers and birth certificate and such. He had that place marked in grease pencil on one of his maps." I didn't mention that I'd broken the law to get a look at that stuff. I knew what Semmes would think of that.

"Very impressive," he said again.

"I got lucky."

"No," he said. "Finding those maps was fortune. Not luck."

Another of Semmes's distinctions. "What's the difference?" I said.

He leaned back in his leather chair and made a half-turn to look out at the bay, which was smooth as a polished jewel. "Luck is random. Pure chance. Sort of thing people who go to Las Vegas believe in. Fortune is not predictable, but it contains elements of character."

"If you say so."

"Not just me. Goethe too." Semmes made a solemn face and spoke in a fake magisterial tone, " 'How closely linked are Luck and Merit is something fools have never known.' "

"OK," I said. "I'll buy that. But what do I do next?"

"Drink a cup of coffee and wait till John Fearson comes in. He'll be along in another ten or fifteen minutes."

"He holding up OK?"

"He's putting on a good show, which is important. But it is a strain."

And you could see the cracks. Fearson's face was drawn, and there were cusps of gray under his eyes. He'd lost weight.

We shook all around and then Semmes said, "Morgan has some good news."

John looked at me and some life came back into his face. "You found Luther?"

I nodded.

He put a massive hand on my shoulder and squeezed. He could have made it hurt, but he stopped just short of that. He looked into my face. His eyes, which were red already, misted over. "God bless you," he said. "God bless you. Tell me about it."

I did. When I was finished, he said, "So he's safe and doing all right?"

"He looked fine to me. Didn't smile much. Quiet. Kept to himself."

"That's the way he is."

Fearson shook his head with relief. "I've got to admit," he said, "I didn't think you could do it."

"The truth is," Semmes said, "he's good. But that's old news. Let's sit down and talk about what we're going to do next."

Fearson and I took the chairs facing Semmes's desk. Semmes made a steeple of his fingers and rested his chin on it. "Let's talk about the boy first. Should we try to get him out of that swamp and away from his father?"

Fearson shook his head.

"Why not?"

"He's with his father and his father wants him. It isn't what you would call a normal home situation, but how many of those do you see? Anyway," Fearson said slowly, "Luther probably has a better chance with his father than he does with me. If I get closed, my boys go to foster homes."

"All right, then," Semmes said. "Let's talk about that, about keeping Sweetwater Ranch open and beating Rick Hewes till he's a wet place on the floor."

Semmes tapped one temple with a long, bent finger. "I want to talk straight. It will all stay here, in this room."

Fearson stiffened in his chair. "All right, Nat."

"You've seen what Morgan can do, John. He found Luther, and he found people who knew Rick Hewes and could tell stories about what kind of kid he is. That's good for us. But Ed Straylow is going to have his investigators out there too. They may not be quite as good as Morgan, but they'll be good enough. They'll talk to the kids you threw out of Sweetwater and the ones who ran away. They'll find them in jail or drug rehab, and they'll get them to tell their stories."

Fearson was looking straight into Semmes's eyes. A knot of muscle quivered in his cheek; otherwise, he was still as stone.

"We're going to have a tough time. No way around it. You'll make it tougher if you hold out on me. So I want you to think back and tell me about any kid you hit."

Fearson's lips hardly moved, but the words came out with force. "I *never* hit one of those boys."

"Not one?"

"No, sir."

"Four years, all those boys that came through there, and you never lost your temper and punched one out?"

"Lost my temper, sure. But never punched one out."

"You did punish them, didn't you?"

"When they needed it."

"Did you ever lock a boy up and not let him have anything to eat for an extended length of time?" Semmes sounded like he was reading from a script.

"Where did you get that?" Fearson said, pushing the words through his teeth.

"The papers this morning."

"Come on, Nat," Fearson said, almost pleading, "didn't your parents ever send you to bed without your supper?"

Semmes smiled with one corner of his mouth. It was the smile he used when he'd trapped a witness in his own lie. "What about 'physical punishments that were straight out of military boot camp or old-fashioned football practices'?"

"I made 'em run laps if they got into fights."

"Ever run them in the rain?"

"That's when you get most of your problems. When it's been raining for a couple of days and the boys have been inside."

"So you did send them out in the rain to run laps?"

"And made 'em take a hot shower and change into clean clothes when they got back. It seemed to settle 'em down, Nat. Everyone understood it. They even made jokes about it."

Semmes nodded. "All right. Well, what about the strap?"

"What?"

"The leather strap you beat your boys with."

"You mean my belt, don't you?" Fearson said.

"Belt, strap, you call it by any name you like. Let's just say it was a flat length of leather that you would lay against some little boy's flesh in order to make him feel pain. You agree with that description?"

Fearson hit the arms of his chair with his hands. The sound was like a shot. His face was red, and he rose out of his chair with his eyes on fire.

"Now you listen—"

I was reaching to hold him back when Semmes held up his hands with his palms facing Fearson. He smiled.

"Easy," he said. "It's me, old Nat Semmes, not some halfback from LSU."

"Nat, you got to *believe* me," Fearson said, still crouched half in and half out of his chair. "I wasn't trying to hurt those kids. I *love* those boys." His voice cracked.

"I hear what you say, John. And I believe you," Semmes said. "Now you listen to what I say, and you had *best* believe me. I'm speaking as your lawyer. You and your lawyer are discussing a trial. You will be a witness, and what you say and how you say it will decide whether you win or lose and might even decide whether a civil suit turns into a criminal action. You understand?"

"Yes," Fearson said. He was sitting again. There was something small about his voice now. Small and almost meek.

"You are going to have to answer questions that are a whole lot tougher. And Straylow will insinuate that you probably did things we'll never know about to those kids. Unspeakable things. He's going to try to make you look like a drooling, raging fiend. If you lose your temper, then you'll just be helping him. Understand?"

"Yes," Fearson said softly.

"Straylow and I will ask you about the same events. What he'll make sound like a savage beating I'll make sound like a routine spanking."

Fearson nodded.

"He'll find his expert witnesses—psychologists and the like—who will come in and say that any physical punishment amounts to abuse and inflicts permanent emotional damage and so on and so forth. I'll bring in my tame psychologists with all the same degrees, and they'll say that firm discipline is necessary and good and all that. The jury won't know who to believe when they're through."

Fearson shook his head helplessly.

Semmes smiled ironically. "It's called expert testimony in the trade. The idea is to give the jury unbiased, technical information that everyone can agree on. But you can find people with degrees to argue either side of anything in this world. With two good lawyers—and that's what we've got here—one side's experts just cancel out the other's. That leaves the jury trusting its own instincts."

"So I have to make a good impression," Fearson said.

"On twelve strangers."

"I can't believe this."

"Most people who find themselves in court can't believe it. They say it is like a dream. They become very passive. Just lie down on the track and let the old train run over them. I want you to convince yourself that this is real, John, and start getting yourself ready for it, just like it was a big game. For the national championship, say. Prepare yourself, psych yourself up, visualize yourself on the stand—get *into* it, all the way into it. Do that and you'll be all right."

Fearson nodded again.

"OK. Now did you bring that list I asked you for?"

"Yes."

"Good. Let's get a copy and give it to Morgan so he can get started."

The list ran to about three dozen names in two columns. There were phone numbers and addresses next to some of the names but not all of them. The names in one column belonged to boys who had been at Sweetwater and were now somewhere else and doing all right. They were in college or the service or simply working and staying out of trouble. The other names belonged to boys who had run away from Sweetwater or had been kicked out for breaking the rules. Some of them were in places unknown, if, indeed, they were still alive. A couple were in jail or some other kind of custody. The rest were, when last heard from, back at home or in a foster home.

When I'd gone over the list, asked a few questions, and made a couple of notes, Semmes got up to walk Fearson out. I went with them. While we waited for the slow elevator, Semmes put his hand on Fearson's shoulder and said, "Hang in there, John. We'll beat this thing."

Fearson nodded. "I got confidence in you, Nat. If you tell me something, then I'll believe it. But there's something I know that you aren't telling me."

"What's that?"

"Even if we do beat them, like you say, a lot of people will still believe the things that boy is saying about me. It's not ever going to be the same again."

"No," Semmes said. "It won't. I wish I could tell you different, but I can't."

Fearson sucked in a huge breath. "Well, nothing to do but play to the gun. I appreciate what you're doing, Nat, and what you've done, Morgan. No way I could ever pay you back for that."

He shook Semmes's hand. Then mine. He stepped into the elegantly paneled car. He was smiling when the elevator doors closed, but it was not the smile I'd first seen out at Sweetwater. This was a salesman's smile, the kind you see on the face of a man trying to convince himself that his own line of goods isn't a lot of worthless junk.

"Can you stick around for a while?" Semmes said after the elevator doors had closed.

"Sure."

"I've got some people coming in—the directors of Sweetwater and somebody from their insurance company. They're going to want to know how it's going. And I expect they'll be thinking about a settlement."

"I see."

"You don't approve, do you?"

"No," I said. "It makes good sense, I suppose, but I don't like it."

Semmes smiled. "No more than I do. I can promise you that. Clean conclusions, that's what I want out of life, but they get scarcer and scarcer. Up or down; yes or no. Spare me this endless ambiguity. Gets so it's like swimming in muddy water."

"I know what you mean."

"Well, nothing we can do about it, standing out here in the hall. Let's go back inside and drink a cup of coffee. Those boys will be along in a few minutes. We'll tell 'em what we have to tell 'em, and we'll listen to what they have to say. Then we'll see if we can find a way, between us, to cut this thing nice and clean."

The meeting started about fifteen minutes later. Semmes knew all five of the directors of Sweetwater, and when he shook their hands and asked about their wives, children, golf games, and such you could see why his family had once pushed him to go into politics. All these men felt comfortable with him and trusted him. Nat Semmes radiated a kind of confidence and toughness that made you feel like whatever happened he would deal straight up and he wasn't starting out with some secret agenda. To my mind, his family had it wrong. He was way too good for politics.

The chairman of the board of directors was a big-boned man with pale skin, thinning blond hair, and a mouth crowded with oversize teeth. His loud, hearty voice filled the room. According to Semmes, he was one of those restless, gregarious men who go through life making deals and friends compulsively. He'd started out buying and selling timberland back when they were still turpentining trees, and when he'd made a little at that and they quit cutting trees for sap, he got into banks and farms and oil leases. When they came in, he did shopping centers and suburbs. Then condominiums. Along the way, he'd raised his family, performed his civic chores, and generally lived a blameless life.

"Nobody ever got hurt by getting too close to Charlie Blanchard," Semmes had said. "He sees life pretty simple and doesn't understand why everyone isn't the same way. Something like this Sweetwater thing just bewilders him. He'll want to see if there isn't some way we can't just fix it, clear it up like it was some kind of minor family misunderstanding."

Blanchard shook my hand heartily and said, "How you doing, son? Nat here has told me a lot about you, and I'm glad to finally meet you."

"Pleased to meet you too," I said. And I was.

"You helping out on this thing with Sweetwater?"

"Yes, sir." It was easy enough to call him sir.

"Call me Charlie, would you please? Doctors and IRS agents call me sir."

"OK, Charlie."

"Hell of a mess," he said. "Just a *hell* of a mess."

I agreed that it was a hell of a mess.

"I don't see why it has to happen to someone trying so hard to do some good, you know what I mean?"

I said I knew what he meant.

"I just hope old Nat can clear it up so Big John can get on with what he's doing. And I'll tell you what, if Nat *can't* do it, then the thing just can't be done. You know what I mean?"

Exactly, I said.

"So I got to believe Nat will do it," Blanchard said confidently. "Especially with you on the team."

Blanchard introduced me to the other directors.

They all looked like sober businessmen, prosperous by the standards of their part of the world but certainly not hog-rich Wall Streeters. These were middle-aged men in nondescript business suits, physically soft and instinctively amiable. None of them had more than a fraction of Blanchard's aggressive good cheer, but they were all the sort you would have been happy to trust your estate to or sit next to on an airplane.

The last man Blanchard introduced me to was thinner, more precise, not so easy to read, and harder to like. He was with the insurance company. His name was Bill Tinker, and he wore a seersucker suit and bifocals in aviator frames.

Blanchard sat directly across from Semmes's desk. The other directors took chairs to either side of him. Tinker sat on the couch, and I found a place next to the bookshelves, out of the main orbit of action. After everyone had declined coffee, Blanchard said, "Well, Nat, we all know why we're here. It's a bad situation and no one likes it, but I think I can speak for everyone when I say we're glad you're handling it."

The other directors nodded. Tinker remained motionless on the couch, a briefcase in his lap and his hands folded on top of it.

"Now, we understand that it's still early in this game. First series after the kickoff, if you know what I mean. Right now, you're representing all of us, as the board of directors of Sweetwater Ranch. You want a retainer, or something, to make it official?"

Semmes shook his head. "No need, Charlie. I've got your letter."

"Fine," Blanchard said. "I think you know we're good for the fee, and we don't expect any special discounts."

Semmes smiled. "And I know where to find you if the check doesn't clear."

Blanchard liked that and smiled big enough to expose about half his teeth.

"All right, then. Now, the time may come when all of us in this room might need to be represented separately. But let's hope not. Better for everyone if it's done quick and not too complicated. You'd agree with that, wouldn't you?"

Semmes nodded, making it plain that his agreement was equivocal. Blanchard, who probably noticed, went ahead. He wasn't the kind to get bogged down in preliminaries if he could help it.

"Then, why don't you take over, Nat? You talk and we'll listen."

Semmes rocked back a little in his chair and said, "Let's start with what lawyers call matters of fact. The truth, in other words. Matters of law are tougher, so we'll take them later."

"Fine," Blanchard said. "Always best to start out with an accurate survey."

"You've all met Morgan Hunt, here," Semmes said, nodding in my direction. "He's my investigator, my eyes and ears on this case, and I believe he's as good as there is. I'd like for him to tell you what he's found out about the plaintiff."

The men in front of Semmes's desk turned slightly to look at me. Tinker's eyes remained on the wall opposite the couch where he was sitting, as though he were deeply engaged by the Audubon print of an osprey that hung there.

I spoke for about five minutes, recounting what I'd learned about Rick Hewes on my trip to Columbus. When I finished, no one said anything for a few seconds. Then Blanchard, who wasn't comfortable with silences, said, "Sure takes all kinds, don't it?

Big John tried to *help* that boy, and look what he gives him back."

"He's a slug, Charlie," Semmes said. "He leaves a wet trail behind him everywhere he goes, and it would be a shame to make him rich just for leaving some of his slime on John Fearson."

"Absolutely," Blanchard said. "If there's anyone in the world who doesn't deserve this, it's John Fearson. You know how I feel about him. Hell, we all feel that way. That's why we backed him."

"I know," Semmes said. "You've been good to John. He couldn't have done what he's done without you."

Blanchard appreciated that and said so. Then he asked if this meant that Semmes thought he could win this thing by showing the Hewes boy to be a liar.

"It means I can ruin him as a witness. I'll know more about the specifics of his case once we get into depositions. But in a courtroom, I'll skin him."

"That's in a *trial*, right?"

"Correct."

"You can't stop it from going to trial, Nat?"

"Maybe. If I can make his lawyer see what kind of client he's got and what I'll do to his credibility. But I'd call it a long shot."

"Why's that?"

Semmes explained that if the lawyer had gone this far he probably would not be inclined to drop the case cold. "He's got to believe that the case is worth something." When he said this, Semmes looked in the direction of Tinker, whose eyes were still on the painted osprey, which held a struggling fish in its talons.

"We're all grown men, here," Blanchard said, "so we know what that means."

Semmes nodded.

"Everyone here has had to make a settlement he didn't like at one time or another. Except maybe Mr. Hunt there." Blanchard nodded in my direction. "Most of us aren't willing to pay the way he did. It comes down to figuring costs. If you've got to pay one way or the other, then you might as well get out as cheap as you can and plan on knowing better next time."

Blanchard spoke more softly as they got closer to the core of the conversation. "You need figures before you can decide if the price is too high."

"I haven't had any offers . . . yet."

"You think you'll be getting one?"

"Any day now."

"Then, maybe you should know what our thinking is."

Blanchard turned slightly to Tinker, whose eyes left the print he'd been staring at so intently and shifted focus. Otherwise, his face did not change. He had no personal stake in any of this, came at it with all the passion of a body man appraising a crushed fender.

"The board has a policy with us. The maximum coverage is for five million. The deductible is a hundred thousand dollars."

"We'll be out a fair amount," Blanchard said, "even if this thing never goes to trial and we do settle."

Semmes nodded, and there was a touch of sympathy in the way he did it.

"If we go to trial," Tinker said, "the company may want to retain you, or it may prefer to use other counsel."

This time when Semmes nodded, it was quick and curt.

"The question the company has to ask is, When do the legal expenses begin to outweigh the costs of a settlement?"

"Do you know the answer?" Semmes said.

"Not precisely. But it seems reasonable to think that in a case of this sort—with the number of witnesses who'll have to be deposed, the requirement for an investigator"—Tinker looked at me without interest, as though he were merely taking inventory —"the research, and expert-witness fees plus the billable hours—that we would be better off settling this case for one hundred and fifty to two hundred thousand than seeing it through to a verdict. No matter how good your evidence is or how well it is presented, child abuse is a touchy issue with juries. These days, especially."

"Cost you fifty thousand, then?" Semmes said.

"Plus or minus."

"What do you get for your money?"

"Plaintiff waives all claims, past and present, against our clients."

"What about a statement, for public release, to the effect that John Fearson never treated the plaintiff—or any of those other kids—with brutality?"

Tinker said nothing.

"That's not part of the package, then? Even though Hewes and his lawyer will be getting two hundred thousand—*plus or minus*—for three weeks of easy work? Nothing but telling a bunch of bald lies, baiting the press, filing a few papers, and promising to find another mark before they do it again? Seems like you could raise the ante just enough to cover some kind of statement that would give John Fearson his reputation back. Part of it, anyway. No way he can get it all."

"That sort of statement is not one of our conditions."

"What would it be worth to you?"

"Nothing. It would be an abandonment of our fiduciary duty to our stockholders to increase the size of the settlement merely to secure such a statement."

"What if I talked the Hewes kid's attorney into throwing a statement like that in for free?"

"We'd have no objection, of course."

"Of course," Semmes said softly, looking straight into Tinker's calm eyes.

"I have a heart too," Tinker said. "I do this every day, and I might like it less than you."

While Semmes was still staring at Tinker, Blanchard spoke up. "Listen, Nat, *nobody* wants John Fearson to get hurt any more by this thing. You do what you can to settle up with this other lawyer. If he wants more for a statement clearing Big John and Mr. Tinker here can't come up with the money, then I'm good for it. You can go as high as fifty thousand without asking me. Any more than that, I'd like a call."

"That's awfully generous, Charlie."

"You know what it costs to keep one inmate down at Raiford for one year? John Fearson is doing something wonderful and doing it mostly by hard work and sweat. I don't mind giving him money."

"All right. But I'll try not to spend that much."

"Whatever you think best, Nat."

Semmes looked across the room to Tinker, whose eyes were once more focused on the print.

"Am I authorized to negotiate a settlement?"

"Preliminary discussions only."

"Oh, absolutely."

That ended the meeting. We stood and shook

hands all around. I waited while Semmes showed everyone to the door.

"I'll be getting a call from this Straylow any day now," Semmes said when he came back to the office.

"Will he make the deal?"

"I expect. I would if I were in his position. I *think* I would, anyway. But I can't be sure because I can't imagine being in his position. Don't believe I could live with myself."

"No chance of fighting him out in the open?"

Semmes thought for a moment. "If he's just looking for a quick deal and he gets it from the insurance company, he's not going to care about going to court with John. So if we separate the cases against the board and John, Straylow will just take his money and let the case against John die."

"That doesn't do anything for John's reputation."

"No. It doesn't."

"How about fighting him in the papers and on television, then? Give some reporters what I've learned about Hewes."

Semmes shook his head. "You're trying to prove a negative and that's almost impossible. Straylow used the papers to scare John into thinking there might be a criminal case down the road if he doesn't settle quickly. It is also a good way to make the insurance company real nervous.

"We can try to get John's side out there, but unless John wins in court or the kid and his lawyer retract the charges a lot of people are still going to think John is guilty. Some will no matter what we do."

"Seems to me like we need to burn that kid and his lawyer."

"Exactly," Semmes said. "And it will be a pleasure. In the meantime, do me a favor and check out the kids on your list and any other leads you've got on Sweetwater. I don't believe Big John is lying to us, but I don't want to join the legion of lawyers who wish they'd checked out some client's story."

"All right."

"And," Semmes said, "you probably ought to ask around a little about Edward Straylow. It's never a bad idea to know your enemy."

Chapter Eighteen

For three days, I talked to boys who had been with John Fearson. They were hesitant, most of them, and what I got from them came slowly. They did not volunteer anything, and I learned most of what I was looking for in what they did *not* say. None of them showed me scars or told me horror stories. I called Semmes every night and reported. He was reassured by what I told him. Fearson was what he seemed to be, as much as anyone ever is.

I asked the boys if they'd talked to anyone else about these things, and one of them said he had. An investigator had come around to the garage where he worked. They'd talked for a few minutes, and he'd told him the same things he told me. I asked the boy if he remembered the man's name.

"He gave me a card to keep," the boy said. He wiped the grease from his fingers and pulled out his wallet. The name was Jack A. Riordan. There was a phone number in the 904 area, no address, and the single word INVESTIGATIONS printed in the lower corner. I'd never heard of Riordan, but that didn't necessarily mean anything. I wrote the name and the number in my book, thanked the boy for his time, and drove to Tom Pine's office, where I found him with his feet up on the desk reading an official-looking report.

"Sit," he said. "What can I do for you?"

"Do you know an investigator named Jack Riordan?"

Pine shook his big head slowly, side to side, in a weary sort of way. "Never had the pleasure."

"If he'd been around to talk to someone in the jail, would you be able to find out?"

"If the phone is still working, I would."

"You mind?"

He thought for a moment. "Don't see why not."

He picked up the phone, dialed, and then identified himself and asked a few quick questions. He put the phone down.

"He was over there day before yesterday to speak to one of our tenants. Fellow by the name of Reese, who is eighteen and staying with us while he waits to see the judge about stealing a car and then holding up about ten different convenience stores with a nickel-plated, slide-action shotgun.

"We had a better description of that shotgun than we did of the punk. One cashier said it was like looking down the mouth of a piece of three-inch pipe. He made an impression, Reese did, with his choice of ordnance. Me, I thought he was kind of overdoing it. Like wearing a tuxedo to a dogfight. You want to see him?"

"I probably should."

"Then I'll walk you over," he said. "I can use my influence to get you to the head of the line."

We walked to the jail, which was a block from Pine's office. It was a new, three-story building, mustard in color and surrounded by a high chain-link fence with loops of concertina running along the top. The razor edges of the wire glittered like shattered glass.

Pine spoke to someone at a desk inside the front door. The man nodded, picked up a phone, and called for a turnkey. When the man arrived, Pine said, "Enjoy your visit," and went back to work.

The turnkey led me up a flight of stairs and then down a long concrete deck. Jail smelled just like I remembered. It was the smell of rot, a special kind of decay that is so constant and oppressive that you begin to think that even the steel and concrete are in a state of decomposition.

Near the end of the deck, the turnkey stopped in front of a small cell where the boy I was looking for lay on a dirty mattress, looking at the ceiling and listening to a big, loud radio. It was a two-man cell, but he had it to himself.

"Someone here to see you," the turnkey said.

The boy on the bunk did not move or take his eyes off the ceiling. "Yeah? Well, who the fuck is he?"

"Ask him yourself. You've got ten minutes."

The turnkey walked away, and the boy rolled over on his bunk and looked at me with one bleary eye.

"You from the public defender?" he said. "How come you ain't wearing a suit? Lawyers all wear suits, even the babes."

"I'm just a civilian," I said. "I'd like to ask you a few questions."

"Talk to my lawyer," he said and rolled away, showing me his back.

"It isn't about your case."

"Go fuck yourself."

"I want to ask you about someone who tried to help you."

"No such person."

"John Fearson?"

"That prick." The boy laughed in the convict way, all mouth and nose. He sounded like he was trying to get rid of something before it gagged him. "Man, he put me through some shit, but now he is going to get his."

The boy rolled off the bunk and stood to look me over. He was average height, thin and flabby at the same time. When you are inside, the flesh goes white and spongy if you don't exercise. He had eyes the size and color of old pennies and homemade tattoos on his skinny forearms.

"Preacher John and his camp for lost boys. What a load of shit. Preaching and coaching. Always slinging this old shit about how if you worked hard and you didn't quit, you could make it in the world. Told us how hard he'd worked when he played football and how it had paid off for him. All bullshit."

"Didn't inspire you, huh?"

"Hey, man, you ever *seen* him? They call him *Big* John for a reason. Body like that, he was going to make it as a football player. He had it right from the jump, and he's telling a bunch of kids who've never had any luck that they can make it if they do right, work hard, and pray. That is just a fucking lie."

"Is that all you've got against him, or did he do something to you?"

"Son of a bitch whipped me with his belt. Like I was some kind of fucking kid."

"What did you do?"

"I should have killed him."

"I mean, why did he hit you with his belt?"

His eyes shifted slightly to one side. "Fuck, I don't know. Broke some rule. You couldn't turn around without breaking some kind of rule."

"Which one did you break?"

"I don't remember."

"Stealing?"

His eyes moved to the side, slipping out of contact with mine. Even in jail his kind can't call a thing by its name. He didn't think of himself as a *thief*, and what he did wasn't *stealing*. He makes it sound like combat, something tough, not furtive. He *knocks over* a store, *hijacks* a truck, or *boosts* a TV. Better for the image. Convicts are long on image and sensitive to any slight. Men get shanked over slights a free-worlder would miss entirely.

"Big John and his fucking rules. Make a mistake and you pay. Well, guess what? Now he's going to pay. He broke the rules, and now he's going to get his. Wait long enough and everything comes back around. I love it. What I want to see is Big John in here for a few nights. That would be just fucking wonderful. And I'm going to help make it happen."

I didn't say anything.

"You're working for Fearson, aren't you?" He was smiling, showing a mouth full of bad teeth.

I still didn't say anything.

"Tell him it's payback time. Tell him I remember that belt."

"Tell him yourself."

"Maybe I will, in here."

"Don't hold your breath," I said. The turnkey was at my shoulder and we left together. Behind us, Reese shouted the old line about payback.

* * *

There was a message for me at the gate. Pine wanted to meet me at a place out on the bay. I drove out there, parked, and took a beer out back, where you could sit on a seawall and watch the boats pass and the gulls feed. Today, there was a mullet fisherman wading the flat, throwing a cast net in limp circles on the still water. He would study the surface with the patience of a raptor, then wind up and throw. There would be two or three struggling silver fish in the net each time he brought it in. He was good, and I watched until Tom Pine came up behind me.

"You expect it could get very goddamned much hotter?" he said.

He carried two cans of cold beer, and he handed one to me. "Sorry I'm late."

"No problem," I said.

We sat at a picnic table that was shaded by a canvas awning that had been bleached by the sun until the original blue was almost gone.

"I called that guy Riordan," Pine said.

I gave him a look.

"Must be I'm bored," he said. "Maybe it's the heat. Not enough trouble of my own, so I've got to go fooling around in yours."

"You talk to him?"

"Nah," Pine said. "The only number listed is for the law offices of Edward Straylow over in Panama City. So I checked to see if Riordan is licensed with the state. Bonded and all that. He's not, but you don't have to be as long as you just work for one lawyer."

"I know," I said.

Pine took a swallow of beer, then exhaled with a kind of animal satisfaction. "I was so eat up with curiosity by then that I talked to a friend of mine in

the sheriff's office in Bay County to find out what he
knew about Riordan. What he told me might be interesting to you.

"Seems Riordan was a cop up East somewhere.
One of those New Jersey towns; I can't keep them
straight. Anyway, about a year ago, they came down
on the whole department with one of those corrup-
tion investigations. Guys wearing wires, special
prosecutors, planted evidence—the whole nine
yards. Riordan was one of the dirty ones, but he
won the race to the prosecutor's office and made
himself a deal, testified against all his old partners
and buddies in exchange for immunity and helped
send a lot of them up. They offered him witness protection, a brand-new identity, and a job to keep
body and soul together, but he turned them down.
Came here, instead, to hide out in the backwoods
among the hicks. My buddy talked to somebody
back where Riordan comes from. He said Riordan
turned down the witness program because he'd gotten used to the good life and didn't want to go back
to living hand-to-mouth off diddly-assed paychecks.
He also said that Riordan's going to be looking over
his shoulder for a long time now, after what he did."

"He won't be putting down deep roots here," I
said.

"Doesn't seem likely."

"Did your buddy know how he got hooked up
with Straylow?"

"Nope."

"What did he tell you about Straylow, then?"

"Nothing much. Far as he knows, Straylow is just
another hustling lawyer, practicing alone and taking what comes along. He said he couldn't see
where Straylow could afford to hire a full-time investigator and pay him the kind of money Riordan's

gotten used to making from payoffs and shake-
downs."

I finished my beer and thought for a minute. Pine
stared out at the water and looked contented.

"Well, I suppose I ought to find out more about
those two."

Pine nodded and said placidly, "Talk to Joe Carroll. He's a bailiff over at the county courthouse. He
was a cop—pretty good one—until he got his leg
broken so bad they almost had to take it off. A guy
he pulled over on a traffic charge ran over him, and
then while Carroll's lying on the side of the road,
the guy backed the car up and ran over him again.
The driver happened to be one of the state's ranking
psychopaths, and he'd been spending the morning
shooting Methedrine.

"Anyway, Joe talks to the lawyers, and he's thick
with a bunch of them. They do a lot of gossiping
about their brethren. You know, who's getting the
good cases and pulling down the big fees, who's on
the ropes. Girlfriends and boyfriends. All the good
stuff."

"I'll talk to him today," I said.

"Tell him I said hello."

"I will. And thanks, Tom. I owe you."

Pine waved that away like it was a fly pestering
his sleep. "I'd just like to see you and Semmes win
this thing. Be a real shame if you don't and Big John
goes down. How's it looking?"

"They're talking settlement."

Pine shook his massive head. "Now, ain't *that* a
bitch?"

"I'll buy that."

"Why don't you just flip a coin; pick odds or evens
or something? Save all this running around." He
drained his beer and put the empty down with dis-

gust. "When they get around to making me king, we'll have us some new rules, and you know what the first one's going to be?"

"What's that?"

"From now on, we play 'em all out to the end. No tie games and no settlements. Everything is win or lose, live or die. No more of this half-assed, halfway bullshit."

"You'd make a good king, Tom."

"Damn right. Everyone would call me You Blackness, and I wouldn't take no shit. Not even from white boys like you."

I found Joe Carroll in the bailiff's room at the old county courthouse, an indestructible-looking, quarry-stone building that sits in the middle of town surrounded by empty shops. The lobby smells like an old, airless attic, where dust particles fill the air like swarming insects.

There were three steel desks in the bailiff's room, and a man sat behind one of them reading a newspaper. He wore a uniform but no side arm. That must have been hard on the self-esteem, I thought. These days, even part-time security guards at third-rate country clubs carry guns.

"Help you?" the man said.

"Looking for Mr. Carroll."

"You found him," he said cheerfully. "What can I do for you?"

"Tom Pine said you might be able to help me."

Carroll smiled. "How is old Tom? Ornery as ever?"

"I'd say so."

"Good. We need more like him." The man folded his newspaper and stood up. He walked three or four steps in my direction, dragging a useless leg behind him. He stuck out his hand and we shook. I introduced myself.

"Pleased to meet you," Carroll said. He had a strong, slightly puzzled face, like a college kid still learning his way around, and a good build that had started to sag.

I told him I was doing some research for a lawyer, helping him prepare for a trial.

"Which lawyer?" he asked quickly.

"Confidential?"

"My word."

I told him I was working for Semmes, and he studied me closely for a second and then said, "OK. Now I know you. You're the vet Semmes finally got out of the slammer, right?"

"Afraid so."

He smiled. "Well, I *am* glad to meet you. I always thought you got a raw one."

I nodded.

"You just tell me what you want, and I'll do what I can to help you. I've got a lot of respect for Mr. Semmes. I mean, a *lot* of respect. I see a lot of lawyers, know more of them, probably, than is good for me, and he is one of a kind. They broke the damn mold."

I nodded again.

"Is this about the thing with that ballplayer and his camp?"

"Yes, it is."

"Sounds to me like he's getting a raw deal too."

"Semmes is trying to fix that."

"OK," Carroll said, "come on in and sit down, and tell me how I can help."

He led the way across the room and sat in a steel chair behind a desk. I pulled a chair away from one of the empty desks and sat across from him. Carroll picked up a pencil and tapped it nervously on the surface of the desk.

"OK," he said. "Let me have it."

I asked him what he knew about Edward Straylow, and he smiled knowingly. "Sizing up the opposition, huh?"

"That's right."

"Well, I'll tell you, he's not in Mr. Semmes's league. But not many of 'em are. You see a lot of hustle and drive around here. Most of them are hungry and plenty willing. They'll do what it takes to win, but they don't have the same confidence that Semmes has. When they stand up in court, it's like they're trying to sell themselves while they're selling the jury. They want to believe in their clients and all the things they're saying, but what they really believe in is winning the case. They're like preachers who know all the words in the Bible but still aren't sure any of them are true. Deep down, they think the whole thing might still be a big fairy tale. But they've got a church full of paying customers looking to them for the word, so they take a deep breath, and they start preaching and sweating and calling on the name of the Lord, and it's pretty good. They get most of the front pews going, but way back in the church, and deep down in their own hearts, it just isn't taking. That old poison of doubt is still inside eating away. You know what I mean?"

I smiled. "Exactly."

He smiled back. "I was raised on revivals. Couldn't wait until I got old enough to stop spending all my Sundays being saved.

"Anyway, Mr. Semmes doesn't have that problem. When he starts talking, you want to believe what he's saying because there isn't any question in your own mind that he believes it. Believes *hard* and in a way that just makes you want to believe along with him. I don't know where it comes from. I know a lot of it is that he won't take a case just for business, but I think some of it is just something you either have or you don't. Comes to you when you're born, you know, like red hair.

"Straylow didn't get it. Not any of it. So, like a lot of these boys, he tries to make up for it by hustling. He works hard. He's got plenty of hungry, and he doesn't mind a good fight. Like a lot of them, he believes he's better than he really is. You know how that goes—the reason he hasn't done better, in his mind, doesn't have anything to do with how good he is; it's all a matter of not getting the breaks. He missed the good cases because of bad luck, lost his appeals because some judge was against him personally, couldn't push some new argument far enough because he didn't have the money. I'd say he's almost as bitter as he is hungry.

"But he hasn't done too bad. He is in the top half of the middle third, maybe. And in the last year or so, he's been moving up."

"Winning more?" I said.

"Winning *bigger*, I'd say. He got a couple of pretty healthy personal-injury settlements that had everyone talking. Most of these boys, what they think about and talk about all the time is money. You don't hear them discussing the fine points of case law more than ten percent of the time. When they hear somebody won a judgment, or settled, the first thing they want to know is, How much? Straylow brought in a couple of big ones lately."

I asked about the cases.

"One was a kid on a jet ski who got run over by a barge and killed. Straylow got a settlement from the barge owner's insurance company that was supposed to have been pretty sporty. The other was a drunk-driving case. Some boys drove their car up into the trees one night. The driver got killed, and one of the passengers was crippled. The driver was in the high-risk pool, and his insurance was only for ten grand. So Straylow started looking around for a defendant with some real assets, and he found out the kid's old grandmother had given him the money to buy the car. She was one of these country widows who got an insurance check years ago when her husband died, and she just put it in the bank and left it there collecting interest. Straylow's argument was that the old woman was negligent in letting the boy have the money since she knew he had a bad driving record and was a drinker. He was representing the kid who was crippled in the wreck. There was a private settlement, and the word around here is that Straylow got most of what the old lady had."

Carroll shook his head and smiled thinly. "A lot of these cases come down to finding somebody to sue who has got some money."

He tapped his bad leg with the pencil. "My guy wasn't insured, and there wasn't anyone on the sidelines we could go after. We thought about naming the parole board, since they'd let him out after he'd done three years on an eight-year sentence because they needed the space and he'd been a nice boy in prison. But we ran up against sovereign immunity on that one. I get disability, workmen's comp, and this job. In September, I'm going to Tallahassee to start law school. I've studied the people around here who are making it all right, and I figure if they can so can I."

"Good luck."

He nodded, a little grimly. "Never thought about it as long as I was still a cop. What I thought about lawyers back then was that there ought to be a bounty on all of them. But things took a turn, and now I've got to start over."

"Sometimes that's not all bad."

He smiled. "Well, you'd know. And if you say so, I'll just have to trust you."

"One more question?"

"I'm not going anywhere."

"Do you know anything about the investigator Straylow uses?"

"Riordan?" He shook his head.

"Yes."

"You know about his background?"

"Yes."

"Then you know about as much as anyone. I've heard that he's tough. And scared, too. He's supposed to be real careful about the way he moves around. Looks under his car before he gets in, sits facing the door when he eats out—that sort of thing. And I've heard he changes his address and phone number a lot."

"And doesn't work for anyone but Straylow?"

"That's what they say. With his record, he couldn't get licensed. If he could, he'd have more business than he could handle."

"Why's that?"

"He might be a snake but he's good. Word is Riordan made those two big cases for Straylow, and now Straylow's getting rich."

"How rich?"

"Nobody knows for sure. Like I say, the terms of the settlements weren't released. He's doing all right, but like most of them he doesn't waste any time spending it. He's wearing better clothes and driving a better car. But he's still bitching about money the way they all do no matter how much

they're making. Last time I saw him, he was in here
bitching about how much his kid was costing him.
He just opens up around me for some reason. A lot
of them do. Anyway, he's going on and on about
how much he's spending on his kid, and I said
something about braces, you know, trying to be
friendly about it.

"Well, Straylow practically bites my head off.
'Braces, my ass,' he says. 'I'm paying for private
drug therapy at the most expensive hospital in this
part of the state. One month of it. I could get a
whole floor at the Royal Sonesta for what that
worthless little shit is costing me.'

"Said it just like that," Carroll said. "Talking that
way about his own kid, and you could tell he meant
every word."

Bingo, I thought, in spite of myself. And then, trying to sound offhand, I said, "Well, that's got to be
tough on a parent. Tough as anything."

"I know," Carroll said. "I've seen enough of it.
But Straylow wasn't exactly torn up because the kid
had a problem. It was the money. Some of these
guys, they make so much that it winds up hurting
them, and they don't even know it."

I thanked Carroll for taking the time, and he said
it was no trouble, glad to do it. When I got up to
leave, he stood, too, slowly and painfully, then
walked me to the door of the courthouse.

"How are you and Mr. Semmes doing on this
thing?" he said when we were standing at the door.

"Hard to say. It's still early."

"Straylow's putting on the heat, though, isn't
he?"

"He sure is."

"I expect he's hoping for a settlement. But I'll bet
part of him would like for it to go to trial."

"Why's that?"

"Oh, they'd all like to go head-to-head with Mr. Semmes. He's got the reputation and they all resent it. They all think they can knock him off. Be interesting if it did go to trial. Straylow might think he's red-hot, but if he got into a courtroom with Mr. Semmes, he'd get an education real fast."

I smiled. "I believe he would."

Carroll and I shook hands. I thanked him again, and he said there was no need, he'd enjoyed talking. Then he limped back into the gloom of the courthouse, and I stepped outside into the bright, stifling heat of the July afternoon.

Chapter Nineteen

It was about time, I thought, to get a close look at the enemy. I wanted to see Edward Straylow up close, so I got on Highway 98 and drove east, across the Pensacola Bay Bridge, past Hurlburt Field and the rows of military housing, through Fort Walton Beach and Destin, where the condominiums had sprouted like mushrooms from the scoured white sand, and on to Panama City, scene of one of the world's gaudiest honky-tonk beaches.

The beach is a strip, probably twenty or thirty miles, of T-shirt-and-sunglasses shops, barefoot bars, raw bars, miniature golf courses, water slides, go-cart tracks, souvenir stands, and all manner of other small, seasonal, salt-water businesses. Panama City Beach draws them down from Dothan, Valdosta, Waycross, Evergreen, Birmingham, and hundreds of other landlocked places where people sweat and daydream about two weeks at the beach.

The traffic along the beach road had seized up like an overheated piston, so I got off and drove past the strip shopping centers and the acres of used-car lots until I was in the old town of Panama City. It felt quiet and slightly weary, as though all the beach combers had just worn it down. The old streets and the old houses, half-concealed behind their vast live oaks and magnolias, were out of a time before water slides, time-shares, and Wet T-Shirt Night at the barefoot bar.

I found a pay phone where the book had not been stolen or ripped apart and looked up Straylow. His residence was on Agua Verde Street, which turned out to be in a little development east of town, just off Saint Andrew's Bay. The development was old enough to have been built when it was still possible to dredge canals, so the lots that flanked them were "waterfront." The canals were lined with boat-houses and a variety of boats, everything from small ski rigs to sixty-foot sport-fishermen.

I found Agua Verde and Straylow's house. His boat was modest enough by neighborhood stan-dards—a fifteen-foot Robalo. The house itself was a two-story place of old brick. No two bricks were ex-actly the same shade of red, so the house had a kind of interesting mottled look. The grass was cut and the hedges were trimmed. A purple Suzuki Samurai and an aging Volvo wagon were parked in the drive.

I considered simply parking the truck and watch-ing the house for a while. But in this neighborhood, somebody would probably notice me and call the law. So I drove around the golf course in the center of the development. It seemed a little forlorn, with only one twosome out playing in the heat. From there, I drove on to Edward Straylow's law offices. They were in a small building in an old part of town that had gone through one of those lavish restorations financed by tax write-offs. This one featured a lot of stucco and wrought iron and some very old, white clapboard buildings that had been around from the time when the French, the Spanish, and the English had all cast a greedy eye on this coast. I'd always thought this place had paid them back for their sins. No gold, no exotic spices, not even any skins worth setting up a trading system to exploit. Nothing but malaria, snakes, hostile Indians, and the sudden storms that sunk at least one treasure fleet.

It was fairly late in the afternoon, and I decided to wait around to catch a look at Straylow and follow him wherever he went. I couldn't think of anything better. It was a fishing expedition and I was casting blind.

I read a day-old copy of *The Wall Street Journal*. Beans were up another three cents in the scorching summer weather. Good news for me. I thought about cashing in but guessed that the worst had not yet arrived, and my instincts are fairly good on that, if nothing else.

It was an hour before Straylow emerged. There was another man with him, who wore rumpled cotton pants, a bright purple T-shirt, and a safari jacket. He carried a notebook and wrote hastily as Straylow talked. A reporter, no doubt, getting his daily briefing. They stood on the sidewalk for five minutes, with Straylow doing most of the talking. He didn't smile or make any gestures, and there was something serious about the way he talked. The reporter wrote rapidly and must have turned a dozen pages in his notebook while I watched. When he finally closed it, Straylow nodded and turned away without shaking the man's hand. He walked half a block to a small parking lot and put a key in the door of a blue Mercedes. When he pulled out of the lot, I followed him.

He went north, out of town, along the bay for about ten miles until he came to a bar called the Crow's Nest that was built out over the water.

He parked and walked inside. I drove past, then came back, parked in a different section of the lot, and waited ten minutes. I went to the front door hoping that I wouldn't have to be dressed like Straylow before they'd let me in.

But the Crow's Nest was a casual place. There was a dock out front with a couple of sailboats moored to it, and most of the people inside were dressed for boating. If anything, Straylow was over-dressed.

I took a stool and ordered a beer. Straylow sat at a table with a woman. She was young and blond, and she had an ample, well-exercised body. She was drinking from a tall, frosted glass that had a large slice of pineapple hanging over the rim.

Straylow sat across from her, smiling like an actor at an autograph party. She looked impressed.

I didn't want to stare, so I turned back around to pay for my beer.

When I looked back at Straylow's table, he and the woman were holding hands and looking into each other's eyes. I finished my beer and drove back into town. It was early evening. The family hour.

When I was back near the south end of the bay, it occurred to me to stop near Agua Verde and watch for one of Straylow's cars. It was a dead-end street, and there was a convenience store on the corner where it ran into the main road. I decided to sit there and drink a cup of coffee while I waited. The coffee was strong enough to peel paint.

After almost half an hour, I'd seen only three cars come out of Agua Verde: two Mercedes and a Porsche. I was ready to give up and go look for a place to eat when the purple Suzuki pulled up to the stop sign. I couldn't see the face behind the wheel— there was too much glare from the headlights.

I slipped in behind the little car. As the driver pulled into the traffic, I hung back and kept an eye on him.

He drove across the bay bridge and then out to the beach, where he pulled into a bar with a neon sign that read SURFIN' SAFARI. When I turned off my engine, I could hear the thudding bass of a rock band.

I parked fairly close to the Suzuki. A boy about seventeen got out and locked up. In the glow of the sign, I was able to get a good look at him. He was a younger, more petulant version of his father. I waited until he was through the door before I locked up and followed him.

Inside the Surfin' Safari, the noise hit you like a punch. The people were packed in tight, the way they used to cram them into ships to bring them across the Atlantic to do hard labor. I paid a door charge and got the back of my hand stamped and then made my way to the bar, slipping through the creases in the crowd.

I ordered a beer and watched the Straylow kid, who now had joined a group of young men. Two girls approached the boys. From the look of things, the girls wanted to dance. Two of the boys nodded in an offhand, bored way and followed the girls to the dance floor.

When the band took a break, Straylow followed

his friends outside to the parking lot. I waited a minute, then followed.

I didn't see them at first. So I wandered through the lot, taking slow, careful steps like someone who'd had too much to drink but was trying hard not to show it. I wanted to look like a drunk who had lost his car.

I overheard an argument between a man and a woman. Evidently, she didn't think he ought to be dancing with someone named Rachel as much as he had been. He, on the other hand, didn't think she should be so "needy." They were getting loud.

In another car, a troubled female voice was saying, "I don't know where else I'll get the money."

A panicky male voice answered, "I'll get it. Don't worry. Just don't tell your parents."

I was beginning to feel like a Peeping Tom, and I didn't like the feeling. Then I saw the five boys, clustered around a Jeep Renegade with huge, off-road tires. I crouched behind a car and listened.

The only sound for a minute or two was a strenuous sucking of air, repeated after a few seconds. Go powder. The boys were doing a little friendly cocaine.

"Any of you guys know where I can score more of this stuff?" one boy said.

"How much?"

"Just enough to get me through the summer?"

There was some murmuring. Nobody seemed to have a reliable source.

"Well, keep your ears open," the Straylow boy said. "If you find any, call me."

More murmuring, more sniffing, more talk about what good stuff it was. Then they moved back in-

side, where the girls would be waiting to ask them
to dance.

I stood up, walked straight to my truck, and drove
home.

Chapter Twenty

I worked on the River House the next day, since there wasn't much more I could do for Semmes while he waited for Straylow to call and make some kind of offer. It was hot, and the farm reports had started to use the word *drought*. My fall contracts had gone up a nickle in one week.

I was working on the porch, laying a new floor, and I'd been at it most of the day and was about ready to quit when Jessie came up the drive in her Alfa convertible, with her hair trailing out behind her in a way that always did something to me.

"Don't stop on my account," she shouted from the car. "I like to watch a man work."

"It's quitting time," I said.

She came over and kissed my sweaty cheek. "Boy," she said, "you taste good."

I went inside and got something cold for us to drink. She had iced tea with bourbon and mint and

I had a beer. Two, actually. One for my thirst and one to sip.

When I handed her the drink, she looked at me and said, "God, Morgan, you look *great*. I might have to just throw you on the ground right here."

I was wearing very old blue jeans and a pair of jungle boots. No shirt. I was covered with sweat and sawdust.

"I look like a sawmill hand," I said.

"Well, it turns *me* on."

"Something wrong with you, then."

"Nothing wrong. I just like men who sweat when they work." She smiled and pushed her tangled hair back, keeping her eyes on mine. There was something eager in her eyes, along with the usual deep stare, and I got the message. Felt it in my stomach.

She laughed and hugged me in a close, serious way, and her body felt soft yet firm. When she pulled away, she was breathing heavily and her clothes were damp with my sweat and flecked with sawdust.

"Right here in the *grass*," she whispered urgently. Her fingers were inside the waistband of my jeans.

First we were kneeling, and then we were lying on the grass. We got our clothes off, and her skin was strikingly tan against the green grass. She moaned something that I didn't understand and probably wasn't meant to. My ears were pounding, and I could hear my own breathing and, for some reason, a single mockingbird in a tree close by singing like a fool.

We lay there for a while afterward, holding each other and listening to the mockingbird. I could feel her breath in the hollow part of my neck, then her voice saying, "This is sure fine, Morgan."

"Sure is."

"But this damn grass itches."

"It was your idea."

"And aren't you glad I had it?"

"I sure am."

"But now I itch. If I promise to feed you, will you let me up off this grass?"

We went to her house, where she made crab salad while I watched and listened to her talk about her day. She ran a local preservation group that was trying to save a swamp from a developer who had it in his sights. His vision included a hotel, shopping mall, marina, and golf course.

"Seems like we've got enough golf courses," I said.

"Can't have too many, Morgan. Especially not with the Japanese going so crazy for golf. All them Sonys and Mitsubishis need 'em a place to play. No room in the sacred home islands. They're all filled up."

"I see."

We took our plates out to the porch, poured wine, and watched the sun set. The river was low and dark as ink, moving so slowly that it seemed to require an effort to flow at all.

"This developer," Jessie went on, "is banking on a world full of rich Japanese golfers, and he's got him a line of credit from some bank in Chicago.

"But I don't see what in hell a bank in Chicago is doing messing around down here. Pretty soon, there won't be anything around here *but* hotels and marinas and golf courses. What I don't understand is, Why do we need another when so many already went broke? That's what the S and L boys over in Louisiana liked back in the high-rolling oil days— marinas and hotels.

"You know what S and L stands for, don't you, Morgan?"

I shook my head. When she was like this, I loved listening too much to talk.

"Stealing and looting."

I smiled.

"It's the same kind of thinking behind this hotel and marina and golf course for rich Japanese. Gobble gobble. Just get it all, and don't worry about what mess you leave behind. But we got a pair of nesting eagles back in that swamp and a lot of other things, too, and we are going to tie the developer's ass *up* on the permits."

"Can you win?"

"I don't know." She sighed. "He might get tired and quit. Or the bank in Chicago might get restless and put its money somewhere else. But you kill one and two more come along. We need to find somebody to buy that land and take it out of circulation."

"Any luck?"

"We got a nibble from the Nature Conservancy."

One of my beneficiaries. I liked the idea of my money going to help save a swamp—especially Jessie's swamp—after I'd departed this vale.

She took a sip of wine and said, "I've been running on too much. Tell me what you've been doing. You and Nat going to save that boy's ranch for him?"

I told her about what I'd been up to, following Straylow and then his son. Her eyes narrowed as I told it.

"So," Jessie said, "you know that Straylow likes ladies he's not married to and his son is fond of cocaine, like about half the rest of the kids in the world." Her face was drawn with disapproval. "I don't see why you bothered to even find out about that stuff or what good it will do you now that you know."

"Straylow is going to ruin John Fearson," I said. "He's already got the child protection unit at Health and Rehabilitative Services breathing down his neck. They could close him down, and the attorney general's office could decide to prosecute him for child abuse and send him to prison. And then, there's the civil suit."

"I know, Morgan. But that's all courtroom stuff. It's done out in the open."

"It all started with Rick Hewes, and he's a liar. Straylow is the engineer, and the train is running on lies."

Jessie studied my face for a moment, like a doctor looking for symptoms.

"So you think it would be all right to use some of this other stuff on him to make him quit?"

"I don't know," I said. "Semmes is in charge. I'm just out there scouting around, finding out what I can to help him."

I was evading and she knew it.

"But you wouldn't mind using stuff like that, would you?"

"I wouldn't mind putting the blocks to Straylow."

"You'd *love* it," Jessie said fiercely. Her temper was rising. It made her face glow.

"He's a creep."

"Well, boy, if you make it your business to start stomping creeps, then you'll be busy till kingdom come. Why don't you just do your job, what Nat Semmes needs you to do, and leave all the rest of it alone? How come you have to fight somebody else's fight, unless you just like it?"

We were back to that.

I didn't say anything, and after a few moments

Jessie stood up and walked into the kitchen. I wondered if she was leaving me for good, but then she shouted, "You want coffee?"

"Sure." I went into the kitchen to help her.

She had her back to me and didn't turn around. There was something tight and furious in her posture, but then she sighed and relaxed and said, still without turning around, "I don't want to do this again. Not tonight."

"Me neither."

"I'm trying to understand the way you're thinking, and sometimes I think I do. You like a fight, Morgan. You get restless when you go too long without one, like some of these barroom Don Juans when they've been too long without seducing some new secretary."

I didn't say anything.

"I don't like it," she said, turning around now so that I could see that the look on her face had gone from anger to the kind of deep concern that comes with caring about someone more than you'd like to. "I don't have to like it, either," she said. "I guess I can understand it. But you've got to understand the way I feel too."

"I do," I said.

"One of the worst things a woman can do is start trying to change a man. That's what wives always do, you know. A man marries a woman because he believes she thinks he's just perfect. He thinks that because she keeps telling him so. And then, once they're married, she starts right in trying to change him."

"What about husbands?" I said. "What do they do?"

"Start hating their wives, I suppose. You see it all the time."

"Well, I sure don't hate you." Couldn't imagine it, in fact.

"And I don't want to change you, either. But you've got to understand the way I'm thinking. I can't keep it a secret. I don't do good with secrets."

"I understand."

"All right. I can live with that. You're a good man and you'll consider what I'm feeling. Only one more thing I'll ask."

"What's that?"

"Be careful. Think about what you're doing, and don't just do it because you're all full of fire. Think about it cold."

"OK."

"That's a promise?"

"Yes."

"OK, then," she said, and smiled feebly. "Now, do you want something in your coffee? Cognac or bourbon or something?"

"Just black," I said gratefully, feeling like I'd just been given some kind of reprieve and knowing that if she'd asked, I probably would have changed. Or tried to, anyway.

We took the coffee to the living room and talked about other things. A little later, we did the dishes, and then Jessie said she wanted to watch the news. She thought there might be something about her fight to save that swamp. But by the sheerest coincidence, this night I was one of the stories. I would have gladly missed it.

I was barely paying attention when somebody named Robert Hartley, a man with a lot of jaw and the kind of insincere eyes you see on someone trying to sell you life insurance, came on the screen and said, "Tonight, this reporter has learned of an interesting new development in the child-brutality case surrounding the Sweetwater Ranch and former football star John Fearson."

He paused to let that sink in. The color was perfect on Jessie's set. Hartley's skin was the color of mild mustard.

"As reported here earlier, the most serious charges against John Fearson made by attorney Edward Straylow, who represents a boy who fled Sweetwater, include several alleged beatings and other forms of mistreatment at the hands of Fearson. Straylow and his client are asking for several million in damages, and in what is perhaps a more ominous development for Fearson, Straylow has urged the state attorney general to conduct a sweeping investigation of Sweetwater.

"John Fearson is represented by Nathaniel Semmes, who has made a career of unpopular and unusual cases. Semmes has so far refused to comment on the case.

"But yesterday, while inspectors from the state Department of Health and Rehabilitative Services were going over the premises at Sweetwater, this reporter learned that Semmes is being assisted in this case by one of his most notorious former clients."

With those words, my picture appeared on the screen. It was a very old picture, but I didn't look younger. My eyes were squeezed into slits, and my cheeks were hollow. A series of numbers, seven digits, ran under my neck. It was my mug shot.

Hartley went on in his steady, grave voice, telling his audience how I had done time in Alabama for murder. I suppose he had his facts right, but I couldn't be sure. When I saw that picture of myself, with the numbers under it, my memory sailed back like an old clipper ahead of a strong trade, until I wasn't in the room with the television and the news program and Jessie anymore. It was another time, another place, and another life entirely.

I had finally quit soldiering for wages. I had been guarding oil and decided that shabby as my life was, I wasn't going to risk it for the sake of a bunch of Mercedes-driving Arab princes. Soldiers have died for a lot stupider things, I suppose, but I'd had enough. I was going to go home and spend the wages I'd saved on an education. I was going to be a college boy.

I had a ludicrous vision of myself: studying the classics in small, dusty rooms with wooden walls and ancient desks, taught by a professor who smoked a pipe and wore tweed jackets with patches at the elbow and forgot the name of everyone except the characters in the *Iliad*.

I arrived at the university late in August, about two weeks before the fall term began. I had my things in an old canvas duffle with my serial number stenciled on it in fading black ink.

First, I found a place to live in town, a mile or so from the campus. A garage apartment in a quiet neighborhood. I unpacked my duffle and then went out and bought the things I needed to cook and keep house. I could have lived in a dormitory, but I didn't think it would work. I wasn't a real college kid. For all my ignorance, I knew that much.

I registered for my courses and bought my books. School started, and I went to my classes and read the assignments. I ignored football games, fraternity rush, political rallies, and all that sort of thing. I came to love the library. Especially the periodicals room. After years when a two-week-old *Time* magazine was some kind of treasure, that big, quiet room with the shelves and shelves of magazines and papers was a gold mine. I can't say it would have lasted, but for a while life seemed good.

Then my sister called. She was in trouble and needed help. The call set off all my alarms. She was the only person in the world I could call family. We'd been orphaned when a 727 had not quite made it to the end of a runway in marginal weather. We were young when it happened, still in grade school, and we grew even closer when we were split up. I went to live with an uncle in the country, and she moved in with an aunt. We grew up different and sentimentalized each other. We always wrote, and whenever I was in the States, I went to see her.

We'd seen less of each other after she married a man who cut a wide path through Atlanta. He was about my age and liked to remind you that he was "into" a lot of things. He was "into the arts" and "into real estate" and "into politics." They had a lavish place in Buckhead and played golf at the Piedmont Driving Club. He had friends in Washington and business in New York and contacts in Los Angeles, so he traveled a lot. Lucy stayed at home, in Buckhead. He seemed to think she lacked the kind of lightning-quick mind it took to know what was going on, but she was more than smart enough to know she had been abandoned.

I'd visited a couple of times, and it was hard seeing what had happened to her. She had lost weight, her eyes had lost their vitality, and her mouth was pinched with pain. When we talked, her mind seemed to wander, and the conversation trailed off into silences that said everything.

She wasn't crying when she called, but even through the long-distance lines I could tell that she had been. She was leaving him, she said. Could she come stay with me for a few days? I wondered why she needed me for that, assuming she must have friends in Atlanta who could make it more comfortable for her. But I said sure and gave her directions.

A little after dawn, her BMW eased to a stop in front of my garage apartment. I waited a long time for the door to open and finally walked out to meet her. In the feeble light, the swelling around her eyes didn't show any color. It could have been caused by a reaction to something. But the torn lip was unmistakable evidence. She had been beaten.

I wanted to get in my truck and drive to Atlanta, was trembling with the urgency of it, but she pleaded with me. That would just make it worse, she said. So I promised I wouldn't, though I wasn't sure I meant it when I said it. We went inside, and I put clean sheets on the bed. She slept all day while I prowled my little rooms, feeling the most personal rage I'd ever known.

She told me about it that night, after she woke. I could hardly look at her distorted, discolored face while she talked.

Things had been bad, she said. He had girls; she had guessed that easily enough and endured it until people began to treat her with a kind of ostentatious pity. The worse it got and the less he was around, the more money and jewelry he gave her.

"I learned to loathe diamonds," she said with a painful smile.

She threatened to leave him, and he gave her a demonstration of his temper. He didn't hit her; he merely smashed some crystal. Then a day or two later, he made some promises, and for a while things had been better.

"Tolerable, Morgan," she said. "Not ideal, but tolerable. I decided to see if they'd turn into something else. If maybe he'd grow up."

They talked about a child and decided that it was time for one. But it didn't work. She went for an examination, and the doctor said she was fine; maybe her husband should come in. When she suggested it, he put on another display of temper. But she held her ground, and he made an appointment. Turned out he was the problem.

That made things worse. Everything regressed until she threatened, again, to leave him. He exploded and said if she ever left, she would regret it for the rest of her life.

"I thought he was talking about his money," Lucy said, shaking her head. "That didn't mean anything to me. I hated Buckhead. How can you take an aristocracy built on Coca-Cola seriously?"

They talked one last time about a reconciliation. He said that if she would just take the diamonds and appear cheerfully at the charity functions, then he would provide her with comfort forever.

"I guess he meant I could find a boy if I wanted one and would keep it discreet."

She said she wanted a real family, with a baby, even if they had to adopt one. Without a word, he hit her.

"He was wild, Morgan. He hit me until I was out, then he locked me in a room. I had to go out the window."

More than ever, I wanted to drive to Atlanta and find him.

"That won't solve anything," she said. "Just let me stay here a few days and make some phone calls. There is no permanent damage, and believe me, I'll be out of it, clean, in no time."

She called a lawyer and some friends, and her

face began to heal, though she still winced every now and then from where he had bruised some ribs. When that happened, I'd feel the heat rising, and she would look at me and say, "It's all right, Morgan. I'll be fine. I'll be out of it soon, and anything you do will just screw it up. I should have done this a long time ago."

After a few days, I decided that she was right at some pragmatic level where I'd never operated. Before you leave on a journey of revenge, some Chinaman once said, you must first dig two graves.

I went back to my classes. She stayed at my place and used the telephone. We were actually managing some pleasure in each other's company.

But you don't get out easy. Not as a rule, anyway, and I should have known that. The husband tried to call one night. I answered the phone, and when he asked for her I gave her a look. She shook her head. I spoke very slowly and distinctly into the mouthpiece and told him just what would happen if he ever came near her again.

He drove over the next day, and when I came home from class he was there, in my house, talking to her. Her face was drained, translucent with rage. He shouted at her. It was the degrading things he seemed to feel he was entitled to scream at her face that made me come loose, I think. If he'd quietly asked her to come back, I may have been able to keep it on a leash.

I didn't try to kill him; in fact, I probably wanted him to stay alive in order to feel the pain. But I wasn't sorry when he died in the emergency room. It was a hematoma. His head had hit the floor too hard, and he was one of those men who take a lot of aspirin. He had thin blood.

He also had tapes of the threats I'd made. His

divorce lawyer had suggested that he record his conversations with Lucy. The tapes were useful for the prosecution at my trial.

I regret what I did only because Lucy killed herself with pills after I'd done less than a year.

So I did time until Nat Semmes took an interest in my case and, with the help of people like Jessie Beaudraux, got my pardon. Not a parole, but a full pardon from the governor. I could vote and buy a pistol like any other citizen.

But the television reporter still saw me the way the prosecutor and the jury had seen me. And I was a sinister element in his story.

"What is known, at this time," he said ominously, "is that this man has become a player in this unusual and controversial case. At the very least, the presence of a man with his background raises questions about John Fearson's choice of friends and allies in this difficult time for him."

In other words, Mr. Hartley didn't really have a story to tell. Replaying the old news about me was just a way to give the folks watching at home a few cheap thrills.

I turned the set off. Jessie stayed on the couch and took a dainty sip from her wine glass.

"Does it bother you?" she asked.

"Some. But I can't do anything about it."

"I don't understand why they did it. There was nothing in that report that was new."

"I expect Straylow fed that stuff to the television boy," I said.

"Seems to me," she said, as though she hadn't heard me, "that you could get out of this Sweetwater thing. It's in the courts now. The lawyers have it. Why don't you leave it to them? Go back to fixing up your house."

"I'll think about it."

"Think about it *seriously*, will you, Morgan? I think you owe it to yourself. You've got some peace due you in this life. More than anyone I've ever known, you've earned that."

And I did think about it, while I was lying on my back, looking up through her skylight at the stars, waiting for sleep. I saw myself on a small river, with the water breaking around the smooth rocks. The water was cold, and the meadows running down to the banks were green. The leaves on the distant aspen trees trembled. I would cast a fly until I'd had enough and then lie on the bank with my face toward the flawless, blue sky and not think about a single thing.

That was my idea of peace.

Chapter Twenty-one

Semmes called in the morning while Jubal and I were eating breakfast. Jube barked when the phone rang.

"Scuse me, Jube," I said, and went inside to get it.

"Are you busy this morning?" Semmes said. He doesn't like to impose.

"What do you need?"

"You mind coming in here? I had an interesting conversation last night. We need to discuss it."

"Give me an hour."

I finished my coffee and took a cold shower for a few minutes of relief from the heat, which was already punishing. I dressed in cotton khakis and a light poplin shirt and felt like I was wrapped in furs. The truck was hot, and the highway shimmered ahead of me like desert sand.

* * *

"How about something cold?" Semmes said when I sat in front of his desk and looked out at the gulf.

"Water," I said.

After he'd handed me the glass, he sat and rested his forearms on his desk. He seemed a little less calm than he usually does in office meetings, where he is the chief source of calm and reason.

"Well," he said, "I finally heard from our friend Straylow yesterday. He called here late in the afternoon. I was just finishing my reading. Fascinating, all this stuff going on in Russia. I can't seem to get enough of it. Who'd have guessed?

"Anyway, I'm about halfway through this long *New York Times* story about the black market in Moscow when the phone rings. My secretary had already taken off, so I answered it myself.

" 'Mr. Semmes,' this voice says, trying to be very formal even though you could tell the woman had grown up eating grits and going barefoot. 'Please hold for Edward Straylow.' "

Semmes shook his head. "I guess they go for that routine because it makes them feel like movie producers or something. I told the grit eater I'd be in my office for another hour or so and if Mr. Straylow wanted to talk to me, he could call himself, but I wasn't holding for anyone. She seemed to take it personally.

"But she passed on my message, because he called himself, about five minutes later. I'm surprised he didn't go out and use the car phone, just so I'd know he had one."

Semmes made a quarter-turn so he could look out at the water.

"He sounded a little irritated at being reduced to punching buttons on the telephone. Introduced himself and said he thought it might be a 'good idea if we talked.' I told him that would be fine, when did he want to have this conversation? He said he happened to have some business in Pensacola this morning, would I have some time? He'll be coming by in another fifteen minutes."

"Do you want me to sit in?"

Semmes shook his head. "He wouldn't tolerate it. Anyway, it's not necessary. It won't be a long conversation, and I can give you the high points. But I'd like for you to stick around."

"Sure."

"Have you found out anything about Brother Straylow in the last couple of days?" Semmes spoke in a way that made the man's name alone sound devious. His contempt was never mild or muted. In his own way, he was as much a hater as I am.

"I know a little about how he lives."

"Tell."

So I ran down what I'd learned, keeping it brief and factual. Semmes already had opinions; he didn't need to hear mine.

"Yes," he said when I'd finished. "Yes, indeed. I believe I know Brother Straylow without ever having laid eyes on him. Know him well. Been in over his head so long now he wouldn't remember what it felt like if his feet ever could touch bottom. Loaded up to the limit at the bank and with the credit-card people. Cars are leased. Took all the equity out of the house. And he'd rather cut his own throat than cut back. Probably gets cramps every time he sees the letters *IRS*. He doesn't see this case as a matter of truth or law or such nonessential stuff as that. To him, it's a lifeboat."

I nodded.

"The wife and kiddies are just chains around his

neck, the way he looks at it. Dragging him under.
That sweet thing you saw him with, she's probably
the one solace in his life. She doesn't know, and she
treats him like a big man. So he probably goes into
hock to impress her too. I wouldn't be at all surprised if he was buying her some clothes and a little
jewelry."

I nodded again.

"What a dismal, goddamned story," Semmes
said. "Old too. Old as creation. But tell me a little
more about this Riordan."

I told him what I knew, which didn't seem like
much.

Semmes shook his head when I'd finished.
"Straylow, Riordan, and Hewes. Three bottom feed-
ers."

The buzzer sounded and Semmes picked up the
phone, listened briefly, then said, "Thank you. Send
him on in."

He hung up the phone and looked at me.
"Brother Straylow is here. Duck out and read a
magazine. This will probably take thirty minutes."

I decided against sitting in Semmes's cheerless
waiting room, even though it was cool, and went
outside, where the air felt like steam. I walked one
block to a little park, sat on a bench under a live
oak, and stared at the mottled green statue of a Confederate colonel. I cleaned my nails with my pocketknife and watched an old man in rags make the
rounds of the trash baskets searching for salvage.
After thirty minutes I went back, rode the elevator,
and got out on Semmes's floor. I almost bumped
into Straylow, who was plainly angry and almost
distracted enough that he didn't recognize me.

Then his eyes narrowed, and he looked me up and
down with the kind of professional disdain that all

lawyers learn. The look was meant to remind me that I was an insignificant obstacle in the path to his objective.

I nodded at him, and I suppose there was something mocking in the way I did it.

"I don't like being followed," he said.

"Speaking to me?"

"Don't give me that shit. I remember you from the Crow's Nest the other afternoon."

"Nice place," I said. "You go there often?"

"I won't be harassed by some ex-con," he said. "You tell your master that if he wants to play that kind of hardball, then I can play too. I'll file a complaint with the bar."

"Which bar is that?"

"Cute," Straylow said, barely opening his mouth. "Just tell him. And you be advised that I'll go further than that. If I catch you snooping around my personal life again, I'll be sure you learn to regret it."

"You'd better hurry," I said. "You'll miss this elevator and it moves slower than moss."

He stepped into the elevator without taking his eyes off me, and before the doors closed he said, "I mean what I say."

I went into Semmes's office without knocking.

"How did it go?"

"About like I expected. He said he thought it might bc in my client's interest to avoid a trial, and I said that it might be in *his* client's interest too. Then we danced the old lawyer fandango for a few minutes until he let it slip that he might be willing to settle for seven hundred and fifty thousand. Impossible, I said. My client couldn't possibly go higher than ten percent of that. It was bullshit and we both knew it."

Semmes picked up a pencil and dropped it on the desk. Picked it up and dropped it again. "God, but there are days when I hate the law."

"Can you deal?"

"Oh, sure. As long as we're both talking *money*, we can come to a price sooner or later. The longer it goes on, the more it costs us *not* to settle. He knows about insurance companies. He may be common as sin, but that doesn't make him dumb."

"So?"

"He's thinking about the money. Our side has something else in mind."

"Big John?"

"That's right. When I told him that any settlement would include some kind of statement from his client, he wasn't buying. The way it usually works, the defendant says, when he settles, that he is making no admission of guilt. Straylow said he'd go for that but no more."

"Doesn't do much for John."

"Just about nothing, I'd say."

"Why wouldn't he go for a statement from his client?"

"Because it would make him look like a fool, I suppose, and even Straylows have their pride. Or their vanity, anyway. Also, he knows that time is on his side, and he probably knows that I'm not the insurance company's first choice to handle this thing. If he doesn't like what I'm offering, then he can just wait for the next fellow to come along. And then," Semmes sighed heavily, "I think he turned me down just because of who I am and because he knows that clearing Big John means a lot to me. Turning me down gave him a cheap, nasty little rush."

For a few moments, neither of us said anything.

Then Semmes spoke softly. "The money is an aggravation, but it doesn't make any difference. It won't even make any difference to Straylow—not as much as he thinks it will, anyway. But John Fearson's reputation is different."

We were sitting there silently thinking around the problem when the phone buzzed.

"Yes," Semmes said.

He listened, then cut his eyes to me and said, "Put Mr. Fearson on."

After a second, Nat said, "Good morning, John." Then he listened for a minute or two and said, "John, I'm just as sorry as I can be."

He listened for another minute or so, then said, "Well, I've got Morgan Hunt sitting here with me now, and I think we'll drive on out there. I'll see you in a little bit."

Semmes hung up and looked at me bleakly. "The state, in its wisdom, has just closed down Sweetwater Ranch. Big John sounded like he wanted to cry."

Semmes drove even faster than usual and didn't say much. At one crossroads, while we were waiting for a light, he shook his head and said, "I feel so goddamned bad for John. And I feel worse for those boys. What I'd like to do is take that sorry Straylow and tie his ass to a post and horsewhip him. But that's not acceptable practice anymore. We're too civilized."

When we got to Sweetwater, the boys were being loaded on buses to leave. We watched.

They carried small nylon duffles and backpacks that held everything they owned. They wore T-shirts, jeans, and running shoes. Some carried radios or baseball gloves. Most of them turned and

waved to Big John just before they climbed on the
bus. A few of them were crying.

Jimmy, the boy Semmes liked so much, recognized him and broke out of line to come running
over. He hugged Semmes and then Fearson, then
stuck out his hand to me and said, very seriously,
"Good to see you again, sir."

His face was red and he was sniffling.

"Mr. Semmes, you're going to fight them, aren't
you?"

"You bet I am." Nat's voice was a little thick.

"Well, kick some ass." He looked quickly to Fearson.

"Sorry, Big John," he said.

"You watch your mouth where you're going,"
Fearson said. "You understand me?"

"Yes, sir."

"All right. Now you'd better get on the bus."

"You can beat 'em though, can't you Mr.
Semmes?"

"I can beat them."

"Then suck it up and beat 'em good. It's not fair."

"I'll do my best."

"OK. Well, 'bye. Love you, Big John." He picked
up his small red duffle, turned, and ran for the bus.

We watched until the buses had pulled out, then
Fearson and Semmes went inside to talk. I stayed
outside and walked aimlessly around the grounds.
They felt almost unbearably empty, like a city cut
down by a plague.

After an hour or so, Semmes came out of the little
office, and we started back. The day had turned so
hot that the air seemed to scorch your skin. Nothing
moved, not the birds, the bugs, or even the few
small white clouds that hung high overhead.

*   *   *

Semmes said nothing on the way back, and it was not until we were sitting in his office and he had gone through his phone messages and checked his calendar that he opened up.

"We don't have much time," he said, looking out at the bay like one of his beleaguered clients.

I nodded, feeling the same way.

"I'm going to have to talk to Charlie Blanchard about Straylow's offer. The insurance company will be getting itchy, and now that HRS has closed Sweetwater down, the attorney general will be feeling the pressure to come up with some kind of criminal complaint. We might have a grand-jury investigation. That's a lot of momentum, and we need something to stop it in its tracks."

I nodded again.

"Straylow is the key. He's pulling the strings, and we need to break his goddamned fingers."

That was music to my ears, but I didn't have any ideas. So I waited to see if Semmes did.

"He's crooked as a snake, Morgan. I've been around long enough that I can see it with my eyes closed. With enough time, I could break him into little pieces, but we don't have that kind of time. Unless you can come up with something."

"I'm game," I said. "But what am I looking for?"

"I'm not sure. We need to play offense. Maybe he needs to think that he could lose something a lot more important to him than just this one case. He's about to wipe Big John out, and he needs to think the same thing could happen to him. Somewhere there is something that could do it."

"You thinking about a countersuit?"

He shook his head. "Takes too long. Anyway, lawyers are always suing and countersuing. Nobody pays any attention. We need something that people would notice. Something that would make them think that John is a victim."

I thought for a minute. "What does it take to get someone disbarred?"

Semmes smiled and lifted a document from the surface of his desk, forty or fifty sheets stapled at one corner. *"The Florida Law Weekly,"* he said. "It's an abstract of the state supreme court decisions, including all the disciplinary cases against lawyers. Every issue has two or three of my brethren up for professional execution. What gets them is money."

Semmes explained commingling of funds and I listened.

"Comes down to having access to other people's money. You are supposed to hold it in a trust account. The bar gets the interest, which might be the reason it's so tough on people who misuse the funds. Incentives again."

Semmes smiled.

"You're talking about stealing?" I said.

"Most of the people who do it probably don't think of it that way at all. More like *borrowing.* The money is there, and you need it, just temporarily, until another big check comes in. So you use the trust-account money to pay some bills or to take advantage of an investment opportunity that won't wait. Then, later on, you put the money back. Unless you're audited pretty close, nobody ever knows. It's an awful temptation."

"And awfully hard to prove," I said.

"Unfortunately, yes."

"Anything else we might use?" I said.

"Oh, I suppose Straylow could be disciplined if he knew that Rick Hewes was lying under oath. But we'll have to wait on that, and anyway, that's even harder to prove."

"What if there is a grand jury, and Hewes lies when he's questioned?"

"Straylow won't be there. Grand-jury witnesses are not represented by counsel. He can insulate himself from Hewes's testimony. And that's a ways off."

We sat there in silent frustration until Semmes said, "Sometimes, there just isn't any good solution. You know what a smart man once said about that?"

I shook my head.

" 'When there is no solution, there is no problem.' Hard-nosed but true."

"You aren't giving up?"

"No," Semmes said. "But we may be looking at rehabilitating Big John instead of saving him if we don't come up with something real soon."

I couldn't remember seeing Nat Semmes this way, and there was something about it that shook me. The rational part of me knew that he could be outmaneuvered and beaten—he was an unusual man but still just a man—but the other side of my nature expected him to keep fighting and always pull it off, somehow, at the last minute, just like in the movies. We all have our last line of illusions, and that, probably, was mine.

"There has to be a way," I said.

"If you think of something," he said, "I'd like to be the first to know."

"How much time do we have?"

"It's Friday. I can wait until Monday morning before I call Charlie Blanchard. He can take a couple of days to think things over. But it probably comes down to this weekend."

I said I'd be in touch and left him there looking at his desk like a chess player trying to discover the inspired solution hiding somewhere in a hopeless board.

Chapter Twenty-two

Traffic in Panama City moved like opposing streams of laboring ants. It was Friday night, and people were out looking for action. I fell in line and rode the clutch past the T-shirt shops, the raw bars, the go-car tracks, the ceramic sharks, and the flimsy motels. The Gulf was less than a hundred yards away, but even with the windows down I couldn't smell the water, only the vapors of the trapped cars.

It was still early when I pulled into the parking lot of the Surfin' Safari and killed the engine. It ticked with exhaustion. No sign of the Straylow boy, so I walked to an outdoor pay phone and called the Dahlgren kid to ask him, once more, if he'd check on Jubal and make sure he got something to eat.

After I'd made my call, I sat in the cab of the truck, watched the parking lot fill up, and tried to convince myself that I really wanted to go through with what I'd come here hoping to do.

It came down to how far I was willing to go. When I argued from one side of the line, it was easy: just how much mercy had Straylow shown Big John; how much had he let his scruples—such as they were—get in the way of a ripe, easily plucked settlement? We were playing by his rules.

When I took the other side, it was harder. The Straylow kid was a careless, unrepentant junkie, and sooner or later he would get caught and burned. But I didn't like being the rat. It was a role more than any other that I found insupportable.

So look at it from another angle. Consider the objective, nothing else. If you gain the objective, then the tactics are legitimate. And the tactics you are willing to use tell you something about how badly you want the objective. How much did I care about Sweetwater, Big John, and his boys?

A lot, I told myself. But maybe not enough.

What if I made destroying Straylow the objective? How much did I hate him?

Again, a lot. He was the reason my old story had been dragged out on television the night before, diverting the people watching the local news and maybe giving the station a little help in the ratings. If Straylow thought he could trifle with my life like that, no reason for me to feel squeamish about giving him some of the same. He'd asked for it and he richly deserved it.

I kept at it, thinking around the edges of the problem, the way you worry a bad tooth, touching it with your tongue because you can't help it, not because it does anything to relieve the ache. I'd been at it for more than an hour and had succeeded only in agitating myself and multiplying my confusions when the Straylow kid pulled up in his little Suzuki, locked the car, checked his hair one last time in the side mirror, and walked to the front door of the bar like a man expecting good things from the night ahead.

I followed from a distance, and it was largely a repeat of the first night I'd spent shadowing him. He met his friends inside, where they drank beer, danced in a bored way with a couple of young women who were probably strangers, then stepped outside with the boys for a friendly toot. It all felt sort of routine. Strange that you could go to prison for it.

It was early, ten o'clock, and the likelihood was that the Straylow kid would be at that bar with his friends for at least another two hours. That gave me plenty of time. When he and his friends were back inside, I started the truck and drove to Straylow's house. Simple deal, I told myself, his kid for Big John. The only question was, Would I go through with it if Straylow said no?

If I wouldn't, I told myself, then best turn around now and drive on home, because Straylow had to believe me when I said I would send his kid to jail.

I didn't drive very fast, but I did make it all the way to Straylow's house.

I parked on the street and walked to the front door, past sprinklers lazily watering the thick centipede grass. When I pushed the button, chimes went off inside. I waited, and then, after a full minute, the door came open in an impatient sort of way, as far as the night chain would let it.

"Oh," the woman said. She'd been expecting someone else and was alarmed to see a stranger.

Before she could close the door, I said, "Mrs. Straylow?"

"Yes?"

"I'm looking for Mr. Straylow."

"I thought you were him," she said, befuddled. I could smell the bourbon.

"He's not in?"

"Not much," she sighed. "Who are you?"

"It's about a case he's·working on. May I come in?"

"Not unless you can do better than that," she said.

So I handed her the things I carry in my wallet. While she studied them, I said, "I have some important information."

"What about?" she said, trusting me enough now to sound defiant.

"Mrs. Straylow," I said, "I do undercover narcotics work. You can call Lieutenant Tom Pine in the Escambia County Sheriff's Department to verify that."

"Narcotics," she said bleakly. The meaning of that was plain enough to her. She unfastened the chain and held the door open for me to come in.

She was wearing a pair of white pants and a blue denim shirt, knotted at the waist. A pair of old Topsiders. Her hair was brown and dyed to keep the gray out. There were creases around her eyes and her mouth, the signs of early wrinkles in her neck. She was an attractive woman by any measure, except the one they use in the movies and the magazines—she wasn't young anymore and couldn't compete with this year's crop of fillies, like the one I'd seen with her husband at the cute little nautical bar.

Her eyes were brown and seemed to hold an equal measure of curiosity and pain. Each year, I imagined, there would be less curiosity, more pain. Just now, there was also a portion of fear.

* * *

She led me down a hall to a small room with a sofa, a pair of wing chairs, some bookshelves, and a television. The television was on, and the VCR. She was watching *The African Queen.* The half-filled glass on the table next to the couch was her date.

She turned to me and said, "Sit down if you'd like." Her face was pale and her lip trembled.

I thanked her.

"This is about Jason, isn't it?"

"Yes."

She wrapped herself with her arms and squeezed tightly. "Oh, God," she said, "Oh, *God.*"

She sat down on the sofa and idly picked up the remote, turned off the television, and looked back at me.

"Is he under arrest?"

"No. Not yet."

"Not *yet?*"

That was my cue. The next line out of my mouth should have been "No, but unless your husband does what I tell him to, your son will be in jail before midnight, and he might be there for a long time."

Why couldn't I say it?

Lots of reasons, I suppose. I talk a good game, especially to myself, but I have a way of flinching. Some part of my mind keeps seeing things—wanting to, anyway—from that other angle.

This time, it was the kid. I didn't know Jason Straylow, but I knew enough from two nights of watching him to know that he wasn't my kind. My kind lived with John Fearson—or had, anyway. But I remembered another kid, this one from inside. A nothing kid, not very bright and nowhere near tough enough to make it where he'd been sent. He had these deep, frightened eyes, the eyes of a trapped animal, full of panic. He'd been dealing a little at some rinky-dink junior college and got himself busted. Talked too much, no doubt. He came up for trial during one of those fevers when all the newspapers and politicians start howling for a war on drugs, and he pulled a judge who wanted to send a message. Twenty-five years with no parole. He had to do more time than he'd lived, and he couldn't make the mental adjustment. Didn't have the tools. He was dying and going crazy at the same time. I tried to help him, tried to get him to take some college courses, start reading some books, lift weights, run the track, *anything* to help chip away at that big rock of time. But he couldn't do it. He tried to hang himself, but he couldn't do that either. Living next to him made doing time that much harder, and I knew if I put Jason Straylow in Raiford it would make living that much harder.

And maybe part of it was talking to his mother, who looked sick with fear.

"No," I said. "Not yet. But he's still doing drugs. He's doing them tonight."

"But you didn't arrest him?"

"No. I thought you ought to know about it. Maybe you can do something before he gets in too deep to dig himself out."

She looked at me, and the curiosity in her eyes, which had been dulled by the whiskey, came alive. She seemed to study me for a long time, as though I might be somebody she had known once and she was trying to remember my name.

"I'm sorry," she said. "I didn't ask you if you wanted something to drink."

"No, thank you."

"You're sure?"

She gave me another long look. There was intelligence and something else in her face. Sympathy, maybe.

"I wasn't thinking clearly at first," she said. "Too much bourbon. I know who you are."

I didn't say anything.

"I know who you are, and I *think* I know why you came here."

I nodded.

"But you changed your mind, didn't you? You didn't come here to warn me about Jason. You weren't following him because you do undercover narcotics work. You're working on that case of Eddie's, the one with the man who has the boys' ranch."

"I'm sorry," I said. "It was a bad idea."

"Why did you change your mind?" She said it calmly, almost as though she felt bad for me that it hadn't worked out.

"It's not your boy's fault. He's got a problem, but it doesn't have anything to do with me. I'm sorry. I got carried away."

I wanted to get away from the house and from her, so badly that I felt like running. I stood up.

"No. Wait a minute. Please."

"The part about your son is true, Mrs. Straylow. You need to do something about him. It was a bad idea, but maybe you can use it."

"How?" she said bitterly. "Should I go out to wherever he's snorting coke with his friends, put him in the car, bring him home, and put him to bed without any supper?"

"I'd go with you," I said. "I could make him get in the car."

She smiled mournfully and shook her head. "I'm sure you could. Then what?"

"I don't know."

"Nothing," she said. "I don't know why Jason wants to do this to himself. Maybe it's because he's been unhappy at home for so long. That's reason enough, isn't it?"

"I don't know."

"You know what Eddie probably would have told you tonight, *if* you had been able to find him at home? He'd have said, 'No deal.' He thinks this case is his big chance, and Jason . . . Well, Jason has been a *problem* for a long time now. Lately, it's gotten worse, until it's more like a cancer than a problem. I don't know who Eddie hates seeing more when he comes home, me or Jason."

She stared at me, and her tone changed from self-pity to something almost prosecutorial. "If Eddie had been here tonight and he had said no to your deal, would you have really had Jason arrested?"

I shook my head. I despised myself for being one of those men who make threats they can't back up.

"Why not?"

"Because he's just a wasted kid," I blurted out. "It would be like running down some animal just because it got in your headlights."

She smiled and I saw the look of sympathy again. "You draw the line at kids?"

"Yeah, I suppose." God, I wanted to get out of there, but I felt like I had some kind of duty to stay. I'd brought her this grief, come in out of the night with it when she was consoling herself with Bogart and bourbon. Now I had to stay and take my licks.

"I do too. I feel like I'm responsible in some way for what's happened between Eddie and me. You know what I mean?"

I nodded. Now, I thought, I was going to get the short course in marriage dynamics, condensed from the works of Phil Donahue. Real punishment.

"I don't have any right to bitch," she said. "I went into it with my eyes open and all that other bullshit. I married Eddie because he was attractive and smooth. We were going to make it. I helped him through law school, typed his papers and worked to pay the bills. We had some good years, but I knew what he wanted all along, and I just wasn't smart enough to see that I wouldn't always be part of his plans. So I've got no bitch.

"But Jason is different. He didn't choose us. Eddie has made his life hell, and that's not Jason's fault. He's a gentle boy, always has been; even when he was a baby, you could tell that if you took the time. Eddie never took the time.

"So when Jason didn't like sports, Eddie couldn't understand. He kept pushing the boy, raging at him, making him feel like he was a failure. He did the same thing when Jason had trouble in school. Jason is creative but he isn't brilliant. The tests show that, but Eddie didn't pay any attention to the tests. He just kept saying Jason wasn't tough enough, didn't try hard enough, couldn't 'suck it up and fight.' God, I hated hearing that. Poor Jason, for the longest time he just wanted to do something to please his father, but nothing seemed to work. So he finally quit trying and then he quit caring. I think he actually enjoys doing things that disappoint his father now. It's a way of getting back at him. He got in trouble before with drugs, and we had to send him to one of those hospital programs. The doctors wanted to talk to Eddie about his problems with Jason, but Eddie wouldn't even meet with them. He kept saying, '*I* don't have a problem. It's the spoiled, soft kid who has the problem. That's what I'm paying them to fix.'

"Jason was in the hospital for a month, and Eddie

went to see him twice. On weekends. He stayed an hour, both times, and he was furious when he left. He talked the whole time about how much that hospital was costing and how it was just 'money down a rathole.'

"Jason never had a chance, and Eddie wouldn't have given him one if he'd been here tonight to do it."

I nodded. Nothing in the world I could say.

"What do you need?" she said abruptly.

"Beg your pardon?"

"What do you need?" she repeated. "For your case. What did you come here hoping to get in exchange for not putting Jason in jail?"

"I wanted your husband to drop the case. And make some sort of statement about how John Fearson wasn't guilty of any of the things that he's been accused of."

"He's not guilty, then?"

"No. Not as far as I can tell, and I've spent a lot of time looking into it."

"Then you need something on Eddie, don't you?" She said it calmly. As though she were asking me, again, if I'd like something to drink. "Since you can't bring yourself to deal for Jason, you need something on Eddie to make him quit and release that statement."

I stared at her.

"Well, why not? Jason is my child. I'll make the deal you came here to make. If you won't have him arrested, then I'll give you something you can use. If saving my child means ruining my husband . . . Well, that's just a lucky bonus."

"I don't know the law," I fumbled, "but I don't think you can testify against him."

She waved her hand at me and smiled. "I don't

intend to. But I know about Eddie's work. I was his secretary when he started out and was too strapped to hire one. God, but we were poor. Worked all the time on little hopeless cases. Ate tuna fish and spaghetti until I just can't stand the thought of it anymore, even when you call it pasta. I knew everything that went on in that office.

"Eddie's done better lately, and he doesn't need me the way he used to. He doesn't seem to need me at all. But I still know what goes on. He may not know it, but Eddie can't keep any *professional* secrets from me. Not many of the other kind, either."

I nodded again, feeling like a dumb boy being seduced by a mature woman.

"If you knew something that could get Eddie disbarred, that would probably help you, wouldn't it?"

"Yes," I said.

"Then let me explain how he's been stealing money from his clients. If you've got a notebook, you might want to take notes."

Chapter Twenty-three

It was late, and I had more business in Panama City in the morning. So I spent the night in a decaying motel east of town and woke up early, eager to escape from my tight, moldy room. After breakfast, I bought some things at a drugstore and went back just long enough to shave and check out. Then I drove north, into the rural backwater of the county. It took me about an hour to find the two-bay garage and salvage yard filled with wrecked cars and pickups. The sign said TRAWICK'S AUTO.

I parked and went into the nearest bay, where a man had an old Blazer up on a lift. He was underneath, changing the U-joint.

"Mr. Trawick?"

"Uh-huh."

"Wonder if I might talk to you for a minute?"

"Just as soon as I bust this sumbitch loose and get a new one in," he said. "About ten minutes."

"Take your time."

I walked out of the bay and wandered around the garage. It was one of those operations where tools get put down instead of put away; old tires lie around waiting to be stacked; seized-up transmissions and rusted-out mufflers are pushed to one side until someone gets around to hauling them off, which might be a long time yet, from the look of things.

The office wasn't much better. The furnishings consisted of a metal desk piled with old orders and invoices, a couple of folding chairs, and on one wall an out-of-date calendar from a feed store, with a picture of a woman wearing overalls in an interesting way.

"What can I do for you?" Trawick asked when he came into the office, wiping his hands on an oily rag. He was short and wiry, wore coveralls, and one cheek was full of tobacco. He spat before he came into the office. "If it's trouble with that truck, I can't get to it before Monday."

"No," I said, "the front bearings might need packing, but they can wait. I'd like to talk to you about something else."

He looked at me suspiciously. "I hope you ain't going to tell me you're one of them environmental inspectors coming to check on how I get rid of drain oil or old batteries."

"No," I said and tried to smile. "Nothing like that. You were involved in a lawsuit a while back."

"Yeah?"

"I'm an investigator," I said. "I work for lawyers."

He turned and let a load of juice fly. "Everybody's got to do something, I guess."

"I'm looking into the way that case was settled."

"Uh-huh. Well, we won that suit, fair and square. I'm sorry the old woman got hit up so hard, but my boy is in a wheelchair for the rest of his life. He ain't but sixteen. There wasn't no insurance. We didn't get rich. Otherwise, I wouldn't be out here busting a hump on Saturday morning. That money will make it a little better for my boy, but it ain't going to start him walking again. You going to try to get that money back?"

"No. The money is yours. And your boy's."

"Then what?"

"I'd like to know how you got paid. And when."

"Why?"

"Well," I said, "there is a way that sort of thing is supposed to be done."

"And if somebody done it wrong?"

I shrugged. "Then there may be another lawsuit. You might be entitled to another settlement."

I wasn't sure of that, but it surely worked on George Trawick. A look of larcenous interest passed over his face. "I *thought* he was screwing us. Thought it all along."

"Tell me what you remember," I said, taking out my notebook. "Exact dates and amounts if you can remember them."

He turned to spit, then faced me again. He remembered it all, in detail.

Before I left Panama City, I called the number for Straylow's office and got his service. I left my name and number, said it was important, and got back on the road for the River House.

I'd been home for less than an hour and was still sitting on the porch with Jube, drinking a beer and trying to decide whether or not to call Semmes and tell him what I'd found out, when the phone rang. I hoped it was Jessie but expected that it wasn't.

It was Straylow.

"You said it was important," he said impatiently.

"It's about commingling of funds," I said. "Yours and Trawick's. I thought maybe you'd want to talk about it."

There was a long silence followed by a sigh and then his voice, in a new and weary register. "Not over the phone."

So we agreed to meet somewhere around halfway. I got back in the truck and drove through Pensacola and down 98 to a place by the side of the road where there was a view of the Santa Rosa Sound and a few picnic tables. Straylow was waiting for me, and we had the place to ourselves.

We didn't shake hands or exchange idle pleasantries. The tension in his face had turned his eyes into slits the width of a nickel.

"How much do you know?"

"Enough to get you disbarred."

He thought for a moment, then spoke in a soothing, "trust me" tone. "Then you know that Trawick got everything that was coming to him. And more."

"But he didn't get it on time or in the proper way," I said.

"That's a technicality," he replied, trying to sound unconcerned but failing utterly.

"Not for me to say. Or you."

"I know how it *looks*," he said, trying now to come across as accommodating and misunderstood. He was stalling while he searched for a new line of argument. I was a jury of one, and he needed to find where I was vulnerable.

"But there are things you don't know. Especially if you've been talking to George Trawick. He couldn't wait to get his hands on that money. He fought every single expense, and he never said thank you or 'good job' or anything else, even though he and that boy of his wouldn't have gotten a cent if I hadn't kept pushing that case until we found someone with exposure who could pay. Trawick is a mean, bitter redneck. We made the standard contingency arrangement, and then he complained that the fee was too high. He made it sound like I was stealing even though he wouldn't have gotten a dime without me."

I waited for him to go on. He had a story to tell, and he was setting me up.

"I did good work for Trawick and that boy of his. Real good work. Nobody else would take his case. And he got everything that was due him. And I'll tell you something, even though it doesn't have anything to do with the law or that case, something that might make a technical mistake a little more understandable."

I nodded.

"You probably don't give a good goddamn—and I'm sure Trawick doesn't—but I've got a son too." He shook his head and worked an expression of pain into his face. Either he was good or the pain was genuine.

"My son needed help too."

He searched my face the same way I'd been searching his. Whatever he found there, it was enough to make him push on with his story. "You don't know about families and kids," he said. "But you know about drugs and you know about prison."

I nodded.

"Well, my son was on drugs. Bad. There isn't anything worse. You think you know your kid and you think he loves you, and then one day you realize that

you don't know him and that he hates your guts.
You try everything. You try talk and understanding.
You try getting tough and scaring the hell out of
him. But nothing works. You're dealing with a
stranger, and you're fighting something you just
can't beat.

"My wife and I tried it all, and when nothing
worked we started blaming each other. My son
didn't just ruin his life, he ruined his parents' marriage too. It was the worst thing I've ever gone
through in my life."

We'd been sitting across from each other at one of
the picnic tables. He got up and walked a few feet
away and stared at the water for a while. He
touched his face once or twice, but I couldn't tell if
he was crying or if he just wanted me to think he
might be. He was doing his best to look like a man
bearing up under a heavy load of trouble.

He turned around and came back to the table but
didn't sit down. "My son got busted," he said,
"holding enough to make him a dealer. He was a
juvenile at the time, but there was talk of trying him
as an adult. It would have ruined his life."

Straylow straightened himself and took a deep
breath. "If you are any kind of parent at all, you just
cannot let that happen. You do everything possible.
I hired the best criminal lawyer I could find, and he
managed to keep the whole thing in the youth-of-
fender system. That was a break, but we were still
dealing with a judge who wanted to send my son
away.

"We came up with another plan, and the judge
bought it. A hospital with specialized, intensive
treatment. A thirty-day program. It was that or the
reformatory. So we were lucky to get the hospital
program. Very lucky.

"But it all cost money. A lot of goddamned money." Straylow looked at me and held his hands up helplessly, palms extended.

"People think all lawyers are rich." He shook his head. "All those seven-figure judgments. Well, I didn't have the money for the hospital, and the hospital doesn't do charity work. I also had some very steep legal bills.

"I *had* to pay that hospital." He said the words slowly and deliberately. "And I would have done anything to get the money."

"So you used Trawick's?"

"It was right there. I couldn't sell my house that quickly. Even if I could have borrowed the money, it would have taken time. So I went into the trust account, and then I fed Trawick a story about how the money from his settlement was in an interest-bearing account until some questions about the appeal were sorted out. I don't think he ever believed it.

"I started calling receivables, and I had another fairly big case at the time, with a large settlement. I put the money back in the Trawick account and wrote him one check for everything he was entitled to and another for 'interest.' I think he knew what that check was for."

He paused for a moment, and I waited for the summation—the kicker.

"I didn't like it," he said. "But I didn't feel like I had any choice. And if the same thing happened today, I'd do it again."

We looked at each other for a minute, and then he said, "That's the story behind Trawick's money. And that's what I'll say if you report me."

"It might work," I said. "As mitigation, anyway."

"So you *are* going to report it?"

"Not necessarily. I'll deal."

"What's it going to cost me?" Somehow he managed to sound like the injured party.

"Nothing. I want you to drop the case against John Fearson. And I want you to make a statement saying that your client was telling lies about brutality at Sweetwater Ranch. You do that, and I won't say anything about the way you handled Trawick's money."

"I told you," he said righteously, "I did that for my family."

"And I'm doing this for John Fearson," I said. "He feels like those boys at Sweetwater are his family, and he lost them because you played along with that lying little client of yours."

"I'm only his lawyer. It's my job to represent him. That's what I *do*."

"Well," I said, "your bad luck. *This* is what I do."

"Blackmail," he sneered.

"Sure. You can call it that if it makes you feel better. But the way I look at it is you're guilty and John Fearson is not."

He showed me his throat. "If you report that Trawick business, then I'm ruined."

"Then give me a reason not to report it."

"Drop the case?"

"*And* make the statement."

"I can't."

"Why not?"

"It isn't just *my* case," he said helplessly.

"Riordan?"

He nodded.

"What's he got to say about it?"

"He found the Hewes kid, drinking in a bar one night. The way he sees it, it's his case. He needs money and this is his chance."

"Tell him to piss up a pine tree."

"I can't."

"What can he do to you?"

His face was desolate. "The same thing you could do," he said. "And that's just for openers."

"Tell him there won't be any other cases if you don't get off this one. You're his meal ticket."

He shook his head. "He wants to get out of here. He needs money now."

"Pay him."

"With what?"

It wasn't my problem. So I didn't answer.

"I could pay *you*," he said hopefully.

"I told you my price," I said.

"And I told you," he replied, his voice rising with frustration, "I can't do it. I'd be finished."

"Better you than Fearson," I said.

He looked beaten.

"You need to drop the case and release that statement on Monday morning if we're going to have a deal." I stood up to leave.

"I'll have to get back to you," he said. His voice, like his expression, was barren.

"I'll be home all weekend."

I left him there, by the side of the road, sitting at a picnic table and looking out at the water.

Chapter Twenty-four

There were the usual small chores to do around the house, and I made myself busy by doing them. Edward Straylow would either call before Monday morning, or he wouldn't. There wasn't much left that I could do except stay close to the phone. So I organized my tools, scraped splattered paint from a window, and replaced a corroded junction box. It was routine work and didn't require much in the way of thought. My mind drifted.

Jubal heard the car first and barked. For a moment or two, I thought it might be Jessie in her Alfa, but that didn't seem likely. We hadn't said anything irretrievable yet. But we had come close. The morning after the television news had replayed my old story, we were nearly shouting, and by the time I left her house we'd pretty much decided that it would be wise to stay away from each other until the Sweetwater thing was over. Maybe longer.

"Morgan," Jessie had said, "you keep trying to turn this into some kind of war when it's only a job. You've got to recall, sometime, that life keeps on."

She was right, but that didn't change my mind.

The car was a Lincoln, pearl gray and long as a boat, with darkly tinted windows and polished chrome. It eased to a stop, and a man got out slowly. He adjusted his sunglasses and smoothed his thinning hair, then flipped his cigarette onto my yard.

He was dark and stocky, wearing white pants and a golf shirt that would have looked better on a thinner man. The expensive linen sport coat probably covered a gun, either in his belt or in a shoulder holster. He looked like the kind of man who would feel undressed without a gun.

He glanced around the grounds and house like he was trying to figure out why anyone in his right mind would want to live this way. You could tell that he liked the feel of pavement under his feet.

He walked up to me. There was something belligerent in his stride, but he kept his eye on Jubal: they're always afraid of dogs.

"He bite?"

"Not so far."

He looked at me. He had a sly, weary face, a heavy beard, and a few acne scars.

"You Hunt?"

"Who are you?"

He sighed. "Riordan. Jack Riordan. You and me gotta talk."

I didn't like having Jack Riordan on my porch. He was one of those men—and I'd known a lot of them —who seemed to take up more than his share of space. He was a crowder, instinctively aggressive and acquisitive. It was easy to see how he would have been a good big-city cop before he turned crooked. He would have been everywhere, in everybody's business, and he would have known things without realizing it or knowing how he knew them.

"You know who I am, don't you?"

I nodded.

"OK. And I know about you too. For a guy who didn't go to one of the big schools, you're pretty good. But a guy can learn a lot in the can, I guess. I don't know, and I don't intend to find out, either."

He ran a thumbnail across his chin. It sounded like sandpaper.

Jubal sat down next to me, and I rubbed his ears. He kept his eyes on Riordan. So did I.

"You work for anybody besides Semmes?"

"No." It was the first word out of my mouth since he sat down and started talking. It seemed like the best word to use when you're talking to a man like Riordan. There were probably a lot of people who regretted the day they'd stopped saying no to Jack Riordan.

"How does he pay?"

"He's fair," I said.

Riordan nodded abstractly. "Yeah. That's his reputation. He's a *fair* man. Always tries to do the right thing. One of those old-school types. Probably got a plantation back somewhere in his family. Where I come from, his type had beach houses in Maine. They tested very high on *fair* too. Easy for them— didn't cost them anything, and they never got their shoes dirty."

A mosquito buzzed his ear, and he waved it away with a meaty hand. I noticed the gold watch.

"I suspect that if you keep running around locating witnesses for him on this boys'-camp thing, he'll pay you a *fair* wage. He'll hand his client a bill that's fair, and maybe he won't even bother to collect. If he wins, he'll think that's a fair verdict, and nobody will be out anything. Fair deal all the way around, right?"

"You don't like it, though," I said.

He shrugged. "Man wants to work for wages when the rest of the world is on percentage, it's no skin off my ass."

"What if it cuts into your percentage?"

He smiled. His teeth were yellow. "That's a good point," he said. "A very good point."

"But not my problem."

"It could be."

"Did you come here to lean on me?"

He put his hands up, palms extended. "Hey, give me a little credit, will you? I came to talk some business, make you an offer."

"Then make it."

"How'd you like to work for me, instead of Semmes?"

"For a percentage?"

"Absolutely. None of this 'fair wage' shit."

"What do I do?"

"Whatever needs to be done."

"Forget about Trawick?"

He drew his lips back from his teeth. It was not a smile. "That would be good."

"And drop what I'm doing for Semmes on Sweetwater?"

"Even better."

"Straylow is not exactly my kind of client."

He shrugged. "He does what he's told and his checks clear. I won't be here much longer. I'd go crazy if I had to live my life in this backwater. When I'm gone, you'll inherit Straylow."

"How much could I expect?"

"How much do you need?"

"Like that?"

"Yeah. Like that. This boys'-ranch thing could be big. Straylow could win it straight up if it ever gets to court. You know how juries are about kids. So the insurance company will pay big to keep it out of court."

He looked around slowly, surveying the big old house that sagged here and there and still showed the years of neglect. It was the other side of the penthouse world that men like Riordan considered "real class."

"What do you owe on this dump? Couldn't be more than forty grand. You could pay the whole thing off. Easy."

I stood up. "OK, Jack," I said. "You made your offer, now run along. Tell Straylow I won't play."

He stood and smoothed the front of his golf shirt over his roll. "Looks like I was wrong," he said. "You may do good work, but you're still just a cracker. A dumb cracker. All you small-time crackers are the same."

"Well, Jack," I said, "that may be true. But you're the one who had to come hide out down here among us. We might be crackers, but we aren't scrambling around like rats trying to get out of the sun."

His face went hard, and he gave me a look that had probably worked on a thousand suspects. "Watch yourself, cracker."

"You got no backup here, Jack. No partner, no badge. And you're on my property. Crackers feel like you can pretty much do what you want to a man who won't get off your property."

He forced some air through his teeth and glared at me.

"I'll make *you* a deal. You quit working for Straylow. Convince him to drop the Sweetwater case and make a statement saying that John Fearson is innocent of all those charges. You do that, Jack, and I won't locate the boys you finked on and tell them where you're hiding."

I saw the look cross his face. I might have given him the first shot, but I knew he was wearing a gun under his jacket. So I dropped a shoulder, and when he took that fake, I pivoted and swung my leg, catching him just above the ankles. His feet went out from under him, like somebody had sprung a trap, and he went down in a pile. He reached for his piece, but I was on him and had the hand before it moved six inches. I used just enough force that he knew I could break his arm. I was a foot from his face, and I could smell his cologne. It smelled sweet and ripe.

"You smell like a twenty-dollar whore, Jack," I said. I wanted to break his arm and then just keep on breaking things. I felt like I was on the curl of a huge wave, and as it broke so did my anger. It was a wonderful feeling of freedom and release and power. I felt a surge of blood and a kind of overall lightness, as though I were flying, bearing down on my prey like a hawk.

Riordan saw my look and he must have known. But he came from a hard school, and he didn't say anything and fought hard to keep his face from showing anything, to hold onto the mask that had always worked when he needed to throw a scare into someone. But I saw the fear pooling in his eyes, and that was enough. I had some will left, and I was able to get a hold on myself. Just barely. I was trembling and my voice sounded high and thin.

"You need to do a few things, Jack. You probably ought to change perfumes, for starters. Get some of that stuff Elizabeth Taylor is selling. I think it's you."

He didn't say anything.

"But what you *really* need to do is get your fat ass off my property. Then you need to go turn over some rocks until you find where Straylow is hiding. Tell him it's time to back off. Then you need to get out of Dodge. Go to Costa Rica or someplace and hide out.

"You understand all that, Jack?"

He didn't say anything and he held onto the mask.

I used a little more force.

"Understand, Jack?"

"Yeah," he said through his teeth, still holding onto the mask even though he was sweating through the layer of cologne. "Yeah, I understand."

"All right, then. Now just hold on while I take this hog leg of yours. That's what crackers call a gun, Jack. A hog leg. A knife is a frog sticker. Might help to know the language, as long as you're here. Which won't be much longer. Right?"

"Right," he said through his teeth.

I pulled the snub-nosed .38 from his belt holster. "I'll leave this with Straylow in a couple of days. After we've settled everything. You'll have to get along without it, but you're a big boy. You'll make it."

I let him up. "Before you run along, Jack," I said, "there *is* one more thing. Pick up that cigarette butt you threw on my lawn. You get in trouble down here when you dump your trash on another man's property."

He straightened himself up and walked slowly across the lawn until he came to the spot. Then he reached over and picked up the cigarette butt. Without looking back at me, he walked around the Lincoln and got in. He started the engine and after a second or two slipped the car into gear and started down my driveway, moving very slowly.

After I'd calmed down enough to think, I went inside and dragged an old footlocker out of a storage room. I turned the key in the padlock and raised the lid. There were boxes of ammunition in the bottom and, resting on top of them, a Ruger mini-14 packed in Cosmoline. I took it out to the shop and cleaned it off with WD-40, then relubed it and checked to see that the bolt moved frictionlessly where metal made contact with metal.

There were a dozen twenty-round magazines in the footlocker, wrapped in oiled newspaper. I unwrapped them and dried them until there was only a thin coat of oil on the surface of each one. I loaded four. The rounds slipped in with a positive, solid sound, and the loaded magazines felt heavy in my hand. There was something satisfying about that.

I fitted one magazine into the rifle, worked the bolt, and watched it pick up a round and guide it smoothly into the chamber. I put the safe on and rested the rifle in a corner where I could get to it in a hurry. If Jack Riordan came back, I wasn't going to duel him with pistols.

It was close to evening. The air had cooled slightly, and I was thinking about a beer and something to eat. I was restless and tired of waiting for the phone to ring. I wanted to be getting ready for an evening out, cleaning up and getting dressed before I picked Jessie up in another hour and took her out for some dinner and then a little music. It was Saturday night. Those rhythms were in the air, and I felt them keenly.

The phone rang, and once again I hoped it would be Jessie.

"Hello."

"He's going after you." I didn't recognize the voice.

"Say again."

"You'd better be careful. He's already come after me."

It was Mrs. Straylow. She was gasping between words.

"Take it easy," I said. "Are you hurt?"

There was a pause, as though she might be thinking it over. "No. I'm not bleeding. Nothing is broken."

"Your husband knows you talked to me?" I said, already knowing the answer.

"I told him," she sobbed.

Naturally.

"What did he do?" I said.

"Oh, he yelled at me a lot, and I yelled back at him. There's nothing unusual about that. Then he slapped me. That was something new. He'd never done that before. Never had the guts . . . or been so afraid. Funny thing, it didn't hurt."

"So, you're OK?"

"No. I'm terrified." Her voice was rising and shrill. "Eddie didn't do that, though. It was his man Riordan. He didn't put a hand on me, or even say very much, but he scared me more than Eddie ever could. I'm still scared."

"They're gone now?"

"Yes. When he left, Riordan said he was going to get you next."

"I've already seen him."

"He'll be back."

"I can handle him."

"You need to be very careful."

"Oh, I will. Now what about you?"

"I'm afraid. Riordan would kill me."

"Where are you?"

"Home. At least it used to be."

"Get out of there."

"Where will I go?"

Come on, lady, I thought.

"Anywhere. Pack what you need for one night, and go to a motel."

"I don't know." Her voice was cracking, and she was about to lose it.

"OK. Listen. Go get in your car and drive west on 98. Don't stop for anything unless you need gas. When you get to the Pensacola Bay Bridge, there will be a little park. It's very bright. I'll be parked there, waiting for you."

"Now?"

"Right now. Hang up the phone and get in your car."

She didn't answer.

"Do it."

"All right."

"Good. I'll be waiting."

She hung up.

After I fed Jube, I took the rifle out to the truck and put it on the passenger side, with the muzzle to the floorboard. I could reach the stock easily, but nobody standing outside the truck could see the rifle.

Just before I reached the bridge, I stopped at a carry-out place for a cup of black coffee and a chicken leg. It was nearly dark when I pulled into the park to wait for Mrs. Straylow. I ate my supper and watched a couple of small shrimp boats dragging the bay. The Saturday-night traffic moved steadily in both directions.

I figured on an hour's wait. After two hours, I started coming up with reasons why she'd be late. She had stopped for gas. Or gone by the bank to use the cash machine. Or taken time to pack a bag.

After two and a half hours, I wondered if Straylow and Riordan had caught her leaving. Or if she had changed her mind and gone to a friend's or to a nearby motel and tried to call me.

I got out of the truck and walked to a phone booth, called the Straylow home, and listened to fifteen rings before I hung up.

I got back in the truck. Should I drive to Panama City?

I wouldn't know where to look for her if she wasn't at home. But I could ask Tom Pine to make a call to the Bay County Sheriff's Department and request that somebody send a cruiser around to the Straylow residence just to make sure there wasn't a woman there who couldn't come to the phone because she was tied up or dead.

The logical thing was to go back to the River House, but to be careful doing it. There was also a possibility that the call had been made to get me away so that somebody could come in behind me and be waiting when I returned.

So when I was still half a mile from my turnoff I pulled over on the shoulder, almost into the ditch as a precaution against Saturday-night drunks, and killed the engine. I got out carrying the Ruger, checked the chamber instinctively and then the safety before I slipped into a little stand of pine, dogwood, and jack oak that flanked the road and spread to the edge of the River House yard.

The pines were tall enough that their crowns made a ceiling that kept out the thin light of a quarter moon. Even after I had my night vision, it was tricky moving. I couldn't see more than ten feet ahead of me, and even then I could only make out large shapes.

I had to move carefully, but I still had an advantage. I *knew* I was out there, and I knew what I was looking for. Knew, too, what I would do if I found it.

The blood pounded solidly in my ears. I picked up one foot, put it down, and then took a breath. Picked up the other foot, put it down, and let out the breath slowly and quietly. It was a deliberate, maddening rhythm, but it was quiet. I bit down hard enough on my back teeth to knot a muscle in my jaw.

An owl hooted. Mosquitoes whined around my ears before they picked a spot of bare, slick skin on my face or neck. I let them drink.

It probably took me an hour to get close enough to check out the house. By then, I knew there was somebody in the woods with me.

I went down on one knee behind a fat pine. You would need a scope, I thought, to pick out my silhouette. I listened, straining to pick up something through the roar inside my ears. The pine sap smelled strong and precise. It occurred to me that this would be the smell inside a no-frills coffin.

I could see the house, and I could feel the river. And I knew the other thing was there. It could have been an animal—a deer or a raccoon—but I didn't think so. In fact, I was sure.

I stayed behind the tree for thirty minutes. A long time to remain entirely still. Too long for most people. But I had gone much longer. I once watched a company of North Vietnamese regulars while they were stopped at a rest station under the triple canopy thirty clicks inside Laos. There had been five of us, nearly two hundred of them. We were less than a hundred feet from the closest of them, with our bodies pressed close to the earth. When my bladder was full, I just let go and felt a warm, muddy puddle form around my cold loins. I was badly dehydrated, and the smell of ammonia was very strong.

In the morning, they pushed on, and when they were a half-click down the trail we called the fast movers in on them. When the napalm hit, we could hear their mortar rounds and grenades cooking off.

Next to that, watching my own house for half an hour was nothing.

For some reason, I was sure there were two of them, stretched out on a mound of earth next to a patch of palmettos. This changed things. I had been expecting Riordan, even though this was not his usual turf. Maybe, I thought, he had hired local help.

One of them was better than the other. When the one who was itchy moved and rattled some dried palmettos for the second time in five minutes, the one who was good hissed at him like a teacher scolding a restless child.

I moved in a little closer, until I could make out their shapes. One was large and stationary, and the other was smaller and moved his head every few seconds. From the way he twitched, I figured the mosquitoes were getting to him and he'd have much rather been inside somewhere.

It would have been easy to get them both with the

Ruger. They were flat on the ground, and there was
no way the second one could get to his feet and
make it to the bushes after he heard the first shot.
I'd drop him before he took a step. I lined the muzzle up on the first man. A spine shot.

I moved the rifle in a short arc until the muzzle
rested on the smaller man. Piece of cake.

I eased the stock off my shoulder and laid the rifle
on the pine straw that covered the ground. I let off
half a breath and went back to watching the two
men. The pounding in my ears settled slowly, and I
began to breathe regularly.

The earth was warm and moist, and it smelled
strongly of rot and decay and the things that fed on
them: worms, fungus, mold, and countless insects.
They crawled over my skin, and their tracks felt
small and precise and seemed to penetrate deeply
into my body. Between the smell of the pines, the
dampness of the earth, and the touch of the small,
earth-dwelling insects, I knew as close as I ever
would the feeling of the grave. Like the poets have
always said, there is some peace there.

But not for my visitors. They were restless. After
another fifteen or twenty minutes, they stood in
front of me, rising stiffly.

"This late," the larger one said, "he must not be
coming."

"What do we do now?" the other one said in a
high, young voice. Not a small man, like I'd
thought, but a boy.

Luther Jordan and his father.

"We'll go to a motel. Sleep on nice, clean sheets.
That sound good?"

"Sure," the boy said.

"OK. Then follow me out of here."

I lay very still while they passed within five feet of

me. Then, speaking softly so I wouldn't alarm them,
I said, "OK, Sarge. Just hold what you got."

They froze and waited for me to show myself.

Luther Jordan was scared. His father was angry
with himself. "You're pretty good," he said. "I never
heard a thing."

"Not as good as you," I replied. "The boy gave
you away."

Luther hung his head.

Jordan looked at him, then put a hand on his
shoulder and squeezed with affection. "It's all right,
son. You did better than a lot of grown men."

The boy looked at the ground, and in the weak
light I could see his throat work as he swallowed
tears.

"You got no reason to get down on yourself, Luther. You hear me?"

The boy nodded.

Jordan looked up at me. I noticed the nine-milli-
meter pistol in his belt. I lowered the rifle. He made
no move for the pistol.

"We ought to talk," I said. "There are things you
need to know."

"OK."

"Can't use the house. I've got somebody looking
for me. You have a vehicle around here somewhere?"

He told me where he'd parked.

"OK. Let's go get it. You can follow me. I know a
safe place where we can ditch it. Before anyone no-
tices it, you'll be a long time gone."

Chapter Twenty-five

Jordan was driving a Mazda pickup with a camper shell. He and the boy got in and followed me to a fish house and ice plant where shrimp boats unloaded and docked. The mates and deckhands parked in a big lot out back, and some of the cars and trucks stayed there for weeks and months before their owners came back to claim them. Some were never claimed. Men changed boats, stayed in other towns, were arrested, got killed. Nobody paid any attention to the vehicles in this lot. I couldn't be sure that Jordan and his boy were not being looked for, that the Columbus police had not sent out the word. If they were being looked for and the car was known and spotted, I would be open to an aiding-and-abetting charge. I wasn't taking any chances.

They had some gear—packs and duffles that smelled faintly of the Eglin swamp where I'd first found them. We loaded what they needed into the bed of my truck, then drove out a road that fed into the interstate, where Jordan checked into a Triple-Six. There was an all-night diner next door, where we got some food for the boy and black coffee for the two of us.

The boy ate his cheeseburgers while Jordan and I talked.

I told him that it was only a matter of time before the police in Columbus connected him with Perkins, if they hadn't already. "There was a man I talked to, name of Valentine, who was smart enough to figure it out," I said.

Jordan nodded. "They might decide to come looking for me. But I ain't going to be easy to find. Not for the police, anyway. But I ain't so sure about you. That's why I'm here."

His face had the old mountain-hollow profile, formed by the anger of some grievance that could never be made right.

"You found me in that swamp. I thought you might have come looking, that you were just slinging bullshit about scouting for deer season, so I asked an old buddy of mine back at Benning about you. Hollibird. You know him."

"Good man," I said.

"Yeah," Jordan said. "One of the best. He had your name. Wasn't hard to find you. Course, you weren't hiding. The way I was when you found me."

"That was just lucky."

He drank some coffee and said, "I spent the last three months I was in the army working up new identities for me and the boy. Figured out a place to go and how we're going to live. No Georgia policeman will find us.

"But I had to make sure about you. If you found me in that swamp, then you might come find me again. I've got to know what you want. Is it the boy?"

I shook my head.

"Because the boy stays with me," he said fiercely. "I want it that way and so does he. What the rest of them want, or the law says, it don't matter. He's my son. I've been screwed around on that one all I'm going to be. You or anyone else wants to take him back, then it's through me."

"I don't want to take him back."

"What about the man that runs that camp?"

"The camp was closed down. And that man thinks the boy is better off with you."

"How come he was closed down?" Jordan asked.

"It's a long story."

"I'm in no hurry."

The expression on his face never changed while he listened. It was both fierce and melancholy. When I finished, he was silent for a moment, thinking. Then he said, "You need a little help? Someone to watch your back as long as this Riordan is loose?"

"I could probably use it."

"Then you got it. Long as you don't expect us to stick around for more than a couple of days."

"All right," I said. "But why?"

He shrugged. "You did me a favor not calling the dogs on me and the boy when you knew where we were. You could have done that. You were taking a chance not reporting us to the law. You're taking a chance now. I feel like I owe you one."

I left the room and waited in the truck while Jordan got the boy into bed and said good night. He was concerned Luther would think he was leaving for good, and he wanted to reassure him.

"He's a good boy," Jordan said when he climbed into the truck. "Hard for him to feel like he can count on people, though. They're always bugging out on him."

We drove back to the River House and slipped through the same stand of trees where I'd found Jordan earlier. He moved fluidly and was quiet as a shadow. It felt good to be in the woods with someone that capable. Like old times.

When we got to the edge of the yard, we knelt and studied the house. It looked indistinct in the gloom, almost as though it were underwater.

We planned to watch for an hour. In two hours, it would be dawn. It was the time of morning when somebody waiting to ambush me would be losing the edge, that time of night when things seemed bleakest and when inevitably I used to come awake behind the wire. I would lie in my bunk with my eyes wide open and think that there was simply no way I could make it until dawn, much less to the end of my sentence. I felt as though there were a cold stone the size of a football inside my chest.

I didn't feel that tonight. Felt good, in fact. Having Jordan along to watch my back made me confident, and I actually hoped that Riordan had come back to settle things. I was ready to destroy him—and Straylow—conclusively. I didn't feel detached or clinical about either of them any longer. I wanted to grind them down like a couple of roaches.

But nothing moved inside the house, and I began to feel that Riordan hadn't come. That what he'd said to Mrs. Straylow was meant to throw a scare into me or her. Maybe he had other plans, or maybe he was going to leave town while he still could.

"I'm going to check out the house," I whispered

to Jordan. "You stay here until I turn on a light or you think I need help."

I handed him the Ruger.

"OK," he said without taking his eyes off the house.

I eased across the yard, trying to use the shadows of the old, sprawling trees for concealment. Still, I felt naked and vulnerable. But nothing moved inside the house. I was beginning to relax when I reached the porch. But as my hand touched the door, a small jolt of suspicion cut through the mental clutter. The house was *too* still. Jubal always heard me coming. And if he didn't always bark, he did come to meet me and I would hear the click of his toenails across the wooden floor.

There was no sound from inside.

"Jube?"

Nothing.

I waited, motionless as the old trees in the yard around me. Still, nothing moved inside the house. I wanted to call once more, but I figured the first time would have given anyone inside a good fix. I dropped to my knees.

After a few seconds, I began moving around the house in a low crouch. The ground was covered with thick centipede grass that soaked up the sound of my steps.

It took a couple of minutes to reach the stump that I used for splitting firewood. I had left an ax notched in there, and when I pulled it free it felt good in my hands. Not as good as a shotgun would have, but it was something.

I picked up a piece of kindling and threw it onto the porch. It landed with a heavy thump, and I fell on my stomach and waited for a second noise, a shot or a shout. But nothing moved inside the house, and the thick quiet returned, covering the night like water.

I waited long enough to rattle anyone inside who did not have good discipline. I suspected that Riordan, if he was in the house, would get jittery. It had probably been a long time since he was on a stakeout.

Finally, I stood up and moved, covering fifteen or twenty feet before I went down again, on my belly. Nothing moved. The quiet seemed to echo in my ears and down my neck.

After another minute, I moved again. I had to make up my mind. Go in alone. Call for Jordan. Wait for the light. I decided to go in alone. I believed the house was empty.

Still, I went from room to room, in the dark, holding the ax like a rifle. I kept listening for the sound of Jubal's breathing in the quiet of the house.

I saw him at the end of the hall, lying in a spot that looked darker than the rest of the floor. I started to call to him, then stopped myself. Too late. And if there were somebody there, then he was probably waiting for the sound of my voice.

So I took another step in Jubal's direction, then fell to the floor and rolled twice for the safety of a wall. When nothing happened, I knew I was alone. I stood up and turned on a light. The ax felt useless in my hand.

I walked to where Jubal was lying in a thickening pool of his own blood. His throat had been cleanly cut. His exposed eye was open and horribly vacant. He hadn't struggled. From the way things looked, he had probably been drugged before his throat was cut and had bled to death without realizing it. But that was not charity. Whoever had done it had not wanted a struggle.

In the middle of the pool of blood, there was a cigarette butt.

I turned away to call Jordan, but before I took a step I raised the ax over my head and drove it through a door.

Jordan offered to help me, but I told him I would handle it. I rolled Jubal onto an old rubber poncho, wrapped it around him, and tied off the ends. I lifted the bundle, which felt absurdly light, and carried it outside and down the path to a patch of soft ground next to the slough. I left the bundle on the ground and went back to the toolshed for a long-handled shovel.

I dug and piled the earth carefully next to the hole. It smelled like the blood I'd left drying on the floor. When the hole was deep enough, I dropped the bundle in. It made a heavy, final sound when it hit. I filled the hole, then smoothed it over with the flat of the shovel blade.

I took a small can of gasoline from the toolshed when I put the shovel away and carried it to the house. The gasoline thinned the blood and covered the smell. I rubbed with old towels until there was only a faint, rusty stain that I would have to rub down with sandpaper and steel wool. I took the towels out to the burn barrel and threw a kitchen match in after them. They exploded softly, with the same sound the bundle made when it hit the bottom of the hole.

Jordan was waiting at the front of the house. He had brought the truck around and was leaning against the bed, looking off at a patch of gathering light, where the sun would be rising in another thirty minutes.

"Was it that ex-cop who did it?" he asked.

"Yes."

"Meant to scare you off, I suppose."

"Yes. I'm supposed to go all to pieces now. I'll figure that any man who'd kill a dog is somebody who'd do *anything*. Worked for Marlon Brando, it ought to work for Jack Riordan."

"You know where to find him?"

"Not exactly. But I know where to start looking."

"You still need me?"

"More than ever."

We drove to Panama City, which looked weary and disheveled on this Sunday morning. I had to watch my speed and occasionally relax my grip on the wheel when I noticed that my knuckles were white. We got to Straylow's house before the paper-boy.

The Suzuki and the Volvo were in the drive. No lights burned and nothing moved behind the windows.

"I'll check out the house," I said. "If there's nobody home, I'll break in. You probably ought to stay here."

"Right."

I walked across the damp lawn and tried the bell. The chimes went off like church bells. After a minute, I tried again. After a third try, I circled the house looking for a window where the curtains were open.

Around the back, in a room at the corner of the house, I was able to see through a gap in the curtains. The Straylow boy was lying on the bed, fully dressed. I hoped that he was passed out and sleeping off a hard Saturday night, and not dead. I rapped on the glass. He pulled a pillow over his head. I rattled the glass again and pounded with my fist on the window frame. Finally, he came to the window. He looked out at me too stunned and bewildered to be irritated.

"Front door," I shouted and motioned in that direction.

He nodded.

I went back around to the front. After a minute or two, the door came open. The boy's face was bleary, his hair and clothes were rumpled, and he smelled like swamp water. The room behind him looked worse. The furniture was overturned, drapes had been torn down, and somebody had hit a wall—or been thrown into it—hard enough to fracture the Sheetrock.

"What happened here?" I said.

"I don't know." Mucus clung to the boy's words.

"When did it happen?"

He shrugged. "I don't know. It was like this when I got home."

"When was that?"

He shrugged again, and I slapped him hard enough to twist his face and bring tears to his eyes.

"Wake up," I said.

He glared at me and I slapped him again.

"I don't have time for sullen children," I said. "This is grown-up stuff. So you take a walk back in your mind and try to remember when you got home last night."

"Three. Maybe three thirty." His lower lip quivered.

"Good. Now, was there anyone here? Anyone at all?"

"No. I saw the mess and figured they'd decided to stop shouting and start hitting. I thought maybe the cops had hauled them off. I thought you were a cop."

"Keep thinking that," I said. "Now, tell me one more thing. Where would your father go if he had to hide out?"

He was about to give me another one of those shrugs but stopped when I said, "Think, now."

"He's got a hunting camp."

"Where?"

The boy wasn't much on directions, but he remembered a couple of landmarks that helped me locate the camp. It was almost to the Alabama line, back in the direction we'd come from.

"OK," I said. "That's good. I'm sorry I had to slap you. Go on back to bed."

"What's going on?"

"You'll find out soon enough."

I left him there, standing in the wreckage of his parents' home, and probably their lives as well, too strung out to do anything even if he had cared.

Chapter Twenty-six

I found Straylow's camp by using the landmarks the kid remembered and by knocking on the front door of a couple of farmhouses where people had come back from church and were getting ready for the big meal of the week. Their living rooms smelled like fried chicken.

They sent me down a two-lane that ran through a wide stretch of bottomland to a sturdy logging road that trailed off into a swamp. Straylow's camp, they said, would be about a quarter of a mile down that logging road.

At the junction of the logging road and the two-lane was another set of ruts leading into the woods. I followed them a hundred yards to an open place where people had once taken dirt for fill and now they left the things they no longer wanted or felt like fixing: a couple of old washing machines, a refrigerator, and several sets of rusting bedsprings.

We crossed the two-lane and started down the logging road. I carried the Ruger. Jordan had his pistol. For the first three hundred yards or so, the road was in good shape. We stayed off on the side, using the trees and shadows for concealment.

The road ended in a wide clearing. Riordan's Lincoln and Straylow's Mercedes were parked there, out of place among the shagbark hickory and white oak. An overgrown road—just a couple of deeply worn ruts—led off from the clearing. The camp would be at the end of that road, and there would probably be a jeep to get from there to this little parking area.

"OK," I said. "They're here."

We were about seventy-five yards from the parked cars, kneeling behind a large blowdown. We couldn't see the cabin from the blowdown.

I handed Jordan the Ruger and said, "I'm going to fix up that Lincoln. Riordan has a belly. If he shows up, don't let him get close to me."

"I'll shoot him in the foot," Jordan said. "You'd be surprised how fast that'll put a man on the ground."

I had to run back to my truck for tools, then back to the Lincoln. Jordan signaled from the blowdown that it was clear, and I ran in a crouch until I was beside the Lincoln. I knelt there and waited a few seconds to get my breath. It was hot and I was panting like a dog. When my breathing had settled, I lay down and slithered under the car. I listened for the sound of a jeep coming up the road but heard nothing and went to work.

The fan belt was easy. I cut it with my pocketknife and threaded a loose end through my belt. I didn't want it lying around for someone to see when Riordan pulled out. Then I found the lead off the alterna-

tor that ran to the warning light in the dash. I
peeled a little insulation back and then used some
tape to ground it out against the engine block. It
took about a minute. I rolled out from under the
car, ran across the clearing, and then made it back
around the blowdown.

Jordan looked at me and said, "So far, you're the
only thing moving in these woods."

"OK," I said. "He's going to keep the air conditioner in that Lincoln cranked up all the way. With
the kind of amps that pulls, he won't get ten miles."

"You figure he'll be leaving soon?"

"I don't know. Right now, I'm going to take a
look at the camp. If he does leave, watch and see
which way he goes on the blacktop. He won't get
far."

"Rahj."

I took the Ruger this time and left him with the
pistol. I was also carrying the binoculars from my
truck. In ten minutes, I was close enough to glass
the cabin.

It was a log construction with a steel roof and
thermal-pane windows. Designer rustic. There were
a lot of hunting clubs that built them like this because the members used the cabins for entertaining.
They told their wives they were going to the woods
for a few days of hunting and poker. They didn't
mention the hookers, who were inevitably called
debutantes by the boys in the club. Straylow figured
to be in that kind of hunting club.

I lay on my belly with my elbows in the soft duff
and my palms covering the lenses of my binoculars
to cut off reflections. I could see movement behind a
window. I knew that Straylow and Riordan were
there. I was hoping for a glimpse of Mrs. Straylow.

No luck.

I was still at least a hundred yards from the cabin and thinking about moving in closer when the front door swung open and Straylow walked out onto the porch, followed by Riordan. The ex-cop carried a leather attaché case. They talked for a few minutes, and even though I couldn't hear a word they said it was plain that Riordan was giving the orders.

After five minutes, he turned and walked across the porch, down the steps, and started up the trail to the clearing where his car was parked. Straylow seemed to watch until he was sure that Riordan was leaving, then he turned and went back inside the cabin.

I circled into the woods and ran for the blowdown. While I ran, I heard the Lincoln turn over and begin up the logging road. When I reached the blowdown, Jordan pointed in the direction the Lincoln had turned.

"Let's go get him," I said.

We crossed the blacktop and got in the truck. Jordan drove, and I lay down in the pickup bed, the way we had planned it. Riordan knew me but not Jordan. I felt the tires find pavement and the speed build as Jordan accelerated. After about fifteen minutes, we went around a long bend, and instead of speeding up again Jordan shifted down and slowed.

"There he is."

I raised my head just enough to see the Lincoln pulled over on the shoulder so far that it seemed to teeter over the ditch. Riordan was standing next to the Lincoln with his hands on his hips, glaring at the car like he might just blow it away for causing him trouble.

"OK," I said through the window. "You're just old Bubba, and you'd be glad to carry him down the road a piece, where he can find a garage and a wrecker."

"OK." Jordan sounded tense.

"Just relax. He's in the bag."

"I'll relax when we got a knot tied in the bag."

Jordan eased the pickup behind the Lincoln and stopped. He opened the door and got out. I lay flat, listening.

"Looks like you got you some car problems," Jordan said.

"Goddamned thing just stopped." Riordan sounded like he took it personally. "I trade every six months. Car hasn't got ten thousand on it."

"You think it might be the thermostat?" Jordan said. "They'll sometimes go froggy on you when it's hot like this."

"Shit, I don't know. I don't know a goddamned thing about cars. I pay for 'em and I drive 'em."

"Well, you want me to take a look under? I might can tell you something. If it is the thermostat, you can sometimes free it up just by hitting it a lick."

"All right. But if it isn't something easy, just let it go. I'll get it towed and rent something."

"Sure," Jordan said. "We'll just have us a look-see. Never can tell. Might be something easy. Course with these new jobs, it's hard to see the engine for all the pollution crap. . . ."

Jordan yammered on like a half-touched redneck while he reached inside the Lincoln to free the hood, then went around to the front to raise it. He stuck his head and hands down into the engine well, and I could hear him moving things around and talking.

"Mercy," he said.

"What is it?" Riordan demanded.

"Mister," Jordan said apologetically, "I believe

you got an oil leak somewhere. This car is bone dry and she's run hot. If you get out with nothing worse than scored lifters, then I'll say you got off real light.''

"Christ," the big man said. "Just what I needed.''

"Well," Jordan said, "there is a garage a little ways up the road. I know the fellow who runs it. He's got a wrecker he could send over for your car and a phone you could use to call whoever you need to call.''

"How much?''

"To ride a man up the road?'' Jordan said, his voice full of genuine country pride. "A man whose car is broke? Nothing. Not a thing. Climb in the cab, and I'll have you there in fifteen minutes.''

"All right. Let me get my case.''

I heard Riordan walk to the Lincoln, open a door, then close it again. Then I heard both of them approaching the truck. Jordan got in on the driver's side and slid across the seat to unlock the passenger door. When it was open, he said, "Climb in.''

Riordan was getting into the seat, with one hand on the dash and the other on the handle of his attaché case, when I came around the cab. Jordan put the muzzle of his pistol in Riordan's ear, and I stuck the point of a lock-back folding knife deep enough into his chin to draw a steady trickle of blood.

"Hello, Jack," I said. "I'd like to talk to you about a dog.''

He didn't say anything. His body tensed, and his face went into the hard mask.

"We *will* kill you. Do it in a heartbeat and not lose a bit of sleep if you don't do exactly what you are told. If you do right, I may only cut you a little.''

I paused, then said, "You understand that, Jack?''

He didn't answer, so I pushed the knife in a little

deeper, and the blood came a little faster, like a thick, red ribbon running down his neck, inside the collar of his polo shirt.

"Understand, Jack?"

"I understand," he said, trying not to move his chin and drive the point of the knife any deeper into the pad of soft flesh.

"Fine. Now I know you're tough, Jack. Takes a world-class badass to kill a drugged dog. Man who would do that is someone you've got to respect. So I can't take any chances with you, can I, Jack? I mean, you make a funny move, I've got to cut your throat.

"Of course, I might cut it anyway. Crackers are funny about their dogs."

I relaxed the knife a little, and Riordan spoke carefully, through his teeth. "You aren't going to kill me over a dog."

I drove the knife up into his chin, deeper still.

"Let me tell you something, Jack. I don't think I could live with myself if I let a man get away with killing my dog. Up to now, it was just a job. But you crossed the line."

"I've got money."

"Money for me?"

"Yeah. In the case."

"How much?"

"Twenty."

"So you killed my dog to terrorize me, and then you were going to give me the money?"

"Yeah."

"You figured I'd be grateful and scared at the same time. Or something like that?"

"Yeah."

"Jack, you're a fool."

He didn't say anything.

"Where's the Straylow woman?"

He didn't answer.

"Going hard on me, Jack?"

Nothing.

"OK. We figured on that. So we're going to take you someplace where we can talk."

It took me about two minutes to get his wrists wrapped up with bare copper wire and secured to an eyebolt on the floor behind the seat. The wire cut and drew blood. If Riordan moved, it would get worse.

"Comfortable, Jack?"

He didn't answer and I didn't push it.

Jordan started the truck and drove it back down the blacktop to the little trail where we'd pulled off before. He parked at the edge of the old fill pit, pulled the emergency brake, and got out. I snipped the wire at the eyebolt. Riordan's hands were still wired.

"Out," I said.

He moved carefully. Any sudden move would sink the wire more deeply into flesh. I saw him wince when he tripped on a root.

"Come on, Jack. You can take it. Tough old dog killer like you."

He tried to glare at me, but his eyes were liquid with pain.

I pointed to a fat pine tree and said simply, "Over there."

He made it in several mincing little steps.

"Turn around and put your back up against the tree."

He did what he was told, and I wrapped a length of wire twice around the tree and his neck. If he struggled hard enough, he would cut his own throat.

He looked at me when I finished, and I could see that he was getting some of his confidence back. He could read me, and he knew that while I might stick a knife into his chin deep enough to draw blood, I probably wasn't up to killing him, or even hurting him very badly, when he was wired to a tree. He knew that if I was hot for blood because he killed Jubal, I would have done something by now. He thought he could handle this.

I wondered. Maybe he could. If I wasn't willing to push it and get my hands dirty, Jordan had even less reason. It's the old problem when you deal with the Riordans of the world. You have to be willing to get down and wrestle with them in the mud where they live.

Still, Jordan and I had a little act worked out, and it might work. If it did, Riordan would break and we could have everything we needed.

"I need to find me a siphon hose," Jordan said from the bed of the truck. It was a line from the script we had worked up on the fly.

"Check the toolbox," I said. "Ought to be one in there somewhere. I don't leave home without my Georgia credit card."

He made a production of fishing around in the steel toolbox that spanned the truck bed. I knew the short length of hose was in there, but we wanted to draw it out for the audience.

"I don't see how you can find anything in here," Jordan said.

"Stir around a little," I said. "It'll rise to the top." Actually, the toolbox was pretty neat.

"Damn," Jordan said. "Just once I'd like to reach for something I need and find it in my hand. Just once."

"There's your problem," I said. "You want things to come easy."

After a little more of this, Jordan pulled his arm out of the toolbox with his hand wrapped around a four-foot section of plastic garden hose.

"Found that sumbitch."

He walked over to where I was standing, next to Riordan, who was watching the show with a look that came close to indifference, even though he had to stretch to his full height to keep the wire from cutting the rind of flesh around his neck.

Jordan handed me the hose and a small metal gas can. "Too bad we don't have any soap."

"What do you want with soap?"

"Stir it up with the gasoline. Make napalm. Burns longer than plain gas."

"Fire's fire."

"I reckon."

I made a production of unscrewing the gas cap and working the hose down into the tank. I put my mouth to the hose and thought about just how dead my sense of taste would be for the next couple of days. Then, one of those vagrant notions passed through my head—I remembered drinking wine with Jessie.

Actually, only a few fumes reached my mouth and lips. I could hear the liquid coming up the hose and I got it out of my mouth in time. The gasoline ran into a dented one-gallon can. When it was full, I pulled the hose out of the tank, shook it dry, wiped it with a rag, and put it back in the toolbox.

I picked up the gas can and walked to the pine where I'd wired Riordan. He was wearing the mask, smart enough to know that he shouldn't look confident even if he felt that way.

I splashed some gas on his pants, from the knees up.

"Jack, I want you to tell us where Mrs. Straylow is. That's for starters. Then I want you to tell me all about Straylow and about the lies you and the Hewes kid cooked up."

He shook his head, and his meaty lips formed a very faint smirk in spite of himself. He simply didn't believe I'd do it.

I threw some more gasoline on him, soaking his shirt this time.

"Think about it, Jack."

He had already thought about it. And he thought he had me.

I started to turn away and leave him there, drenched with gasoline, but Jordan was blocking the way.

"Look what I found," he said.

He was holding a rattlesnake. A small one, about two and a half feet long.

"I figured there'd be one around a place like this. All the junk, there has to be rats, and snakes like rats." One hand gripped the snake, firmly but not desperately, just behind the head. The other held the fat part of the snake's belly.

"He's mad," Jordan said. "Just dying to bite somebody."

"Uh-huh," I said. This wasn't part of our script.

"I was thinking," Jordan went on, "that we ought to drop him down the front of this fat boy's pretty green shirt. *Then* we'll light his ass on fire."

He took a step in the direction of Riordan, tied there and reeking of gasoline, his eyes on the snake and filling with fear.

"How'd you like that, fat boy?" Jordan asked, his voice rising.

Riordan's face went white. If he hadn't believed
me, he believed Jordan. The snake was undeniably
real.

Jordan held the snake up in Riordan's face so that
the open mouth and extended fangs were no more
than six inches from his nose. Jordan released his
grip on the snake's belly, and the creature began
thrashing and rattling. There was something nearly
insane in the wild buzzing sound. It wasn't a loud
noise, but it drowned every other sound, and you
felt like you would have to shout to be heard over it.

Jordan's face was twisted with some kind of old,
primitive rage. He was out of the script but still in
character. I wondered just how far he would go. He
looked like one of his ancestors, back up in some
forlorn, roadless hollow, handling snakes, swallow-
ing strychnine, and ranting in tongues.

"You better answer me, boy," he was shouting. "I
asked you a question."

The man shook his head and the wire cut deep
enough to sever vessels. A sheet of blood ran down
the side of his neck.

"Answer me." Jordan pushed the snake still
closer to Riordan's face. "I ain't going to ask you
again."

Riordan's trembling was almost convulsive now.
His eyes were wide and white, and he drooled like a
baby.

"I'm going to drop him down your shirt, and then
I'm going to light your ass on fire." Jordan was almost screaming. I was afraid Riordan might pass
out and strangle in the wire.

"Wait a minute," I said. "Hold it."

Jordan turned to look at me.

"Just hold on," I said firmly to get him back in the

real world. "Don't rush it. I want to talk to him a minute."

There was something curious and detached in Jordan's face. Something inside him had been released, and it showed in his eyes. He had probably looked just this way, I thought, at the moment he killed Perkins.

"I've got to talk to him," I said. "So back off with that snake."

There was a moment when I wondered if it would register. Then Jordan stepped away. He grabbed the snake's belly and immobilized it. The wild, satanic rattling quieted. Riordan's breathing was suddenly very loud.

I looked at him. He had been a picture of arrogance an hour ago. Lime-green shirt and pewter-gray pants, good tan, shades, Rolex watch, and Gucci shoes.

Now he was a mess. He looked like he belonged in one of those hospitals where they keep you tranquilized and teach you how to finger-paint. Smelled like it too. He had lost control, and you could smell it even over the gasoline.

"Make you a deal, Jack," I said. "You can say yes or you can say no."

He nodded feebly.

"Good," I said. "Here's how it works. You tell us where Mrs. Straylow is and all the other things we want to know. Then, after you've told us, you tell the law. Then, if you get asked, you tell a grand jury. Do all that, and I won't turn my friend and his snake loose on you. Deal?"

He nodded again.

"Smart boy."

Chapter Twenty-seven

I drove down the blacktop to a small country store, where I used the pay phone to call Tom Pine at home.

"Got a customer for you," I said.

"Live or dead?"

"Live, I'm afraid."

"Well, damn it all anyway, Morgan."

"Sorry."

"OK. Where you at?"

I told him and he groaned. "All the way at the goddamned north end of the county. And in this heat."

He said he would be along in an hour, and I said I'd be waiting.

"And Tom," I said, "bring along a bucket and a scrub brush. He's kind of a mess. Got his pants dirty and everything."

"I'll get a wagon, then. He ain't riding with me."

I hung up, went inside, and bought a six-pack of cold beer. I drank one while I was driving back to the old landfill and another when I got there. Jordan joined me.

I told him to take the attaché case full of money.

"What about you?"

"What about me?" I said.

"Don't you want some of this money?"

"No," I said. Hot and dry as it had been—and looked like it would remain for a while—I'd probably do better on my beans in the next two weeks. Even that seemed like cleaner money.

"You sure about that?" Jordan asked.

"Spend it wisely."

We finished our beers, and I told him that Pine was on his way and he'd better take my truck and go get his boy. I thanked him for his help.

"Couldn't have done it without you," I said.

"Well," he said, "I enjoyed it." And I believed he did. Takes all kinds.

Before he left, carrying the attaché case, he said he would call and tell me where to find my truck.

When he was gone, I walked away from Riordan and found a stump to sit against. I opened another beer and drank it. I felt like going to sleep.

After a while, I heard a siren, a long way off, like the sound of rising wind. The sound grew until it was something I felt, more than heard, then it stopped. Pine must have killed the siren when he turned off the blacktop. I was standing when the cruiser pulled into the clearing. It was followed by a van. The lieutenant was alone in the cruiser; two men were in the van.

Pine uncoiled from the cruiser and looked over at Riordan.

"Tied him to a bush, huh, Morgan?"

"Didn't want him to get away."

"Uh-huh," Pine said, looking around the clearing. "I don't see how either of you could get away. You're kind of short on transportation."

"I was hoping you'd give me a lift back to town, Tom."

"How did you get out here, Morgan?"

"Drove."

"Hey, *really*? You wouldn't shit me, would you now, Morgan?"

"His car is down the road a little, Tom. Busted fan belt or something."

Pine chewed on the inside of his lip. "You wouldn't put me in a box, would you, Morgan?"

"No. I wouldn't do that."

He looked at me for a moment, then shook his head and grinned. One thing I do have is some credibility.

"OK," Pine said, "I won't make you walk back to town."

"I appreciate that, Tom."

"Just give me a minute here. I need to talk to this fellow. Inform him of his rights and so forth."

I nodded.

"You want to tell me what I am arresting him for?"

I told him.

"OK," Pine said. "You rest here. Drink your beer. I'll just be a minute."

"You mind a suggestion?"

"Nah. I ain't proud."

"If he stalls, tell him the snake man will be looking for him."

"*Snake man?*"

"That's right."

Pine spat, shook his head, and said, "Well, sure,

all right. I've handled stranger shit than that. 'Snake man' don't rattle me none. No, sir. Take more than that to rattle old Tom Pine. You just relax and I'll go do my job."

He walked off shaking his head.

In a few minutes, he came back. "OK. The boys will put him in the wagon and carry him back into town. We'll get him for conspiracy and obstruction and a lot of other stuff, including kidnapping. That'll be the big one."

I nodded.

"Never seen one of the pedigreed badasses so eager to talk. That 'snake man' stuff really did the trick."

"New kind of voodoo, Tom."

"I'll have to try it. Now we'd better get across the road and get the other one."

We walked down the trail to the hunting cabin. Pine walked in the front door without knocking. Straylow was sitting on a couch. There was a pistol on the table next to him.

"Mr. Straylow," Pine said, "you are under arrest. Please don't try for that piece. In this heat, I might just lose it and shoot you."

Pine recited the charges while I went to the rooms in back. Mrs. Straylow was sitting on the bed behind the second door I checked. Her face was a little puffy, but otherwise she looked all right.

She said she would happily testify that she had been taken from her home and held there against her will.

Pine asked her if she wanted a ride. She looked at her husband, whose hands were cuffed behind his back, and said, "Where are you taking him?"

"County jail," Pine said.

"And where is Riordan?"

"He'll be there too."

"My husband's Mercedes is still outside in that little parking lot, isn't it?"

"Yes, ma'am."

"Then I'll drive myself, thank you, Lieutenant."

She smiled at her husband, who looked back at her, his eyes brimming with hate.

"Good-bye, Eddie," she said.

In the morning, I called the television station and asked for Hartley, the man who'd done the clip on me. I gave him the story on Straylow and Riordan and told him how Rick Hewes had shoved an old man's hands into a vat of hot grease.

"That wouldn't have come out at trial," I said. "It's part of his sealed juvenile record. But you can check it and use it."

When I finished, he said, "OK. I appreciate it. Now you want to tell me why I can't use your name on any of this?"

"All my life I've wanted to be an unidentified source," I said. "Now I am one."

He wasn't amused but he ran the story. I stayed away from it, but Nat Semmes called to give me progress reports.

I got my truck, which was where Jordan said it would be when he called. He didn't say where he was and I didn't ask.

I worked on the house, which seemed bigger and emptier without Jubal Early. I considered getting another dog and decided to put it off until I came back from my trip out West. I didn't have the heart for it just yet.

Semmes came by one afternoon. He was wearing old faded khakis and said he felt like going fishing.

We went upriver to a deep pool full of clear, cold spring water. I paddled and he fished.

Nat went on his first Atlantic salmon trip when he was eleven years old. He handled a fly rod with such effortless grace that you were always amazed to learn that he was rolling out sixty or seventy feet of line.

He talked while he worked the pool.

"Big John wanted me to tell you how much he appreciates all you did."

"Did he open back up?"

"No. That will take time. Nobody in HRS is in a hurry to say he made a mistake. You blunder in like that, it can be hard to backtrack. You know what I mean?"

"Yes."

Semmes picked up the fly and made a couple of short false casts, then dropped it easily against a Cyprus knee. He watched the rings of water expand and die.

"You can get in trouble moving impetuously," he said, as though he were considering an abstract proposition and not talking directly to me.

"I know," I said. I realized I was nervous. Afraid that I had disappointed Semmes. More afraid that he would say he couldn't use me anymore because . . . well, because I was impetuous. Lacked judgment or prudence—one of his favorite words—or something.

The rings died, and he sent a small vibration down the line, just enough to move the bug very slightly. A fish boiled around it and took it in a bulge of water.

He set the hook, and the fish came out of the water and showed its bloodred gills. He played it for a minute, brought it to the boat, admired it for a moment, and released it.

"There ought to be a bigger one up ahead," he said.

I eased us ahead with a single stroke of the paddle.

Semmes began laying out line in clean, sinuous loops.

"I can't afford to be impulsive," he said. Something seemed to fall to the bottom of my stomach. I felt sure that he would be telling me next that he couldn't use me anymore, that I was cut off from the action.

"Hard on me, when you go off on your own," he said, and dropped the bug at the lip of the deep-cut bank.

I said nothing. Backed us down with the paddle and waited for him to go on.

"There ought to be a nice one under that bank," he said. "Cool water, shade, food from the overhang. Everything the prospering largemouth needs."

He let the rings die and then sent a slight pulse down the line. The bug disappeared.

"All *right*, now," Semmes said.

This one was five pounds, and when Semmes had released it, he put his rod up and said, "That's enough. I'm not greedy."

We sat and watched the sunset and Semmes said, "I appreciate the chances you took, Morgan. Without you, we'd still be talking settlement, if we hadn't already settled."

I didn't say anything.

"Be careful, though, will you? Next time. I don't want you on my conscience."

"Sure."

I felt fine, paddling back downstream. He'd said "next time." Pitiful, I thought, how little it takes to satisfy some people.

The rain started the next afternoon, while I was on my way back from the lumberyard. A fine drizzle at first, it seemed to pick up momentum until the drops were the size of buckshot and so thick you couldn't see twenty feet. The road steamed and then, like the air, it cooled. It was a hard rain, more than an afternoon thunderstorm, and I was sure it meant survival for some of the bean farmers whose misfortune had been making me paper rich for the last few weeks. I'd lose a little but not enough to keep me from enjoying the rain for what it was. I sat on the porch and watched the river dance where the drops pounded its surface. The leaves, the grass, even the river and the air itself seemed renewed by the rain. By the time it had slackened to a steady, gentle shower at last light, everything felt cool and cleansed. The evening sounds came up, and a couple of fish began feeding along the far bank of the river.

The phone rang and I went inside to answer it. I don't know who I was expecting, but it was not Jessie Beaudraux.

"You want to come to supper?" she said.

"Now?"

"Sure. What's wrong with now?"

"Nothing. Now is the best time. Always."

"How you coming, by the road or the river?"

"By the river," I said. "This rain is too good to pass up."

TROUBLE ON THE REDNECK RIVIERA

You won't find northern Florida's steamy Panhandle on a
picture postcard. But its sluggish streams and piney
woods suit Morgan Hunt just fine. Some hard time in the
slammer has left him on a short fuse. He needs slow
afternoons fishing and lazy evenings lovemaking to cool
down. He doesn't need ex-football star "Big John"
Fearson's case. Any P.I. knows that missing kids are pure
heartbreak: they turn up battered, corrupted, or dead.
This boy's a runaway from Sweetwater Ranch, the home
Fearson operates for troubled youngsters. Coupled with
another teen's charges of abuse, Big John looks guilty as
hell...and Hunt's search for a little boy lost may be a dark
road to deadly secrets, murder, and revenge.

SWEET WATER RANCH

ISBN 0-440-21219-7

21219

0 71009 00450 4

GEOFFREY NORMAN regularly contributes articles to a wide range of magazines, including *Esquire, Playboy, Sports Illustrated,* and *Outside.* He is the author of the thriller *Midnight Water,* for which he won an Edgar Award, as well as several other well-received books.